IN HER SIGHTS

LINDA PETRILLI

This book is dedicated to all the people who encouraged me to keep writing and not give up. My book club group. Maryann who pushed me when I wanted to give up, Pam who gave her time, so I got it right. My publisher, Sonja Dewing, who made it possible. Most of all to my husband Lamar Duncan who loved me even when I was crabby and forgot to cook dinner. I miss you.

Cover Art by Leslie Reilly

PROLOGUE

"Never take to sawing the branch that's supporting you unless you're hanging by it." Texas Bix Bender

The small figure appeared to doze in the warm sunlight. The building was in such poor shape no one would be concerned about what appeared to be a young boy hiding in the ruins where the supporting walls were crumbled and in disrepair. A building that didn't appear able to hold the roof up against any assault from the fierce winds that whipped in from the surrounding desert.

It was a familiar scene in the ravaged landscape of Iraq. Morning prayers were over. The inhabitants in the small settlement had already partaken of the ration of tea and bread. The village had started its drab brown existence for another day.

She took a deep breath and prepared to squeeze the trigger. It was time...

1

"You haven't lived until you have almost died. For those who have fought for it, life has a flavor the protected shall never know" -Guy de Maupassant

RACHAEL WATCHED for her targets as she hid under a pile of cast-off debris. The only movement was from the slight breeze that whispered through the bits and pieces surrounding her. The breeze continued to dance gracefully until it too would be swept away by its stronger blowing cousin.

Sometimes she would doze in the warm sunlight. All anyone who spotted her would see was young boy. Her dark hair hid under a cap and the mud on her face was used to blur her fine features. Some would have thought a burka would have been more appropriate, but it wouldn't have hidden her green eyes and fairer complexion. Without it she had the added benefit, had an added benefit of allowing her to move with ease.

Now was that golden time in the morning when the sun drove off the night's cold air, just before it became the blazing orb that mercilessly baked everything within its reach. If she was back home, this was the kind of morning that she would be taking the horses and the dogs out for a run.

She'd researched this area before accepting this mission. Once upon a time this area had been a marsh full of vibrant green reeds, wildlife, and the tribes who had thrown their loyalty to the rebels fighting Saddam Hussein in the earlier desert war. Their repayment from their allies was to be left behind to face an angry and vindictive dictator. One, who in one of the greatest feats of engineering history had built a dam that had drained the marshes of their life's blood. and turned it back into a desert. As she surveyed the dusty streets and the dry landscape, it occurred to her that the destruction one can achieve when one is really pissed off is truly amazing.

Rachael had noted the fact that none of the remaining Ma'dan paid attention to the two men who had taken up residence in one of the homes. The men were quiet and they attended to their prayers regularly, according to custom. She knew the people had learned from experience that the safest course was not to notice anything that could be construed by either side as an attempt to take part in the war on terror. The tired little town had learned its lesson all too well.

The first two men had arrived a few days ago. They had taken over a small home. Its inhabitants wisely left, probably to stay with relatives. They had been convinced that it was a good time to strengthen family ties. A third man arrived this morning. He had been deposited by helicopter right after morning prayers.

Except for the appearance of the helicopter, the morning was the same as all others. The men gathered around a low table and squatted back on their heels. They could stay in that position for hours as they drank copious amounts of tea. They only took a break to go pee or check for any change in the fickle winds. Their heads were covered by the tagiya. The red and white ghutra and held together by a black circular cord. She imagined that they gossiped about common things if anyone could over hear them.

They would only speak softly of things better not known by the general population when they were alone. She knew two of the men had already chosen a path of destroying anyone they saw as their perceived enemy. She had seen the videos in which they defined the enemy as anyone who did not believe as they did.

The surveillance made in an earlier operation, she noted they enjoyed the killing and torture more than the religious doctrines they espoused. They were not so altruistic in their religious zeal. According to intel reports, they were working a deal with the third man. A deal to provide the weapons needed to hasten the demise and demoralization of their said enemy. He was a notorious dealer in death and destruction with no morals to speak of. Money and power were his only gods.

The reason for the assassination order wasn't a vindictive one. At least not so much so that it had flavored the order to kill them. The end goal was to create confusion while their underlings fought for position and disrupt the supply line. Maybe if the stars aligned correctly, it would allow the good guys to get a toe hold or stay at least two steps ahead. Or heaven forbid, be able to take a deep breath before the next catastrophe.

The problem was it was so hard to know who the good guys were in the muddle of Mid-Eastern politics. Rachael believed even if neither of these goals was accomplished, the world was, for a few turns at least, a better place without their existence. She took a deep breath in and prepared to pull the trigger. It was time.

The peace was broken by three shots. The sound tore through the fabric of the hot air as if it was one long sonic boom. It left behind a vibration of currents like those of a thunder storm at its most wicked. The three men fell over quietly. Dead in between one heartbeat and the next. A moment of stillness as the silence following the vibration of the shots rippled over the street. Then there was chaos as the townspeople ran for cover. Rachael used the commotion to cover her exit from the town.

Quiet would descend again in the streets. Soon the army from one side or the other would invade the little town. Again. Attention the inhabitants did not want or need. She was sorry for being the cause of it. Rachael hoped it would be the Americans. They at least tried to be humane. Others not so much. The people here didn't care for outsiders. But at least, in her mind, the U.S. forces didn't bring religious oppression with them.

Hopefully no one would notice the small figure as she ghosted away. She moved from one windswept rock or dune to another until out of sight of any possible watchers.

Rachael only stopped long enough to shed the ragged clothing and don desert camouflage and boots. She checked the path behind her as she shouldered her pack containing water and provisions that she had hidden earlier. The rifle was already broken down and stuffed in a bag to hide it. She transferred it to the pack for transport. She swathed her head in a scarf to protect it from the glaring sun, donned her sunglasses, and started her run at a steady pace. There were over twenty miles to go before reaching the zone where her extraction would take place.

As she ran, any guilt she might have felt at ending three lives was run through her mind at the same pace as her feet thudding the sandy earth. By nightfall any regrets were left behind in braided thoughts. Tossed out to be blown away by the capricious winds of the desert. Death was simply another harsh reality in an unforgiving land.

The only stops she made were short. She could only afford brief delays to eat, drink and get her bearings. Real rest would come after she was evacuated out of the country. Rachael had set up small supply dumps on the way in. They contained some food, but mostly water. Although a strong runner, she had a long way to go and water was a vital but heavy necessity.

Rachael hunkered down beside the rock that was her extraction point. It was one of those rare landmarks that rose out of the sea of sand. She waited patiently. The small sounds of the desert went on without interruption and there was no sense of anyone else at the site. She was ahead of schedule so she would do what every seasoned soldier did when they had the chance. She took a nap.

Later, she checked the time and ate the only type of MRE she had brought with her. It was breakfast. The only one in her opinion on the Meals Ready to Eat menu that was fit to consume. She washed it down with lukewarm water. A cup of decent coffee, revise that, any kind of coffee, would have been a lot better.

It was time to set up the mantle for her ride home. Then sit back and wait some more. The pilot would follow the coordinates he had been given. Once he spotted the mantle with the orange side up, he'd set the bird down. Orange meant it was safe to land. She wouldn't have long to wait if they were on schedule.

Before setting out the mantle, she rechecked the area. Nothing felt out of place. But as she waited something didn't seem right. Rachael caught a movement to her right. A slight sound of a scrape, as if something had rubbed against a rock. A small rodent scuttled out for a moment and then ran back to whatever hole he came from. Nothing else moved or whispered.

Making up her mind she started out to take the mantle down. There was nothing concrete, but there was a code to follow. You didn't put your team in jeopardy. Even if it was just a bad feeling. Better to abort and recon again. Be sure before bringing the bird in.

As she started to come out of hiding, it was too late. The chopper came over the rock and settled to the earth. It sent up a cloud of sand and heat to provide some cover for the team as they jumped to the ground and fanned out. Rachael faded back and stayed hidden as she watched Sergeant Colby and his team deploy. She kept scanning the area. If someone was planning an ambush, now would be the time. Still nothing.

The team followed procedure. The Sergeant leading the left forward side checked the area eleven to seven o'clock. The team on the right side covered from one to five o'clock, both teams always aware of the front and rear rotors. She loved watching good training in action. It was truly a beautiful thing. It showed that they took their job and her life seriously. Rachael remained still. She wanted to think it was just an aberrant sound and that it was safe to come out.

The site would look devoid of life to the soldiers hitting the ground. Hiding was something she was good at. Rachael simply believed in her mind that she was invisible. Sounded silly and a lot like woo-woo-ism, but she had watched her training films. Knew when she moved out of the shadows it would appear as if the large rock reformed and a small figure detached out of it. It was as if her molecules had rearranged out of the rock itself.

An irreverent thought drifted through her mind as she continued to scan. Maybe that's why she never got asked to dance when she went to the old-fashioned sock hops in high school. No one saw her. Forget that, it was an angst from another time.

Nothing moved other than the soldiers. They were alert but not looking concerned, at least from what she could tell by their body language. Maybe she was just antsy and had imagined the whole thing. As she moved out, she kept her hands held out in front so no mistake would be made as to hostile intent. Colby saw her first.

"Well as I live and breathe if it isn't the Kitten. No

telling who they'll send us to pick up. They let you out of your cage to play again?"

"The rat problem was increasing. They needed someone to take care of it. Besides I was getting low on catnip. I was told they grew a great crop here." She shrugged her shoulders, "Just can't believe those infomercials. Great to see you all, too. Just happy to keep you busy and not wasting Uncle Sam's hard-earned money with idleness and sloth. Hope you brought coffee. If not, then I'm afraid my evaluation of you guys will not be stellar. Let's get out of here. I'm starving for some decent food and coffee." Rachael gave them a grin and thumbs up as she headed for the bird.

As she stepped forward, she caught a glint off the face of the rock behind the soldiers.

Her gut hadn't been screwing with her. There was someone hiding.

She was the target, not the soldiers. Yelling out to hit the dirt, she tackled Colby, riding his larger body to the ground. When the bullet sliced through her side, she couldn't help the involuntary jerk her body made.

She rolled off of Colby's body and drew her revolver in one smooth motion. Returning fire as she moved, she sent three shots winging toward the rocks. That gave the rest of the team time to finish taking cover as they laid down a spray of covering fire. They waited for the insurgents to return fire and take advantage of Colby and Rachael's exposed position.

The only noise breaking the silence was whump-whump of the bird's propellers beating against the desert air. She could feel Colby as he waited for a few heartbeats and then rolled to his knees. He was up and quartering the area with his weapon, covering his slice of the site so she could guard hers.

When the all clear sounded, Rachael checked her side where the bullet had crazed her, her hand came away bloody. Colby had followed her hand and started cussing when he saw the blood. Rachael didn't catch all of it. Which was really a shame. He was very colorful. It was always important to add to one's vocabulary. The tirade ended with something about idiots who didn't wear their body armor.

"Not everyone is built like the Titanic. You run twenty miles with all that crap on when you're my size and see how you like it," she snapped back at him. "I wear it when I need to. Besides, it's only a flesh wound. No need to thank me. I just used you for a big cushion. I hate hitting the hard ground."

Colby pointed her toward the team medic. Then swung around and headed for the rocks where the shots had come from. Rachael ignored the medic and followed Colby. The rest of the men were already there. They looked down at the three insurgents sprawled at their feet. "Sarge, you just ain't going to believe this," one of the soldiers drawled, not noticing Rachael behind Colby.

All three of the men on the ground had a small, neat bullet hole between their eyes. Three shots, three T-box hits, three instant kills. Colby turned and looked at her.

She shrugged her shoulders, and spread her hands out. "What can I say, I'm good at what I do. I am sorry, I was having a weird feeling and was just getting ready to move the mantle when you all landed. My bad."

"Not your fault, we didn't see them from the air either. They were well hidden. Must have burrowed under the sand to hide. Our heat detectors didn't pick them up either."

They must have hidden there while she slept. Her senses were usually sharper than that. The only other option was someone had betrayed her. The ambushers had been in place and hidden before she arrived. Meaning the traitor had to be close to her. There weren't many people who knew about the op. The number could literally be counted on one hand. Colby and his team didn't know where she'd be exactly until she set the mantle out to pick her up.

The traitor had to be higher in the food chain then her extraction team. Rachael didn't believe in coincidence. The only thing that finally gave their location away had been the flash of light. Then and only then did she feel the presence of three minds.

Rachael could see the wheels grinding behind Colby's eyes. She didn't have to be a mind reader to know he was thinking that the attackers hadn't been standing up high enough for her bullets to hit their targets. At their feet lay an RPG, obviously to take down the helicopter if the original ambush had failed. Someone had all the intel.

He cleared his throat, as he looked at Rachael and commented, "Maybe Kitten wasn't such an appropriate name for you after all."

Colby and his team had extracted her from wherever she was on each mission. After her first mission, Colby had christened her with her code name of Kitten. She already had an official spy worthy code name but she wasn't really fond of it. Of course, they hadn't asked her opinion. The average height of the members of the recovery team was six-two, at five-three she looked like a child next to them. The name had stuck. Rachael had requested the same extraction team every time she was in country. She always got her request.

After this incident, she knew from experience that they not only would be willing to make the hazardous flight into the desert to pick her up, they would fly through hell to save her. She risked her life. Had taken a bullet for one of their own. It didn't matter that she lived through it. Rachael had made a conscious decision to give her life for Colby's. The fact that she lived was a happy bonus. What the team knew and understood was she was willing to trade her life for one of theirs. There wasn't anything else needed on her resume. She was one of their own. No one had to tell her this. It was simply understood between those willing to lay down their lives for one another and their country.

Rachael turned and started back toward the medic. She overheard Colby's comment as she started down the slope, "Leave them here. We'll send a recovery team out when we land. Grab the weapons. We don't want anyone who's unfriendly to get their hands on them. Let's get our tiger kitten home and put this mission to bed. She can explain what sloth is to us dummies on the trip out." He was trying to lighten up the situation.

Rachael smiled to herself, tiger kitten. She liked that much better. Much better than her official code name, the Gray Paladin. No one who had taken the time to really get to know her would have considered her a soft, fluffy, domesticated kitten. If they did, it would be a stupid mistake. A tiger, now that was something she could go with. Colby and his team of elite Air Force Para-rescue Team, aka, PJ's were anything but stupid.

2

"Sometimes I meet people and feel sorry for their dog." Unknown

THREE AND A HALF MONTHS LATER.

Rachel settled firmly into the warm roofing material and evened out her breathing. One breath, two breaths as she waited for her target to enter her sight picture. A helicopter beat overhead, searching for the thermal signature of a possible sniper. She stayed frozen in place as it continued on its grid pattern. The air conditioning unit's radiating heat covered any body heat she was emitting.

It was odd that Moody had a team looking for snipers. The normal run of the mill congressman didn't usually entertain death threats in their daily routine. They definitely didn't put out the extra money to hire security teams to guard against them. At least not to the extent of air support. When one considered that this was Washington, D.C., a city with the tightest security in the nation, this was the epitome of paranoia. Perhaps the good congressman had a guilty conscience?

The building was chosen by her agency because it didn't have the usual walls surrounding the roof. Just poles with safety cables. A stress fracture had been 'found' in the old brick, and the walls surrounding the roof had been conveniently removed along with any surveillance devices in the area. With its lack of suitable cover, it would not be considered as a site a normal shooter would use. It was perfect for her type of talent. The walls were being repaired, but today the crew was conveniently at another job. That left her a clear field for sighting and no witnesses.

The operation had taken months of planning. It wasn't good enough to terminate the target. She then had to get out without suspicion. The watch strapped to her rifle marked the countdown to when Moody was scheduled to appear. one of the most influential congressmen on the hill, therefore he had a tight, busy schedule.

There was less than one minute to go. Once the bullet left the rifle and Moody was down, she'd be gone. Now everything was condensed into the final minute.

Then seconds. Rachael still had plenty of light. A quick glance at the flag showed that the air was still quiet. The slight wind shear from the street's whirling currents wouldn't make any difference. She had accounted for that in the composition of her bullets. All calculations were good. Time flattened out.

Congressman Moody stepped out of the court house right on time. As he moved to the top step, her breathing slowed and pulse rate dropped. As his foot hit the top step, Rachel was between her breath out and next heartbeat as she squeezed the trigger. Moody was dead before he hit the ground. His heart may have squeezed out a few more beats, but his brain was gone.

She had hit the sweet spot, middle of the forehead and down through the spinal cord between the first and second vertebrae. It would sever the spinal cord on the way through, destroying the brain stem and stopping all bodily functions. Another textbook T-box kill shot.

Even if he had a full medical team with the appropriate equipment standing at his side, the rescue attempt would have been futile. The only thing that might have saved him was a full convergence of the Heavenly Host with the Alleluia choir as backup. The reason he was a target was that his sins definitely put him headed in the other direction. Odds where heavily in her favor of a no show by the Celestial Body.

Rachel was moving almost before the crack of the rifle alerted everyone to the assassination. With her gloved hands, she caught the ejected brass and was out of the unit's housing. Paused only long enough to replace the cover and move to the door of the roof. The maneuver added mere seconds to her time.

Forty seconds gone and she was in the building, breaking down her rifle as she moved and shoving the pieces into her carry-all. The need for speed in breaking down the weapon trumped the need for silence. The sub-sonic boom her rifle of choice made could only be muffled and add some confusion as to where the shot originated from. The extra bulk of the silencer was not worth the trouble. Not to mention the heat it would generate if it had been necessary to fire more than one shot. Another sixty seconds passed and she entered the apartment she had been living in for two and a half months.

As she came through the door, she removed the covering jumpsuit. The shoe and hair protectors followed and were bundled in with the rifle. Only then she stripped off the gloves and stuffed everything into the storage area behind the wall in the hall closet. She was careful not to scuff the dust on the floor, leaving the bundle on a hammock like sling hanging down. If the compartment was ever checked it would have no evidence of any disturbance.

An agent would retrieve the bundle while she was on her "date." A little over three minutes gone and she swung the door shut to the compartment and pulled the coats back in place. It only had a light leather jacket, raincoat and a slightly heavier coat in case the early fall decided to really cool off. Her jump kit was on the floor with a pair of rain boots.

She hustled through her bedroom. As she double-timed it, she took a moment to glance at the clothes laid out on the bed for her "date." Everything was there, including the fuck me shoes. She left a trail of her sensible nursing shoes, scrubs and underwear on her way to the shower. Still under six minutes since the shot.

The shower was heaven. Between work and the heat on the roof, she felt like she had washed away three layers of dirt. Though she was running on a tight schedule, the couple of extra minutes she luxuriated in the hot water was worth the time. It allowed her adrenaline boost to drain down. She was barely dried off when the banging on her door started. Wrapping a towel around her head, she quickly grabbed her robe and tied it as she went to answer the door.

She called out as she unlocked the door. "You're early, I'm not ready yet!" She let out a "Whoops, you're not my date," to the two men at her door.

The younger of the two men had the grace to look embarrassed. They both held up a badges and ID's. There really wasn't a need for the identification. Both of their appearances screamed cop. Even without the ID's, she would have had them pegged in a heartbeat.

One was older, tall with dark hair and eyes. He was also in good physical shape, not bulky, but well-muscled. She bet he would have a cute butt. He had the Sam Elliot vibe going. Yes, she noticed things like that. No reason to let the men have all the fun. A neat mustache completed the picture. He was the one in charge. In the plus column, he didn't have a wedding ring.

"I'm Lieutenant Reynolds and this is Detective Watts. Are you Rachael Cade? We need to speak with you."

So formal. "I'm Rachael. What's wrong? Is it Mrs. Poninski? Let me grab some clothes and my jump kit and I'll be right with you." Her mind was racing. There was no way they could have gotten here that fast about Moody. They had to be here for another reason and a 911 call was all she could come up with. The only other answer was they had been on their way to this particular building and had a list of the tenants.

It would also mean the police had known the shooter was in this building. Worst case scenario was they had a good idea who they were looking for and had come straight to her apartment. She was really hoping for door number one. She also hoped they couldn't catch her concern from her facial expression or her eyes. Everyone had a tell and she was pretty sure the older cop was adept at picking them up in suspects.

"No, it's not that, we just need to ask you some questions. Why would you think there was something wrong with Mrs. Poninski?" Reynolds quizzed.

Well, that shot it down, looked like door number two. "I'm a nurse. I've helped out a few times when she had chest pain and once when she fell. Everyone knows what I do. They usually come and get me to stay with her until EMS gets here. My agency uses this apartment for its employees. The people in the building knows whoever stays here is a nurse."

She tried to keep her conversation coherent while she searched her mind for any chance, she might have left a clue in the apartment. The only articles to link her to a crime where hidden and without a warrant they couldn't search for anything.

"That makes sense. Sorry, we didn't mean to cause you alarm. May we come in?"

The other detective was slightly shorter and didn't keep in shape as well as his partner. He had a wedding ring. Sandy colored hair, light blue eyes and a sprinkling of freckles across his nose and cheeks completed his appearance. Family life was the likely reason the shorter one didn't get to hit the gym as much.

Rachael stepped away from the door. Holding her robe closer to her, she motioned for them to enter. "What's this about?"

As they stepped in, they could see the trail of clothes leading to the bathroom and the outfit on the bed. She blushed and picked up her scrub top and wrapped her bra up in it before they passed it. Looking at the bundle in her arms, she then set it in a chair. The rest of her underwear was further into the bedroom.

Rachael watched Reynolds as he scanned the apartment. She noted the apartment itself was the usual mixture of bland modern furniture used in furnished apartments. It had a simple floor plan. You could see the whole layout from the foyer.

The only personal touches were the books stacked in neat piles on the floor and tables. She had an e-reader but didn't like to use it. If she would use it, then it would remove the need for packing books when she moved around but she really preferred the feel of a book in her hands. There was a colorful, fluffy-warm blanket on the couch with a comfortable pillow to lean against. A book with its place remembered with a marker was on top of the blanket. It was the new Jim Butcher novel. Reynolds walked over and picked up the book. "How do you like this one?"

"I just started it, but it's good so far. Most of his are." She continued to track him as he looked around.

The TV wasn't turned toward the couch for easy watching, indicating she was a reader, not a television junkie. No personal pictures were in the living area. Reynolds hesitated as he caught a glimpse of a frame on one of the dressers in the small bedroom.

He walked into the other room without asking permission to do a quick scan and picked it up. It showed Cade with her arms around a good-looking bear of a man and a woman who could have been her older sister. He looked at her and back at the picture and then set it down. "Your parents?" She just nodded yes. "You look like your mom." He set it down next to another snapshot of Cade standing next to a black horse. Reynolds didn't know anything about horses, but he could tell this one was a beautiful specimen.

"Thanks." She watched him as he continued to categorize the apartment. Unless someone was under the bed or in a closet, it was obvious she was alone. There was nowhere else to hide. No weapons were in sight, and she wasn't wearing enough to hide one. So, they were here deliberately looking for someone in this apartment. She could almost see him thinking that whatever had brought them to this apartment had to be a mistake.

Rachael knew enough about the law that you couldn't arrest someone for simply being home, even if a crime had happened in the vicinity. What was worrying her, was how they found her so fast. There hadn't been hardly enough time to identify where the shot came from, no less hone in on her apartment number.

It was also apparent that Reynolds thought she was either one hell of an attractive lady or a suspect. His eyes kept coming back to her. The look on his face, though, wasn't that of someone studying a violent offender.

She tried to see in herself what he was seeing. The towel covered her hair, but her skin was a light golden color. She was fresh from the shower so no make-up. Even she could smell the faint aftermath of vanilla and green tea from her soap and shampoo. There were small gold earrings peeking out from the edges of the towel and a modest gold cross hung on a delicate chain was around her neck. The high cheekbones gave her face structure. Her eyes were elfin in shape and green. They were a true, emerald green, clear with only a hint of gold, and framed with thick dark lashes.

She stood around five-feet, three inches tall and all of hundred and ten pounds. Although she was slight, it was all muscle. Most men commented that she was put together nicely. The robe was a peachy pink color and short. It didn't do a lot to cover her legs. She had to keep tugging at the collar to keep from showing off other parts of her anatomy that were interesting to the male of the species.

Although he was trying to be professional, he was having a hard time not staring at her. She also saw him look at her left hand for a ring. She decided she needed to say something since she was getting uncomfortable.

"Sorry. Beth, the nurse who was supposed to relieve me, was late. I have a date tonight."

Detective Reynolds again took the lead, "Where do you work?"

"At Arlington General in the emergency room."

"How long have you been there?"

"Two and a half months. I have another two weeks left on my contract."

"Contract?" His eyebrows rose questioningly. His eyebrows were just this side of bushy. A little more hair and he would have twin caterpillars over his eyes to match his mustache. Reynolds had nice eyes, warm brown in color. He reminded her of someone. She knew she had never met him but he really looked familiar. Why did she care? He wasn't here to make friends or set up a play date.

"I'm a traveler. My specialty is trauma and acute care. The hospitals contract with my company for certain time periods to help cover units when they have a shortage. Since emergency rooms and ICU's require specialty training, I get to travel a lot. I usually cover for vacations or a leave of absence. They need the help, but don't want to hire anyone full time. It saves money because I don't get any of their benefits and except for a minimal orientation, they don't have to train me. I'm covering for one of the nurses on maternity leave."

She looked at them with a half-smile, "But you're not here about my working arrangements." She wondered why they were here. If they were it was about Moody, the only way they could have gotten to her apartment this fast was if they had a tip. A very specific tip. In everyone's life there will be a Judas moment when you know, in your gut, that someone has betrayed you. The desert fiasco could have been a fluke, but add this and it screamed traitor.

"No, there was a shooting. We're questioning anyone who might have seen anything."

"Was the person who got shot someone who lived in this building?"

"No one here. It was Congressman Moody. You may have heard of him. He was shot as he came out of the courthouse. If you don't mind Detective Watts will take a quick look around while we talk."

"Sure, go ahead, just don't mind the mess." She knew she had the right to refuse, but if she cooperated maybe they would believe nothing was wrong and leave her alone. Yeah, like that would really happen. A case like this could make or break a career.

Watts headed to the small kitchen area and started canvassing the apartment. Not that there was much left they hadn't already seen. She blushed when he walked into the bedroom and glanced at the floor. The rest of her underwear was in plain sight.

"I may have seen his name in the news. I've been working extra shifts so I haven't watched much TV. I usually only look at the Sunday paper or one of the national newspapers. I'm not from here so I don't relate to a lot of the local stuff. If he was shot at the courthouse, why are you looking here?"

She wasn't lying. She rarely watched TV or followed the local news. It was always better to stick with the truth. You didn't get tripped up that way. Some of the annoyance she was feeling started to leak into her voice. Not enough to increase suspicion but a normal response to someone who had police nosing around their apartment without a reason. Someone who was trying to get ready for a big date and was already running late. Didn't hurt that most of that was true.

"It was a fairly long-range shot. Still in range for most rifles. We think the shooter may have been on the roof. This is one of the few buildings that has a clear sight line to the courthouse. Did you hear anything or see anyone unusual either when you left for work or got home? Any strangers been hanging around before today that you may have noticed?"

"I got in the shower as soon as I got home. I didn't meet anyone in the building as I came through. In fact, it was really quiet, no TV's or any other noises for that matter." Which was unusual. If she hadn't been in such a rush, she would have noticed the lack. No children lived in the apartments but there was always ambient noise from the people who lived there. "As for strangers, I don't know a lot of people here. You would be better off asking the other tenants about that. I haven't noticed anyone who set off any alarms."

"What time did you get home?"

It didn't take Watts long to check the apartment. Gee, what a surprise, no one else was there.

"It was seven-thirty. I remember glancing at my watch because I was running so late. It's some kind of special deal, and I needed to be ready on time. Plus, I was hoping we'd have time to stop for something to eat. It's been a long day and I'm starving. My date should be here anytime. Speak of the devil," her voice trailed off as there was knocking at her door.

"Rachael, it's me." There was the snitch of the key and the door swung open. Jon Masters stepped in. She felt a spike of anger that he used a key to get in. She had never given him one.

Seeing the two men, he strode into the room, becoming the center of attention as always. When Jon entered a room, it was as if all the air had been sucked out with the light and then rearranged to gather around him. "What's going on Rach?"

He moved in to stand close by her side. It was obvious he was letting the two men know who she belonged to. At least in his mind. Some men just had to mark their turf. At least Jon was well trained enough not to raise his leg and pee. It was simply implied. She knew she was being catty, but something in Jon always brought out the worst in her.

"Jon, these are Detectives Reynolds and Watts.

There was a shooting today. They're canvassing the area. This is my fiancé Jon Masters."

You're investigating the Moody murder?"

"That's right. You know this how?" For some reason, Reynolds looked a little ticked off at the way Masters had walked in as if he owned the place and the lady in it.

"I do some consulting work with the city and your Chief called to ask me to take a look at it."

Detective Watts chimed in, "Jon Masters of Godfrey's International Securities?"

"That's us."

Rachael felt uncomfortable in her towel and short robe with all the testosterone floating around her. Self-consciously, she put her hand up again to steady the towel around her head. She was careful to hold the cuff of the robe in her hand so the sleeve didn't slide down. "Is there anything else you need? I don't mind answering your questions, but could I take a minute to change?"

Reynolds turned back to her. "I think we have everything we need for now. Would you mind coming down to the precinct tomorrow to fill out a report?"

"If that helps you, I'll be glad to. But I didn't see anything so I don't know how that will help." That was true in a way, she hadn't been watching herself. Picky but true.

"Just routine," Reynolds hedged. He really didn't

have anything but his gut was telling him he needed to dig deeper into Ms. Cade.

"Um, where's the precinct?"

Jon laughed, "I'll get you there. Rach can get lost in her living room. Her flight instructor used to say that by teaching her to fly he just taught her how to get lost faster and further than anyone else he knew."

Rachel blushed. It was true for the most part, but she always found where she needed to go. She knew Jon was adding another layer to her story to establish her innocence, but it still grated on her nerves. She smiled as if laughing at herself, "Unfortunately he's telling the truth, I'm the world's worst at finding my way around. What time do you need me there tomorrow?"

"Some time after lunch will be fine. We can show ourselves out."

Jon waited until they left and had time to get away from the door.

"Well, that went well," as he watched her head to the bathroom to finish getting dressed. "I assume you covered your ass as well as usual. Although I will admit what you have on is barely doing a lot in the coverage area." He paused, "Good thinking on your part. Show a little leg and breast, and most men forget what they were here to question you about."

"Sometimes you're a real pig. I didn't do it deliberately. This is the only robe I own." Something she was apparently going to have to correct by getting a more modest one with better coverage. She shook her head angrily which caused the towel on her head to finally fall off.

"I don't like it. I'm never involved in an investigation. My name never comes up because I'm smoke, puff, not there. That's the way I want it. This is also the first time I've had a target here in the states. They got here awfully quick. It's as if they knew exactly what apartment to come to. If I didn't know better, I would say they were directed here. This is the second time my location has been compromised."

"The boss wants you involved in this op for some reason. I'm with you. I don't see any reason for it. It's a hit that could have easily been disguised as an accident. This is your tenth mission. No one knows about you because you've never hit anyone in the States. You'd think he'd like to keep it that way."

Jon started pacing and thinking out loud. "You do have a valid point though. They did get here very quickly. They would have interviewed everyone when they found out what building the shot came from as a matter of course. That would have been the end of it. I wonder how these two detectives knew to hone in on you in less than forty minutes from the time Moody was shot. They had to be in the area and know where they were going to get here that fast. Logistics would have played into a longer delay time in just answering the call. They didn't have time to have stopped by the crime scene. They came straight here."

Rachael shrugged her shoulders. "The boss usually has a reason for doing what he does. He may know something we don't. Which is usually the way it goes. I just don't think he thought I would be looked at so closely. I have a pretty good alibi. You could juggle the times around and speculate that I could have made the shot and got back here in the given time frame. Without proof you'd have a hard time making it stick. Getting nailed at one pick up point can be a coincidence. Me, I'm the suspicious type. Two times and I'm thinking we have a traitor."

Jon looked at her thoughtfully. "You may be right. I'll look into it. We need to get going since I know you want something to eat before we get there."

"So, you are getting to know me. Do you know where I go from here? I only have two weeks left on this contract."

Sometimes he surprised her, she knew he was intelligent but he didn't often come off as warm and caring. Her fault really, she hadn't tried to get to know him as anything more than the assignment required. She had never really cared for him all that much at some deep-seated level she didn't understand. The engagement was a cover for work, nothing more.

"So far nada. You need a few weeks off. I know

there's a break between assignments, but you work your butt off at the hospitals in between."

"Maybe that's my Saving Grace."

Rachael retreated to her bedroom and got ready to go out. She didn't know the person who picked out her clothes for special events, but she wished they did all her shopping. Her regular wardrobe consisted of scrubs, jeans and shirts with a few dressier items for church and such.

The dress on her bed was a slim sliver of dark bronze silk that covered her like a glove. It was slit up the side to allow for movement. It showed off her curves in all the right ways. The color also brought out golden highlights in her hair and eyes. The straps were made up of fake gems that were the same color as the dress. Her only jewelry other than a totally ridiculously large diamond engagement ring were two bronze cuffs that covered her wrists. The only problem with it was no place she could hide a weapon. Don't even think about a thigh holster. Chaffing anyone?

Rachael put her hair up. The copper-colored sticks she used to keep her hair in place could double as weapons. Then she added jewelry and the matching pair of shoes. Looking at the shoes, she hoped she didn't have to run anywhere tonight. The heels added two inches to her height. Rachael had laid down the law against anything higher. She was a nurse not a performer who walked on stilts.

One last look in the mirror and she returned to the living room area where Jon was waiting. As usual he was busy with his phone. She wondered idly if he was really working or playing one of those silly games. Then again, Rachael couldn't imagine Jon just doing something for fun. He looked up as she stepped into the room.

"How do I look?"

"Beautiful as always. You take my breath away sometimes. Let's go dazzle the clients. We have a meet with the boss after the gala. Maybe then you'll get your answers."

She smiled at Jon uncertainly. He surprised her once in a while with the way he responded to her. They only had a working relationship, but sometimes he made it sound personal. Hidden under her seemingly gruff exterior, she was actually very shy. Assertive only when she was at work, she said very little at social engagements. Crowds bothered her, and she usually was unsure about what to say.

It served her well most of the time. She was a good listener which was a plus because everyone loved to have somebody who seemed interested in their conversation. Considering they were on the way to some major function, she guessed she'd get to do a lot of listening tonight.

3

“lways look deeper than the beauty on the outside.” Unknown

REYNOLDS LOOKED over at his partner as they left the apartment. “What are you thinking?”

Sam Watts shook his head in frustration. “Don’t know. Is it even possible for a woman to be a sniper? She’s awful petite to hold some large sniper rifle.”

Reynolds “Was your head up your ass during sexual harassment training? Haven’t you heard. Isreal has a whole team of women snipers. Don’t let her size fool you. I’ve known some pretty tough women. And it doesn’t feel right. Seems fishy that Masters would just happen to show up when we were canvassing the building. Add that to the fact Cade was the only person in that apartment complex who was home. What are the odds? The tip to check this building first was just too good to be true. Have they been able to trace who sent it?"

"That'll take a while. Hunting down IP addresses and then finding where they are rerouted from is a bear. It was timed perfectly. Too late to save the Congressman and left us just enough to catch the shooter if he was still here. She would have been hard pressed to get home from work, shoot Moody and take a shower. She admitted to the date and that someone should be there soon. I don't know too many women who can get ready for a date in under an hour."

"The stuff was on the bed for her night out. I'm not a fashion expert, but it was a killer dress. My wife would sell one of our kids to be able to wear something like that. The apartment was clean. No sign of Masters ever staying over if you get my drift. You have to take into consideration she was cooperative. She didn't even blink when I went into the bedroom. The only time she blushed was when we saw her clothes on the floor."

Watts continued, "Masters will be easy enough to check out. If they've been an item for a while, it'll be known. Lady's got an alibi if her story's true. It's not airtight. Close enough though. A lawyer could create doubt. With her looks, she'll have the jury thinking there's no way such a petite, pretty lady would do such a thing. You can bet the lawyer would play that angle up."

"If she didn't do it, maybe somebody has it in for her. Of course, that would also mean she has made an enemy who has a big hard on to hurt her. Taking out a Congressman just to get even with someone is pretty drastic. They would have needed the information to know if she would be home. Nurses work over their shift a lot."

Reynolds thought as they headed for the car. "Well, we've all seen some pretty hairy domestic murders. Just doesn't work for me. They would have had to know she would be home in time to get ready for a date. If she had worked her usual shift, she would still have been at work. Someone knew she was supposed to get off early. No way could they've anticipated her running late. At least that takes one person off the suspect list. If this Beth was in on it, she wouldn't have run late. She wouldn't chance screwing the whole thing up. No ring."

Watts was startled by the sudden change in topic, "What do you mean?"

"She wasn't wearing an engagement ring. With a high-powered boyfriend like that you'd think she'd have a rock on her finger."

"Maybe they aren't formally engaged yet or she doesn't wear it at work. My aunt's a nurse. She doesn't wear her engagement ring, just the band. I was there when she and her husband got in a big fight about it. She told him it gets banged up on bed rails and stuff and tears the gloves when she goes to put them on. They also can scratch the patients. Not to mention the germs. She won the argument by telling him she'd wear it, and when she lost the setting he could go through the dirty laundry, or buy her a bigger rock."

"Okay, makes sense. Just never really thought about it. She doesn't look like your run of the mill assassin." His mind was telling him she wasn't a run of the mill anything. "I don't know why she rang my bell."

"I noticed you were paying very close attention. I think she was ringing more than your bell." Watts waggled his eyebrows at his partner. "You've never looked so interested in a suspect before. I've never known you to be wrong about if someone's guilty or not, but I can't see it this time. You sure it's not something else that's got your spidery sense in an uproar?"

Reynolds was slightly troubled that his partner had caught his fascination with Cade. He simply mumbled a reply and kept on walking. He didn't see Watts grin as he followed his friend out. His partner rarely dated. The one woman that he kept going back to was bad news. It would nice to see him find a nice lady to care about. If she wasn't guilty and that was a big if.

She was a nurse. Cops and nurses usually made

good pairs. They both had weird hours and met unusual people. Unfortunately, it looked like this one was already taken. Be a real shame if she was guilty. A boyfriend could be worked around. A prison sentence for murder would be a deal breaker.

4

"Isn't odd that when people say 'It's an omen,' whether good or bad, the word has 'men' in it? It is also strange that the only difference between omen and Amen is an o and a." Linda P. Duncan

THE LIMO WAS WAITING for them outside the building. That's the way it was when Jon was in charge. Everything in its place. Everyone on time. He was so meticulous it drove her crazy. Everyone needed a little mess in their life. She supposed it was necessary for someone in their world to be anal retentive about the details. After the op was planned, she was more of a wing-it type of girl. Maybe it was a good thing she usually worked alone.

It was probably the reason why they would never have made it as a couple if it had been the real thing. She would never ever stay in her 'place.' Rachael drove Jon crazy with her unpredictability as much as he got on her nerves with his schedules and rules. It was a good thing their engagement was simply for cover.

It gave them both a reason to be in locations they wouldn't normally be if it weren't for each other. The ploy was used most of the time for Jon's sake because assassination was a last resort. There was also the fact that most of her agency work took place where people didn't ask too many questions on the how or why someone got shot. It was just the way business was taken care of. Her jobs at the hospitals were usually arranged for his convenience. Sometimes, rarely like today, it was to cover her activities.

Rachael still wasn't a happy camper. She was so far under the radar that she never even made a blip. Now for some reason someone wanted to make her light up like a Christmas tree on steroids. As they drove up to the hotel, she noted all the lights and photographers. This so didn't look good. "How big an event is this?

"Big enough that there is significant press coverage."

"I don't like having my picture taken. The less I'm known the better."

Jon smiled lazily at her. "Get used to it. I'm big news. The rich eligible bachelor that works for the government, according to my family, in a low paying clerk job.

Since we're engaged, everyone's wondering if I'm going to finally go home to the corporate nest and take my place in the home business. Everyone hopes I'll see the light and want to settle down with my wife and enlarge the family. Since you're the one I'm engaged to, that makes you big news."

"Have trouble getting your ego through the door much?" she muttered under her breath. God, sometimes he was so self-important. She wasn't being fair. Jon's family was ridiculously rich and had tried everything they could to get him to toe the family line. They would have cut off all his money if it hadn't been protected under a trust from his grandfather. A grandfather who had been a man who thought his grandson had balls because he didn't try to do every thing he could to inherit the family fortune. Of course, the fact that he was the only male child in this generation hadn't colored things.

Rachael had met his parents. She knew they didn't like her. They had nothing personal against her. Not much anyway. Although her parents had left enough money for her to be comfortable, she didn't meet their lofty standards of what it took to be wealthy. They thought the only reason she was after Jon was for his money. Their desire was for him to bring home a bride that would add to the family coffers and influence. It was probably in the back of their minds that if Jon decided to go into politics his working for the government might make good political fodder. He needed a wife who could meet their high social standards to add to the shine.

She never understood why people who had more money than they knew what to do with always thought they needed more? Besides what century where they living in? At least in the good old USA dowries were a thing of the past. All things considered, Jon hadn't turned out so bad. At least he had opted out to try to do something with his life other than world dominance through finance, or worse, be a playboy.

Rachael made a face that showed her displeasure. "I thought this charade was so we could stay under the radar, not on it."

Jon made a put-upon face in return. She knew he didn't like it when she didn't act like he was 'God's Gift' to women. "Sometimes the best way to hide is right in front of everyone's nose. If you're right out in the public's face, they don't look at you for the murder around the block because in their collective minds, you have a built-in alibi."

"I've never needed an alibi. I never get questioned... at least up until now."

"Well, I guess the boss or someone else wants that to change. You're supposed to save him a dance tonight so he can speak with you."

"The boss can dance? I hate dancing. I have the rhythm of a rock. It'll be murder in these shoes. What is it with people in the fashion industry? Do they go out of their way to make shoes and clothes uncomfortable? Why can't we use tonight to have a big public break up?"

"Quit being so grumpy. I don't think that would go down well with the powers that be. You know, if you would relax, we could both get a lot of side benefits out of this relationship."

"Sorry. I'm hungry, and you know I get cranky when I'm hungry. The answer to your implied question is I'm old fashioned enough to think you need to care about someone before you have sex with them."

"I didn't say anything about sex. You care about me. I'm a member of the team. One for all and the rest of the code."

"It's always about sex with you. You're a man after all." The comment really wasn't fair. Actually, it was tacky thing to say. An apology was owed She liked men for the most part. She really needed to get some food. The traffic was horrendous. The police still had the streets blocked off due to the assassination. They hadn't been able to stop for something to eat as planned due to the congestion.

"Sorry, sorry, I'm just cranky due to lack of food. Caring about you as part of the team means I'm willing to cover your back. Die for you and protect you, not live for you. Or sleep with you for that matter."

"There's a difference?"

"The fact that you don't understand that there is a difference is why we have a problem."

Whatever his reply would have been was halted by the door opening. The valet waited for them to get out. Apparently, they were holding up the parade. Neither of them had noticed that they had stopped. They had run out of time, and she was going to have to wait on getting nourishment.

"Show time, darling. Think about it. I could make you a happy woman. Smile and try to look happy. I'm not all that bad a person to be with."

She answered under her breathe, as the valet assisted her out of the car, "No, you're not. Just not the person for me."

The flashbulbs started as soon as she stepped onto the red carpet. This was the first time they had gone to a big event together. Even though his family consider his job to be beneath him, he was actually second in command in one of the most powerful agencies to come along since the war on terrorism started. Add that to being the scion of a disgustingly rich family and being well off in his own right made him the darling of yellow journalism.

The need to pay more attention when Jon told her about her social obligations was another minus in their relationship. So far, they had just been small parties and social get-togethers. No biggy. Just needed to smile and pretend to listen. Sometimes she noted the glares from the women who wanted to be the one on Jon's arm. Little did they know they could have him on a silver platter. At least as far as she was concerned.

Jon Masters was considered a real catch. Even she had to admit he was great eye candy. Six-feet-four inches tall with a toned body. A body that she knew for a fact was as great as the outside packaging advertised. They had trained together, worked together and been on missions together. Which meant she had seen him in the buff. It was a nice buff. Blonde hair and laser blue eyes finished the picture. He was a romance cover looking for a place to happen. He was the total package, looks, money, privilege, and power. Unfortunately, he didn't do a thing for her.

Rachael flashed back to Detective Reynolds. Now there was a man who looked like he might be interesting. Her next thought was why she had thought about him in the first place. It could be the feeling she knew him from somewhere, but she would have remembered.

"Your mind just left the building. Am I that bad?" Jon commented as they finally entered the hotel.

"I do like you, but what you want takes more than like." Well, she hedged a little on that replay, she really didn't like him. Didn't know the reason. Just had a weird feeling about him. "Why are we having this conversation now anyway?"

"The difference is the reality. I know I'm not. Right now, that's the way I want to keep it. You are part of the job, not part of my life." Rachael knew her tone was combative, but she couldn't help herself. Her usual self-assurance was taking a hit. Besides that, she was hungry.

They made their entrance. A waiter led them to a table that was on the back wall. They made a great couple. Her dark hair a foil for his light. She made him look even taller and handsomer. He made her look smaller and more fragile. Looks could be so deceiving. Only someone who was watching closely and knew what to look for would notice how they scanned the room like predators. They both located all the exits with one sweep of their gaze. Their awareness of the where and what of their environment went against being just another loving couple out on a date.

A waiter offered them drinks when they were seated. She noticed there were only two flutes still left. Rachael reached for whatever was on the tray. She smiled a thank you and pretended to sip on the flute of champagne. Neither one of them drank.

If you didn't open a fresh bottle and pour it yourself, you could never be sure it was safe. Even then you still had to be careful. It was better if it had never been out of your sight. The fact that only two choices had been available was a red flag. Even if she was dying of thirst, she wouldn't have considered drinking anything offered to her. Not to mention they were technically on duty and drinking was a no-no. Paranoia at its best.

"What is this shindig for anyway?"

"I told you." Irritation spiked in his voice. "It's the first party to kick off the President's re-election bid. He's been getting some flak from his party because he hasn't taken the time to campaign. They want him to get out and press the flesh so to speak." Jon didn't like it when she ignored him.

Rachel smiled at knowing she could get under his skin.

"Tsk. Tsk. Such a bad president to focus on the war and the economy instead of trying to win votes. He might actually set a good example. Whatever is he thinking? So, I guess I get to dance with both the President and the boss tonight." Oh, happy day.

"Most women would be thrilled to dance with the President."

"I'm not most women. Actually, I like the man. I even voted for him."

"You vote?"

"You don't? Mostly by absentee ballot, but yes, I vote and go to church. As the saying goes, I believe in the Bible and Uncle Sam."

"Where did they find you? Under a rock somewhere?"

"Just because I do normal things doesn't mean I don't have the skills to do my job." She was getting testy. Again.

"I saw the body. You definitely can do your job. I

wish you would be as efficient at being my fiancé as you are at everything else."

"What is your problem? You're not a priest or a monk. I'm not depriving you of anything."

"Yes, you are. I don't like having to sneak around for sex or pay for it. Since we are an item, the agency says I can't date or screw up our cover. You don't want to play. So yes, I do have to live like a monk."

Talk about getting testy. Jon must have a lot of frustration building up. She knew he had been a real player before the 'engagement' had taken place. He must be close to the end of his patience because he usually was as reticent about his true feelings as she was.

"I'm sorry, Jon. Talk to the boss. We both want out of this fake engagement. I'm sure they can find a cover for your travels that doesn't include me." She really meant it. Jon had a right to a life of his own.

"What makes you think I want out of this engagement?" he muttered under his breathe.

Rachael gave him a startled look. Surely, he wasn't falling for her. More than likely it was because she hadn't jumped into bed with him while singing "God Bless the King," for the privilege. The way most of the women around him did. She was saved from answering as the President and the First Lady entered the room. She had noted the Secret Service making a sweep of the room while they were talking.

The President had aged since she had seen him last.

He looked more care-worn. The lines in his face ran a little deeper. His hair was a little grayer. Why anyone would want the grief that went along with being President was a cosmic mystery to her. The man was more in the distinguished category, than out right handsome. He had kind eyes and more laugh lines than frown on his face.

The First Lady looked the same as she always had. She looked like you wished your grandmother would. Motherly, neat, her grey-blonde hair cut in a short bob and maybe five or ten pounds' overweight. She had warm blue eyes, a wicked sense of humor and honestly cared for the people around her. The agents that made up her protection detail would die for her even if she wasn't the President's wife. Rachael felt this was more of a statement of her character than any press release.

President Blair and his wife made an attractive couple as they went out on the floor for the first dance. After a few seconds, others headed for the dance floor and joined them in a waltz. Jon pulled Rachael up and tugged her to him.

Jon was a good dancer and made it easy for her to follow, despite the difference in their heights. He held her too close, but it was part of the façade of them being in love. She wished it was true. If their engagement had been the real thing, Jon was the epitome of the fairy tale relationship. He looked the part of someone who could sweep you off your feet. Unfortunately for both of them, she was way too balanced to let his looks fool her. There wasn't a happily ever after in their relationship. They ended the dance in close proximity to the presidential couple. Leave it to Jon, he always had a plan.

After the formalities were over for the meet and greet, Mary Blair took the lead and gave Rachael a squeeze and patted Jon on his arm. "I think I'll dance with the second handsomest man here tonight. You dance with Rachael, and all the men will be jealous."

William Blair laughed at his wife, "I'm assuming I'm the most handsome then?"

"Of course, Dear, as long as you believe I'm the most beautiful woman. Off you go."

The President's arm encircled Rachael's waist and led her into an old-fashioned two-step. "You do look wonderful tonight. I don't think I've ever seen you in anything except jeans or camouflage."

"Thank you, Sir. Just wish you were the one wearing these heels. The only thing they might be good for is if I had to use them for a weapon. Unfortunately, I'd only get to use them once. They might make a good torture device. You could recommend them to the CIA. If anyone had to walk around in these for a few hours, they'd be begging to talk."

The President snorted out a laugh at her comment. "You're the only woman I know who would make a comment about using a fashion accessory as a weapon. Plus, consider all the pros and cons. I'm sure the CIA can come up with enough torture ideas on their own. I thought all women thought shoes were to die for. My wife has a closet full of them and she's usually not stuck on fashion."

"Talking to the wrong girl here, sir. I come from a state where most people assume we only wear shoes in the wintertime. I have running shoes, my nursing shoes, combat and cowboy boots, and a pair to wear to church. They take up enough room in the closet. What else do I need?"

"I can picture you as a grubby little kid running around in cutoff jeans and no shoes. It suits your personality. But I did need to talk to you. Good job today, by the way." He sighed, "Not among my favorite orders to give, but it was necessary. I would have preferred to have it go down somewhere besides here in the states. Unfortunately, he had no plans for travel in the near future. Moody had to be stopped. I tried every political means to hamstring his flow of information, but nothing worked. I don't know who his source is, but it's golden. If we don't find it soon, we may all go down in flames."

"Always ready to do what you need to keep the country safe. Sir, if I may ask, why didn't they want it to look like an accident? Not my ball of wax, but it would have been a lot less of a circus."

"Your boss decided a message needed to be sent. Let them know we know about them. That sort of thing. He hopes to make them nervous enough to make a mistake."

"If anyone can find the traitor, it'll be him. I just hope this doesn't come back and bite him on the ass."

"You and me both, child. How is the engagement going?"

"You know it's just for show. No real feelings going on."

"That's what I heard, but you two fit so well together. We hoped maybe a spark might happen."

"No spark on my part Sir."

"Why not? According to Mary, he's a catch."

"You know when you eat cold watermelon and the first taste is heaven, the second's good and then it's like your taste buds lose interest? That's what is wrong with Jon. He's nice eye candy. No staying power in the interest department. Not in my wheelhouse anyway."

"Well, I guess that's one explanation I've never heard. It must have southern roots. I need a favor from you."

"Whatever you need."

"There have been some threats made against Mary. I would appreciate it if you would become part of her protection detail."

Rachael felt a flicker of anger go through her. She had only met the First Lady a few times and she liked what she had seen and heard about her. Why did people always want to ruin the few good things in the world was a mystery to her. "I would be more than happy to, but the Secret Service is more adept at that than me. I'm usually the type of person they guard against."

The President's lips twitched in a slight smile as he answered, "I realize that, but you have a creative way of solving problems that they don't have."

"How do we work it so no one will be suspicious of me being around her?"

"You need to remember that threatening to kill the president is a federal crime, when you hear the favor. As you know, we only had boys. She's missed being able to plan a wedding." He sighed, "She always wanted a little girl, but after the fourth boy we called it quits."

"I imagine if you had a girl, she'd be spoiled rotten. She wouldn't have stood a chance between daddy and four older brothers. Dating would be a nightmare. What about adoption?"

"You're probably right about that. I had started into politics, and we didn't think that it was a good time to add raising another child at that point. Maybe after my presidency we could think about adopting. That will be an issue in the future and we need something to work with now."

Rachael didn't like where this conversation was heading. "I don't plan on marrying Jon. I will do most anything for you and my country, but I'm not marrying someone I don't love." The President could pick up on the strain in her voice.

"I won't force you to go through with it, but it will make her happy to plan things. It will give you a reason to stay with her. I mentioned to her that your parents are gone and the main reason you haven't tied the knot yet is you're both too busy with your jobs."

The song came to an end, and they walked back to Jon and the First Lady. There was an aide that Rachael hadn't seen before with them.

Mary met them with a smile. "I am so glad we saw you two tonight. I was telling Jon how much I would love to help you with your wedding plans. It's so exciting!"

Jon just smiled at the First Lady as he handed her off the President. His eyes cut to Rachael, warning her to go with the flow.

"We really haven't set a date yet. I don't have any family, so it isn't going to be a large wedding," Rachael answered cautiously.

"I know dear. That's why you need me. The Rose Garden will be the perfect size and we'll be your family. Will can give you away."

"I don't know. You have so many other things that need your attention. Besides I don't know how I'd ever be able to thank you." Just great. Now the President was getting in on the act. If he didn't quit grinning, she was never going to vote for him again. Ever. She sent him a glare under lowered eyelids and he just grinned harder. Bastard.

"My thanks will be getting to plan it. I have people who are paid to take care of planning what I need to do. They can take care of their jobs. I'll do what makes me happy. In fact, Jon says your contract at the hospital is up in two weeks and you'll lose your apartment. You can come stay with us. We can plan this together. It will be such fun. You'll see. I always wanted a daughter. Now I won't have to wait for my granddaughters to grow up. That is if I ever have any. My sons seem to be following in their parents' footsteps and have had only boys so far."

Rachael was thinking more on the lines of root canal excitement as she struggled to keep a pleasant look on her face. Some people had the weirdest idea of a good time.

The aide sketched out a faint smile in Mrs. Blair's direction. "Sounds like great fun," he added.

What a dynamo. He really needed to learn to keep his enthusiasm under control, not. Actually, that wasn't being fair. To be in his position as the President's chief aide, he had to be good at his job. He touched the President's arm to get his attention, "You need to circulate some now, Sir. We still have three more stops to make."

The President turned in her direction. "Rachael, I don't think you've met Jeff Cody. He took Sam's place when he had to leave." Cody had mouse brown hair that was cut impeccably. Looked like he went to the gym enough to get in shape and wore the appropriate formal tux. He would blend in almost anywhere. He's eyes were arctic blue behind fashionable glasses. For some reason his way of looking at everyone present reminded her of a snake watching his next rat dinner parade by.

Rachael held out her hand for him to shake. "Nice to meet you." She knew as soon as he touched her hand that he was wrong. She could feel the animosity he felt toward the President. It gave her cold chills.

Outwardly he appeared to be pleasant and unobtrusive, as most of the aides around Washington seemed to be. You can't outshine your boss. In this climate, that would be political suicide. Inside he was seething with hate. The kind of hatred born of fanaticism.

Sometimes Rachael couldn't understand how people couldn't feel what she did. The hatred was rolling off of him in waves. She would have to warn the boss about him. His control had to be phenomenal. Anyone who was carrying around that much hostility should have made a mistake by now. That kind of attitude is difficult to hide.

"I'll be in touch with you, dear, so we can talk about the wedding. I understand you don't even have a dress yet," the First Lady trilled on.

"No, I haven't really had time to think about it." Rachael was starting to panic.

The President took his wife's hand, "Come on dear. We need to go make nice. Don't badger the girl. Let them enjoy their date." They left with Cody following in their wake like a small tugboat. A tugboat with torpedoes hidden under the deck boards.

"I see you've found out about your new assignment." Rachael and Jon turned to Don Wilson, the boss, the real head of the security firm. He was difficult to describe. When they put nondescript and average in the dictionary, they were describing Don Wilson. He simply blended into the background. You never realized he was there. It was like his super power. This chameleon-like trait that had made him lethal as an agent and one that led others to underestimate him in the arena of power.

Meeting Rachael's eyes, he offered her his arm and led her out on the floor for a dance. Her heart rate went up slightly. She hoped he didn't notice. She had been in love with him since the day he showed up at her door and offered her a job. There was no way she would let him know that fact. He would never act on it if she did.

"I won't be able to meet with you later. For some reason, the police officers you met this afternoon are suspicious of you. They want to search your apartment. There's enough uproar over Moody's death that the judge gave them a warrant even though they really didn't have enough evidence to get one. Circumstantial or otherwise. We managed to keep them from serving it here or just busting in the door. Unfortunately, they are eagerly waiting for you to get home."

"They already did a walk through. I gave them permission to look when they got there. What is going on? You never want this kind of attention from the authorities. If I didn't live in that building, they never would have looked at me. How did they get to my apartment so fast after the shooting? You have to admit it looks suspicious. This is the second time I've been compromised."

"Those are all really good questions. There is a reason. I just can't tell you what it is at this time. We apparently have a leak. You have my word on it. We will find it. I knew you would be questioned eventually. There was no way to hide where the shot came from. Procedure dictated everyone in that building would be interviewed at some point. I actually thought they would just question you and leave it at that."

"It's what would have happened if it had been any other detective besides Reynolds. Somebody tipped them off that the shooter lived in your building, so he was already suspicious when he got there." He quickly scanned the dance floor to make sure no one had moved too close.

Wilson continued, "It's unfortunate that you were the only one home at the time of the shooting. Statistically there should have been more people around. It is odd that an entire building full of people all decided they needed to go somewhere. We may just have to ride this one out. You really don't fit the profile of a killer for hire."

"Thanks. I'll remember to put that on my next resume. What if they find something?"

"They won't. Benny went in as soon as you were gone and got your bag. I told him to enter and leave the building using the roof and make sure he left marks from the grappling hooks on the wall. Nothing too apparent, something that could have been missed in the first go over."

"He had to wait for the crime scene people to leave. So we used his wait time wisely."

"Broke into one of the apartments where the tenants were out of town. It'll look like someone used it to hide until time to do the job. Then took the roof way out to avoid any cameras. They will have to look elsewhere for their shooter. It's also enough to generate doubt if they try to press charges. It would be hard to prove that you could be in two places at the same time. This is partially my fault. I didn't think they would look that hard at you and didn't have a contingency plan in place. My bad."

"Haven't they already searched the roof?"

"Of course, but Eric Reynolds is a stubborn and thorough man. He's meticulous in his follow up. He'll send them back. It will look like they missed it the first time. Benny won't make it look that obvious. If he doesn't, the empty apartment thing will do the trick. I'll be willing to bet Reynolds is working on getting warrants to search all the apartments."

"That's going to be a little harder since all the regular tenants apparently have alibis of one sort or another. He will get ones for the empty apartments. Benny's red herring will fly. Besides I have another job for you and you'll have such an air tight alibi that he'll have to back off."

"Isn't it risky to pull off another job in the same town?"

"It won't be anything you can't handle. Let's change the subject."

"Before we do that, do me a favor and get someone to look into why everyone else was away. It's too coincidental that they were gone. If I had gotten off when I was supposed to, there wouldn't have been any doubt that I had the time to pull it off. Beth's running late may end up being the thing that saves me."

"I'll have Jon look into it."

"Use Tom Hinkley. He loves working on stuff like that. Puzzles are something he lives for. He owes me one. Tell him it's for me and you want it hush-hush. It'll make his day."

"Do I want to know what he owes you a favor for?"

"Nothing major. His little girl came in the emergency room with an asthma attack. I took care of her. Both she and her mother were freaking out. Tom had a deer in the headlights look of desperation. I got the mom calmed down. The girl was fine after a treatment. All in a night's work."

"I'll get him working on it. Changing the subject, remember."

"In what capacity am I to guard Mrs. Blair? If I'm part of the sniper detail it will only prove to Reynolds that I could have done it."

"You are simply to be with her and plan your wedding. Not many women get to live in the White House while planning their big day. Just go with it. You're a human lie detector. You'll know who's setting her up."

"Speaking of that. Cody hates the President with a fanatical vengeance. He wants to destroy him. Before you comment, I'm actually down grading the situation and not exaggerating. The vibes I felt were fierce. They were coming off of him in waves. I don't know how he's kept it together this long."

"It came through that strongly? He came up squeaky clean on all the background checks. I didn't care for him personally. Couldn't use that as a good enough reason not to hire him."

"I wouldn't hire anyone you didn't like, but that's just me. The man feels wrong. He's up to something. I don't see how everyone's missed it."

"The majority of us don't see things the way you do. Which is actually a good thing. I don't think most people could cope with knowing how other people really feel. My grandmother would say you had the 'sight.' I will look into it and give a heads up to the people around the President. Just enjoy your time with the First Lady."

"That's easy for you to say. You don't know how terrifying girl stuff can be." She changed the conversation's direction. "I won't marry Jon."

"If you keep Mrs. Blair safe and we catch whoever is threatening her, I will help you get out of the engagement gracefully. And you are a girl, so how bad could it be?"

"That's a big if. I won't marry Jon. You can take that to the bank. Is helping me get out of this engagement a promise? And the reason it's bad because I don't do 'girl' stuff well." Once Wilson gave his word it was solid. "The president told me I couldn't threaten him over this. You, I might make an exception."

Wilson laughed. "I promise. Although I am surprised. We all thought you two would hit it off. I think there's even an office pool on when the true engagement is announced. Seems to be a lot of money riding on it. Is there something I need to know about Jon?"

"No, I don't get anything off of him. Maybe that's the problem. I can't feel him. He's almost a null. He doesn't generate any vibes. Which in my case you think it would be a plus. It just doesn't go there. Sorry, I can't force an emotion I don't feel. He leaves me cold." Unlike the man holding her in his arms.

"Well, on that note, I need to leave. You do what you need to. Make nice with the detectives and make them go away."

"I'm not screwing with their heads. They're just doing their job."

"So are you. Moody was giving away secrets that needed to be kept. He got his hands on some plans that took over a year to put together. If he had managed to pass it on to his employers, we never may have been able to implement it. Your bullet will match the other thirteen. You know where that puts you."

"On death row if they find out who I am. The major reason I don't like working in the States is the attention. I'm happier working somewhere the forensics aren't that good. A lot of governments don't really care as long as the person getting knocked off is scum. I change the composition of the bullets for the job. There's no way to change the rifling. Speaking of which, make sure Benny takes care of my weapon."

"He's already cleaned it for you. We'll keep it locked up until you can check it out. He appreciates your concern for your equipment. Now go and try to have a good time. Just don't take too long and keep our detectives waiting."

Wilson left her with Jon and melted back into the crowd.

"What's up? I thought he wanted to meet later." Jon had expected Wilson to speak with him, personally. He just didn't like being left out of the loop. There were times when he was such a prima donna.

"There's been a change in plans. I have detectives waiting for me at home with a search warrant."

"That's not good."

"Tell me about it. I have a feeling they're not dropping in for tea and crumpets. Speaking of which, one dance to keep up appearances and then let's get out of here. We need to go get something to eat. I'm starving, and it's going to be a long night. Everyone might live longer if I'm in a better mood."

"You do know that's not funny coming from you?" Jon switched subjects, "So, we're now planning a wedding?" He tried to make it sound like he was teasing. Jon just didn't do light hearted well.

Rachael smiled as they moved across the floor in time to the music. "Over my dead body. Going to jail may be my way out. At least the fight over extradition might keep me alive for a couple of years. Then I could catch up on all the books I haven't had time to read. See, it can't be all bad news. I have options available."

"Am I that distasteful that going to jail would be a happier alternative?"

She sighed, "No, you're not, but there are times that killing you would seem like a viable course of action."

"Hey now, coming from you, that's not funny. If it

wasn't for that moral compass of yours, I think you would have been a stone-cold killer and would really enjoy your job."

"Don't worry. I haven't planned on it. Yet. You find a place that serves a good hamburger this hour of the night, and I might let you live."

Jon knew a little hole in the wall restaurant that served a great burger and wonderfully greasy fries. She decided for that alone he deserved to live a little longer. It wasn't crowded at that hour of the night. They relaxed in a back booth and enjoyed their food. They were a tad over dressed for the establishment, and drew a few glances. It was a toss-up if the women were more interested in Jon or her dress. It was a no brainer for the men. With the slit up the side, they just stared as she walked by. For once, there wasn't any tension between the two of them.

Apparently, Jon had decided to give their relationship issues a break. He even appeared amused at the male attention she was receiving. Her main concern was keeping all the yummy ingredients from dripping on her dress. She considered using the napkin as a bib and had a secret giggle at the reaction Jon would have for such an unrefined action. Whoever came up with a hamburger bun that didn't fall apart and still tasted good would make a fortune.

Rachael leaned against Jon's chest as they rode up in the elevator. He wrapped his arms around her waist and let her rest against him. She was tired. The emergency room had been a zoo. She had the trauma room. They had three gunshot wounds and a bad car wreck. Although she loved working with difficult cases, it was intense. At least it was when it was true trauma. A lot of emergency rooms had a lot more drama than trauma come through the doors.

Then throw in a small assassination and a meeting with the President, it made for a long day. A soft sigh escaped her as the doors opened. Jon actually gave her a small hug and smile in understanding. He wasn't all that bad. He had his moments. Just not enough of them to make a relationship worthwhile.

5

"Life's not fair. Get used to it." Unknown

REYNOLDS THOUGHT they made a nice-looking couple. The dress and jewelry made Cade look like a warrior princess forced to dress up. She also had all the earmarks of someone who was worn out. She was holding her shoes by the straps. He would place a bet they had come off in the car.

He leaned against the wall next to her apartment as he watched them walk toward him. She looked absolutely exquisite in the dress she was wearing. He knew she would look even more spectacular as it slid down her body onto the floor. He mentally smacked himself on the side of his head. The inappropriate thoughts he kept having about Cade were way too unprofessional. What was wrong with him? He was still in an on again/off again relationship with Lenore and he didn't need any more female angst in his life.

"To what do I owe this visit? I said I'd come down to the precinct tomorrow. Sorry, today."

"We're here to serve a search warrant."

Rachael just stood and looked at him, "What are you searching for?"

Jon tugged her back into him, "It's okay Rach. They want to search your apartment for any evidence that might help in their investigation."

"No, it's not alright, it's been a long day, and I'm tired." Her voice sounded huskier with fatigue riding behind it. "I let you look around when you came before. What else do you need?"

Reynolds straightened up. "I apologize. Your director at the hospital said you had a rough shift, but we have to follow all leads."

"And just what lead led you back to my apartment? I just happen to live under the roof this person used? You think he was hiding under my bed when you came to visit? Your partner checked the apartment. He didn't appear incompetent. What? So, living here makes me an accessory? Is everyone else in the building being searched or am I the lucky one?"

"Just let him in and let's get it over with," Jon advised her mildly.

"Fine!" Rachael unlocked the door and made a little bow to usher in the detective.

"May I change clothes before you start? I don't think this dress will hold up to sitting in the hallway half the night. You can have a female tech stay with me if you like. I will tell you there's a pistol in my bedside table. It's registered and I have a permit to carry. And before you ask, I do know how to use a gun. I am from Kentucky. My Dad started teaching me from the time I was strong enough to hold a weapon. He collected guns and wanted me to know about them. Besides all those pesky revenooers were such a problem." She added the last comment just for spite.

"Do much long-range shooting?" Reynolds headed to the bedside table she pointed out.

"Subtle, detective. Real subtle. I can't use a scope. I never can find the target with them. I don't know why, but I'm the same way with binoculars and microscopes. I shoot off-hand with open sites. I have to be able to see the target without magnification to hit it. Does that put me in the clear?"

Reynolds had secured the pistol and cleared it, but he didn't answer her question.

"I'm assuming since you told me before it was a long range shot that the man wasn't shot with a pistol."

"No. I guess I can tell you that much."

"You're such a fount of information, Detective. Now may I change?"

He nodded and a female tech followed her into the bedroom. She hung up the dress and took off the jewelry. The bronze bracelets that covered her wrists were really nice, she would have liked to keep them. She changed while the CSI oohed and gushed over the gown. She slipped into a pair of sweats that hung down on her hips and a muscle tee that showed off her waistline. Nothing but haute culture for her private wardrobe. She also slipped a pair of leather bracers over her wrists. It was easier than having to explain the scars that formed raised knots on her wrists.

"I'd like to get this junk off my face if it's okay to take the time, and it would probably be a good idea to pee."

The tech laughed, "Just let me check the bathroom and go ahead."

Rachael came out of the bedroom. She had let down her hair. It was more comfortable that way. She hadn't bothered with shoes and braided her hair as she walked to the kitchen to get a glass of water.

Reynolds watched her walk by. The outfit really showed what a small waist she had. What looked like part of a tattoo peeked out under the hem of the shirt. He thought his hands would almost go all the way around without any trouble. There went those inappropriate thoughts again. His head was getting sore from all the times he had to mentally smack himself. He had never had this much trouble detaching himself from a suspect. As a matter of fact, it had never happened before Rachael Cade had shown up at her door in that robe and towel. He had suspects who met him at the door without anything on and it left him cold. What was it about her that was so different? It definitely wasn't her sweet disposition.

"All yours, Detective. Have fun."

"It doesn't do any good to antagonize the police, Rach," Jon told her irritably.

"I'm not antagonizing them. I'm tired and all I want to do is get a cup of hot chocolate, read a few chapters in my book, and go to bed. If that makes me uncooperative, so be it." She headed out the door with what she hoped was her best flounce. There hadn't been many flouncing classes given at the agency. She had never managed to be adept at the girly arts. Tomboy had always been her style.

The officer at the door was young, and he tried not to stare as Rachael leaned against the wall and slid down into a sitting position.

Jon settled next to her. "I gotta say I like the gym punk look."

"Fuck you."

"I am forever hopeful."

Rachael just glared at him for a second and then

snorted out a short laugh. When he was right, he was right. As he grinned back at her she laughed out loud. Sometimes you took your grins and giggles where you could get them. She then leaned back her head and shut her eyes.

6

"I'm up. If you're expecting bright-eyed and bushy tailed, go catch a freaking squirrel." Unknown

REYNOLDS WAS NOT HAVING a good day. Everyone was riding his ass about the shooting. There were more alphabet agencies than he could count trying to horn in on his case. He had been held up over the warrant because the suspect was dancing with the President of the United States. The request that he wait for her to get home to serve the warrant had been more of an order than a recommendation. Now his techs were finding nothing, nada. They had kept the apartment under surveillance since he had gotten the warrant, so there was no way anyone could have snuck in or out without being seen.

There was a slight flurry of excitement when one of the techs found a storage area in the front closet hidden behind the clothes and coats. There was nothing in it but some good quality, well-worn pieces of luggage. A carrying case for a pistol, some boxes for books, but nothing else. The tech assured him that the panel hadn't been moved since Cade had moved in. Something about the dust patterns would have been disturbed if anyone had been in there recently. The apartment was small so it didn't take long to go through it all.

Why did he have such a hunch about the Cade woman? Usually, you could take his feelings to the bank. He had always had a bump that let him know when someone was lying. He knew without even touching them. She had been up front about having a weapon. Cooperative when they interviewed her the first time. When she got home tonight to the apartment, she didn't have enough on to hide anything. Watts was right about the killer dress. It covered everything and alluded to a lot. She wasn't even carrying a purse. All he got from this woman was a wall. Maybe that's why he was so sure she was wrong. He couldn't read her.

So far touching her hadn't come up. Not that touching her would be unpleasant. Okay, enough of those thoughts. He had enough problems in his personal life without adding to them. Up to now, he hadn't had very good luck with his choice of women and Cade didn't look like she would fit into the "easy keeper" category.

The techs were packing up their stuff. He stepped out into the hallway. Rachael had her head resting on Masters' shoulder. She appeared to be sound asleep. Masters was working on his smart phone. He looked up as Reynolds moved into the hallway.

"Done I presume."

"Yes, for now."

"I wouldn't push too hard in this direction if I was in your shoes," Jon added softly.

"Is that a threat?"

"No. Just an observation. I've heard about you. Everyone says you're a good cop. Rachael is well liked by some powerful people and unless you have some real proof, you're going to catch a lot of flak."

"I've been working in this town for a long time. I haven't let rank and privilege change how I work a case." His voice took on a hostile cast.

"Don't get your hackles up. I'm not telling you how to work your case. Just saying unless you have solid evidence to back you up, you may need to back off."

Rachael opened her eyes and stretched.

Jon knew she had been aware of Reynolds since he opened the door. The officer at the door almost had a seizure watching her shirt ride up with the stretch. The cop sighed when she dropped her arms before she showed anything but her stomach.

"So, are you done?" Her voice was surly as she stood up.

Like he said, sweetness and light were so dead on for her personality, not. "For now."

"Oh goody, so, I have more to look forward to?" She was almost snarling.

"Masters is right you know. It's not always a good thing to snarf off at the cops."

"Your fault."

"And why is that?"

"I don't see a cup of coffee with sugar and cream waiting in your hands. If you want to talk to me when I wake up, you better be prepared to get snapped at or have a cup of coffee waiting."

Jon rolled his eyes behind her back.

"I'll try to remember that." Unfortunately, that planted a niggling thought in his head about what it would be like to wake up with her in the morning. That deserved another imaginary slap to the side of his head. At this rate, Rachael Cade was really going to give him not only a headache, but a concussion to boot.

Rachael walked past Reynolds into her apartment. Everything was out of place. Her books had been rearranged and there was a dusting of fingerprint powder everywhere. They had even lost her place in the novel she was reading. The bookmark was lying at the end of the couch. Reynolds must have put out the word to the techs to make it as messy as possible. "Is there a cleaning crew that follows you around to do something about this mess?"

There was a sheen in her green eyes as she glared at him. Reynolds could tell she wasn't about to let him see her cry.

"Afraid you're on your own there. Sorry about the mess." He walked over and picked up her book and replaced her book mark. It was just a conciliated gesture. There was no way he'd know where she had left off reading. "I hate it when someone loses my place. I'm sorry we had to bother you."

"No, you're not. You're hoping you get on my last nerve and I'll say something to prove you right. You can put my gun back where you found it. It wasn't the weapon that was used. You have no legitimate reason to keep it. You people need to bone up on taking fingerprints. Finding my fingerprints here is totally worthless. I live here, so has umpteen nurses before me. No one's using powder anymore except back water police departments, which I had assumed yours isn't. You did it deliberately to make me pissed off. Be happy. You succeeded. Now. Go. Away." Rachael made her speech through clenched teeth.

"You'll get your pistol back when you come down to the precinct. We need to check it to see if it's been used in a crime. You seem to know a lot about police procedure for a nurse," he added.

"Knock yourself out." Taking a deep breath to try to control her temper, she continued. "You probably found my ID and badge. You know I'm an auxiliary sheriff's deputy at home." By now they were standing almost toe to toe. Even angry, he couldn't get a reading on her.

"I read a lot and that includes mysteries. You should try it sometime if your department doesn't keep you up to date on new procedures. You know my gun hasn't been used in a crime, but if it makes you feel righteous, go for it. Now leave." Rachael turned her back on him. She crossed her arms and was hugging them to her body as she looked at her apartment. There was no way she could stay here tonight.

Reynolds left, closing the door softly behind him. He listened at the door for a minute. It was thin enough to hear through.

"Rach, you know that wasn't smart."

"I don't care. This was done for spite. If this Moody person wasn't such a big deal, he never would have gotten a warrant to search my place. If the man wants to do his job that's all well and good, but this is out of bounds."

"You need to understand. You were the only one home when the shooting happened. That puts you high on the list of suspects." He hesitated for a few seconds and looked around. "So, what are you going to do? You can't stay here tonight."

"Your sofas available. It's either that or a hotel."

"You can have the bedroom. I'll take the couch."

"The couch will be fine. I'm shorter than you."

"If you didn't have such a strait-laced attitude toward premarital sex, we could both enjoy the bed."

"Not tonight, Jon. I'm tired. We both know that argument is going nowhere." Besides with his reputation who knew what was on those sheets.

"Go get your stuff. It's late." Jon's voice was sharp. Mr. Cool and Collected was losing his patience. It was nice to know she had that effect on others besides him.

Reynolds stepped away from the door. So, they weren't sleeping together. Cade was an old-fashioned girl or gay. No, he didn't get that feeling from her. Maybe he was wrong and she wasn't responsible for Moody's death. He also had a slight qualm on why the fact they weren't sleeping together made him happy.

These skewed thoughts he kept having about this woman was not like him. Nope a concussion wasn't in the cards, he was closer to subdural hematoma. He headed for his car. As he opened the door, his phone went off. It was Watts.

"Find anything?"

"Nada. What about you."

"Well, you want the good news or the bad news?"

"Give me the good first."

"Your girl definitely has the skills to be the shooter. She got a medal for saving her medical crew and patients in Iraq."

"How'd that happen?"

Watts told him the story. "She was on a medivac helicopter that was picking up casualties, and they were ambushed. They were losing power so the pilot set it down. Unfortunately, it was right in the middle of a small army of insurgents. One of the patients said it looked like a horde coming over the hill. The pilot was killed and the co-pilot and gunner were badly wounded. She stepped over the bodies and took over the machine gun. When she ran out of bullets, she picked up a rifle and started picking them off. One at a time. They were down to handguns and the witness said he thought they would be overrun but she just kept picking them off. The gunner said he heard one of the enemy soldiers say she was a demon and they wouldn't be able to kill her. Apparently, they were becoming scared due to the fact that every time there was a shot, someone went down.

The crew members still able to fight were down to less than four rounds a piece when one of our helicopters came over and finished off the rest of the insurgents. As soon as it was apparent that the fighting had stopped, she put the gun down. Went to work on the wounded. Ours and the enemies.

They reported she never said a word the whole

time. They checked her out, and she finished her tour. The head of the squad talked his commander into putting her in for a medal. She got a Silver Star and there was some noise about a Congressional. Basically, you're taking on a hero. The rumor is that the President's wife is going to plan her wedding because she doesn't have any family."

"What happened to her family?"

"Nothing sinister. She's an only child and her parents were killed in a car wreck. No grandparents, they died in their eighties. She had one uncle and he died young from some type of illness. He was in prison for a couple of years. Her parents were older when they had her, that's probably the reason she was the one and only.

Everything I find on her is good. No real close friends, due, I would assume to her traveling around so much with her job. No problems with work related personalities. Her co-workers like her. All her previous employers say good things. Apparently, her resume glows in the dark it's so awesome.

Even goes to church. The priest says she has been coming regularly since she came to town. He had a letter from the priest where she worked before here and her home priest telling him to look for her. I was lucky, he was still up writing his sermon."

"How did you get all this info?"

"Some of it's on the net. I found an Army Colonel

that remembers the event who was still in his office, her hometown sheriff, who put me in touch with her lawyer. You sure you want all this? There's a lot. Your girl's an open book. She comes from a small town. Therefore there are no secrets. Everyone knows everything about everybody. Especially a home town girl who became a hero. It would be nice if everyone was this easy to dig stuff up on."

"Might as well finish it."

Watts continued. "No record except for a speeding ticket way back. It was a female cop. The Sheriff made a joke about it. Said he didn't want to break his record of never having found anyone without at least one blemish against them. Bet she's sweet talked herself out of a lot more. But we all know there's no law against that."

"So far, her financials are clean. You can follow the money. No apparent hidden accounts. Her parents were well off and had invested well. She seems content to leave the money where they put it for the most part. She's done some re-investing. Uses a broker so that trail's wide open and would be easy to follow. According to her lawyer her new investments tend to be in the area of helping start new businesses or in improving neighborhoods. Which is about all the information he was giving. Nothing that sends up a red flag."

"The boyfriend wasn't kidding about the flying. She owns a couple of planes. One is being stored at a small airport, the Potomac Air Field. It's between Andrew's Air Force Base and the White House. She had to apply for a security clearance and take a test to fly in a restricted area. The Capital is a special flight rules area. The guy there was very talkative. Seems the girl has great taste in planes. She owns two Cessna's that he knows of. One's a small single engine deal and the other's this Turbo Charged 206 that he really wanted to wax eloquent about."

"I had to cut him off. The phone was going to short out duc to thc drool factor. Hc said she used the larger plane when she flew in the first time because she had her stuff with her. It will carry up to six passengers, but she had it configured for four and the rest cargo area. Supposedly it's a great plane for flying over mountains."

"She flew to Kentucky for the weekend and came back with the smaller plane a few weeks after she got here. That's the one she uses to go to and from home. He said she told him she was picking up the larger one the next time out because she would be leaving DC. That matches what she told us about her contract."

"Her only other vice is she's bought a few horses. Seems to favor a breed called Morgan, whatever those are. She has a permit for a concealed and that check came up clean. This kid has more security clearances than the run of the mill Joe Blow from the service and she passed all of them with no problem. It puts her fingerprints in the system. Since she was in the military, her DNA's out there. Sure, we're not looking in the wrong place, here?"

"I guess we'll find out. What's the bad news?"

"Well, actually it's two-pronged. The techs redid the roof like you requested and found marks from a grappling hook and some residual chalk from rock climbing shoes. Looks like someone climbed and then rappelled off the roof recently. Whoever it was tried to hide the marks so that's why they got missed the first time. Jones from the lab said if you hadn't been insistent about redoing the roof, the marks would have been gone with the first rain."

"The check on the vacant apartments was a bust, but one of the ones where the owners are out of town looks like someone might have squatted there for a while. It's been wiped clean. So clean in fact that not even the owner's prints are there."

"And the other?"

"Running the bullet through AFIS raised all kinds of red flags. This is the fourteenth known victim. There's about five or six more that they think he might have taken out. They weren't able to check ballistics to prove it. We may lose the case because there are all kinds of international agencies looking for our shooter. He's taken out some heavy hitters. I'm not sure if they want to find him to prosecute him or hire him to work for them. Then again they may want to give him a medal."

"He?"

"Profile reads a male."

"Could be why they haven't caught him. They have the profile wrong. Although I have to admit despite my gut, Cade doesn't strike me as a killer for hire."

"Well, I guess we'll find out. I do have to say that the kill list is a who's who in terrorism and just general nastiness. Most of the hits took place in Afghanistan, Iraq, and Pakistan. The unconfirmed hits were terrorists hiding behind civilians while they shot at our guys. In two or three cases, they were suicide bombers that were shot before they hit their targets and had a chance to detonate."

"The last hit took out three of the players on the most wanted list of terrorists and their playmates. The one before that was a sniper who was hitting our troops. It was an American female who went over to the dark side."

"So why didn't our guys do the job? We have plenty of snipers in the military."

"Because they were political hot potatoes, and it would have created an incident that we would have to explain. This way no one claimed responsibility so we had deniability. The unconfirmed shootings took place shortly after a big hit, so they think he might have still been around."

"So how does this shoot fit in? Moody wasn't a terrorist or a bad guy from all reports."

"Maybe there's something about him we don't know. The shooter has never varied from hitting someone who had it in for our country. If you follow that logic, Moody was up to something wrong. It had to be bad enough that a hit on our soil was sanctioned. This is the first time he's worked in the States. It's either that or personal. But again, this guy has never taken a shot at anyone who didn't deserve it. The other interesting tidbit of information is they were all T-Box kills. You could place each hit on top of each other and there is no variation in position. One of the techs wrote it was like someone had put an X on the spot. If there's a signature, that's it."

"Before you say anything, I've already started the runs on her professional and private life to flesh out anything I may have missed. It should be ready for you by our nine o'clock meeting or midafternoon at the latest. It's late and some people do sleep at night. Go home and get some rest. Case will still be here later this morning."

"Where's her home of record? Does she still live in her old home town or has she moved to the big city? I know she travels a lot and you mentioned Kentucky. Surely she has a home base."

"Actually, she has two of them. Her main home is a farm in eastern Kentucky. It's a small town south west of Lexington. She keeps a couple of horses that I mentioned earlier there. The place has some caretakers who stay there the year-round. They've been there since her parents were alive. They were her appointed guardians until she became of age. That's where she was raised which accounts for her accent. So, she did stay in her old home town."

"Like I said, I spoke with the Sheriff, and everyone thinks highly of her. Oh, and you're going to love this, she's an auxiliary deputy sheriff in the county where she lives. Which means she's technically a member of the law enforcement community. One of the reasons I got so much info on her, is she's well known and liked. As I said before, she's a local and a war hero. I am quoting here, 'You all are barking up the wrong tree.' Got the feeling if we went there, we might get met with shotguns, dogs and dueling banjos."

"We'll cross that bridge only if we need to. I can handle everything but the banjos. I found her ID and badge. Where's the second place?"

"Cute, boss, real cute. The second one is on the coast of Maine. It's a small cottage. The place is tiny, and the locals knew her parents. She only comes up a couple of times a year, usually early spring and for a week in the fall. She must like leaves. She goes hiking a lot when she's there and likes the beach. Sheriff there knew her parents and knew Cade from her visits there. Said she was a good kid and didn't get in trouble. Like I said her parents were well off, and they left her the property."

"The only property she's bought is a small condo in Durango, Colorado. She likes to ski. The agency that takes care of the place says she lets them rent it out in the summer and a couple of times in the spring. She likes it empty in the winter so she can come when she's off to hit the slopes."

"Well-rounded girl. Correlate the hits with the locations of where she was working at the time. Oh, and you were right about the ring."

"Lost me there."

"She was wearing a rock when she got dressed up. It was definitely out of my pay grade. I can see why she doesn't wear it to work. I guess you were right about her reasons for not having it on."

"I have my moments. I don't know about you, but I smell a set-up. Real odd she was the only one home."

"It does seem strange. She'd be an easy one to try to pin anything on. She's new to the building, from out of town, and no real friends. Under normal conditions it would look like a no brainer. She'd be on her own. Guess no one knew she was friends with the President of the United States."

"Well, this is D.C. Ya got to love it. Go home. We'll talk in the morning."

7

hero is a knight in blood-stained armor.”
Unknown

It wasn’t an act, she was worn out from work. Close to exhaustion from everything else. The wound she had received on her last mission had been more than a flesh wound. Then had started in her new job just weeks after getting shot. Nursing took a lot of pulling and tugging on patients. She kept aggravating the scarring. That, plus to the long day, she was totally bone weary.

Then, add to the equation she had killed a living soul. It didn’t matter that it was necessary or even that the person was evil incarnate. It took a piece of you to kill someone. It wasn't an issue of a guilty conscience. In the vernacular of the south, some people just plain deserved killing. Considering the values she was raised on, maybe the reason she felt guilty was because she didn't feel guilty. It was a convoluted dilemma with thorns sticking out in all direction. Maybe it was the lack of culpability was what she really needed to process.

The agency she belonged to didn't believe in psych evals after a shoot. The only time you saw a shrink was to evaluate you for the job or to decide if you were still capable of doing the job. With the type of wet-work she did for them, the number of people in the need-to-know column was minimal. There was no one she could talk 'shop' with and get their take on the operation, unless you counted Jon or Wilson.

Wilson was the boss. You didn't talk to your boss about any qualms you had with your job. Jon would tell Wilson anything she told him, so back to point number one. The agency employed other snipers. For some reason Wilson kept her separate from them and didn't encourage any comradery. She only knew a few by sight.

Church was her confessional and allowed the peace of the place of worship to seep in to quiet her soul. Some researchers are of the opinion that places absorb whatever emotions occur in that place. Maybe that's why she felt a sense of forgiveness and calm in churches. It was between her and God. There was no confession to a priest. She would never put a priest in that dilemma or danger for that matter.

Often, she wondered how someone who had trained to save lives could be so damn good at taking them. Then again, maybe that was why she could. If you knew how to save a life, you also knew how to end one. She was definitely a two-headed hydra.

Whatever her bosses where up to, it precluded her following her normal routine. So, she packed a small bag. Remembering the appointment at the police station, she added appropriate clothing for that. She slipped on some shoes and followed Jon back down to the limo. Once there, she put her head back on the seat and closed her eyes.

Rachael wondered if this night could get any worse. She shouldn't have asked. The fates have a habit of answering when you least expect them to. Or when you feel the least able to cope. She didn't know if it was to let you know you could handle anything, that or just to kick you in the teeth for the grins and giggles.

The driver let them out in front of Jon's building. He drove off in a hurry. Probably anxious to get home. Jon had a classy, upscale brownstone townhouse in Foggy Bottom. It wasn't in Jon's nature to live in a run-down part of town. He was all for old money and keeping up appearances.

Rachael later blamed what happened next on her

being distracted. Plus, she didn't expect to get attacked on an affluent street in this part of town, at this time of night. The bad guys needed their beauty sleep and usually gave up their trolling earlier than this. It was always the things you weren't prepared for that usually bit you in the ass. After the car pulled away from the curb, she watched it turn. It was only then she caught a movement out of the corner of her eye.

There were five of them, all armed with knives. They had guns to back up the hardware, the bulges in their clothing gave them away. They must have wanted to make it look like a mugging gone south.

Jon had made the same assessment of the situation she had. They shifted their positions so they stood back-to-back. No need for talk, they had worked together long enough they didn't need to go over their battle plan. The attackers hesitated for a second, they had thought Jon would position himself to protect her. That second allowed both of them to settle in a little tighter for the fight. She had a brief thought that she was glad she still wasn't wearing her gown. Poor Jon was still in his tux. Three of the assailants took on Jon thinking he was the more dangerous of the two. Apparently, they had never read any articles about female tigers or watched National Geographic. Most thugs just weren't literary.

Rachael took the feet out from the first attacker and

then grabbed the second one by the wrist, extending his arm out and back. The movement pulled him forward, allowing her to step behind him and put all her weight into her hand. She broke his arm at the elbow and kneed his jaw as his head angled toward the sidewalk. One down and out, one to go. The first one was starting to get up so she kicked him on the side of the head, and he was out of play.

Jon was holding his own. He was efficient in a fight. He was very good and he knew it. There was a mean streak in the man. He liked to draw the fight out before he went in for the kill. Rachael was tired. She just wanted it finished. She took out the third thug's knee from behind, and as he went down, smashed in his nose with her knee. Jon had the other two down and out for the count.

"I had it. You didn't need to help."

"I know. You like to play with your food too much. Hate to spoil your fun and all. I'm tired. Actually, it felt good. Sometimes it takes beating the shit out of someone to help you let off steam." What could she say? She liked a good fight as well as the next guy. "So, what are we going to do with these guys? Call the cops or have our crew mop it up?"

"Rachael, there are times you're a rare bird. Might as well call the cops. These idiots won't know anything. They're just thugs for hire. Unless you got anything else off them, we just act normal. The boss will get everything he needs to know from the police report."

"Nope. Didn't get any evil vibes, merely avarice."

"You really need to work on your vocabulary. These guys wouldn't even understand that word. Greed would have worked just as well."

"Picky, picky. I bet if I wrote you a letter, you'd correct it with red ink and send it back." He just gave her the patented male look that broadcasted that he was so trying to be patient and she was being difficult.

Jon pulled out his phone to call 911 while she checked them for weapons. When she was done, she had a small mountain of various forms of means to wreak violence, from guns to brass knuckles. The soup to nuts of the violently inclined. Then she called the boss. Wilson asked her what she thought about the attack. "You have to wonder what this was about. Unless somebody doesn't want me around the First Lady, there was no reason to attack us."

"You really think that's what this attack was about? You don't think it was a mugging? You know, looks like a duck, quacks like a duck sort of thing."

"Nope. Might be my suspicious nature but I got the feeling they were waiting for us. Considering the hour, that stands out as odd. They had to know we were coming here. It also looked like they had every intention of killing me, but only incapacitating Jon. Which in the scheme of things, you would have thought it would be the other way round. I got bad vibes off of Cody. He didn't like the idea of anyone being close to Mrs. Blair. It's either that or someone, somewhere wants to get rid of me. I think my feelings are hurt."

"Doesn't seem plausible. You don't appear to be a threat. Could just be what it looks like, a run-of-the-mill mugging."

"That depends on what kind of information Colby has. He is close to the President. People talk sometimes and don't realize who's listening. Aides and secretaries tend to blend with the wall color. He could have picked up on the fact that they want me near her and decided to take care of the problem."

"For now, you and Jon act like everyday citizens who have just been mugged."

"We've called the cops. But I don't do hysterical and normal citizens don't send their attackers to the hospital."

She heard Wilson sigh, "Be the nice victims, and I'll check into it." then the click of the disconnect. That was her boss, all warm and fuzzy.

"What did he say?"

"That he'd look into it. Play nice with the cops."

Jon made a face, mirroring Rachael's feelings. "Then I guess we're letting the boss take care of it."

The sirens were close, "Oh goody. We get to play with the police again. The fun and games just never end."

"Chill. We're the victims this time. They're supposed to be on our side."

"You think I can blame Reynolds for this? We wouldn't have been here if it wasn't for him and his gang messing up my apartment. You also need to ask how did they know to wait for us here? Normally would have headed home by yourself. Or maybe stay the night with me. How did they know our movements?"

"Don't I wish," he muttered under his breathe. "Leave Reynolds alone, it doesn't do any good to antagonize the police. By the way, you have blood on your arm. Is it theirs or did one of them get you?"

Rachael hadn't noticed the blood dripping down her arm. There was a gash across her forearm. Being so tired her reaction time must have been off. Those bozos hadn't been good enough to wound her. She was pissed at herself for letting him get through her guard. She reached over to where Jon's shirt had pulled out of his pants, tore a piece of the shirt off and wrapped it around her arm to slow the bleeding.

"Hey! That's a hundred and fifty-dollar shirt!"

"You shouldn't be paying that for a lousy white shirt, and it was ruined anyway. Now you can say I tore your clothes off. At least the tux looks salvageable. Quit griping. At least look like you really care that I'm hurt. A little empathy here would look good. You are supposed to care about me."

By then the police had arrived and were swarming

the area. EMS was called to take care of the wounded. The thug with the broken elbow regained consciousness and was screaming his head off. Maybe she could ask the paramedic to give him some morphine. Give him anything to shut him up. Her head was starting to pound again and she was cranky. Her empathy level was generally higher. It's hard to feel sorry for someone who just tried to kill you and was now crying about the consequences.

The bad guys would go to the hospital and then to jail. She had checked them out after Jon bandaged her arm. Most of the injuries were minor bruises and possible concussions. There were only a few broken bones. Other than the elbow, nothing major. They were all awake and alert by the time the ambulance hauled them off.

The guy with the broken elbow was in for a longer stay and probably some rehab. Rachael was sorry the taxpayers were going to have to foot the bill. She had been trying to disable, not kill. Sometimes that was harder than out and out mayhem.

Jon had his arm around her and was putting pressure on the wound. He acted like he really was concerned. The slight vibe she got off of him was that he was distracted. The police offered to get another ambulance, to take them to the hospital. Rachael declined. She assured them that she was a nurse and knew what she was doing. It only needed stitches. Jon could take her. No need to waste the money or personnel on an ambulance. Thank you so much for your concern and so on.

Rachael sat on the curb while Jon gave his report. He got up to sign some paper work. She lowered her head to her knees and closed her eyes. She was so tired she was nauseous. Would this frigging night ever end? She felt someone sit down on the curb next to her. She knew without opening her eyes that it was the pain in the ass, Detective Reynolds.

"You okay?"

She left her head down. It was too much effort to look up. "Detective, I would have thought you would be home by now. The little woman will be upset."

"I was on my way when I heard the call. I don't have a wife. The officer said you were injured."

"Just a cut. Needs a few stitches. I'll live. So, no wife, girlfriend?" Why did the fact that he wasn't married mean anything to her?

"No girlfriend."

"Boyfriend?"

He gave a short, sharp laugh. "Lord, no! You do just say what pops into your mind, don't you? Any idea why you were attacked?"

"Expensive townhouse in Foggy Bottom. Late at night. A couple alone, duh. What do you think, Detective?"

"I think they picked on the wrong couple."

"You know what Jon does for a living. I was in the military. Besides, there's the fact my parents wanted me to be able to defend myself. I'm sure it's in my file that I have two black belts and martial arts training."

"Ms. Cade, you are more of a puzzle every time I meet you."

"Is that a come on, Detective? Remember, I'm an engaged woman."

"Yeah, I wonder about that too. Here comes your fiancé. You need to get that arm looked at. I'll talk to you later today."

He stood up to face Jon. "I'll get both your stories later. Get her to the hospital before she bleeds out all over the street."

Rachael looked at her makeshift dressing. It was saturated. There was a small puddle of blood on the street. The wonder of gravity at work. The cut must have been deeper than she thought. Well, that explained why her arm throbbed in pain with her heartbeat. The idiot must have gotten lucky and hit a bleeder. She elevated it by bending it up and resting it on her knee. It needed the bandage changed and some pressure applied. She needed to change the leather cuff as it was saturated with blood. The thought of her wrist not being covered made her feel naked and exposed.

There was a mob of people at the scene. She saw one of the agents from the company and even someone from the Secret Service. She had noticed him earlier at the dance. He had a white streak through the middle of his hair. Unusual in the agency, which was why he had caught her attention. Most men tried to hide their age. It was a game for the young and virile. His had to be inherited. No one normally turned white in one area like that naturally unless they were a skunk. Yeesh, she must be tired. Her mind was wandering. Jon saw her note the arrival of the agent.

"That's Johnson, the head of the White House security detail. The President heard of the attack and sent someone to see how we were. I guess he thought he'd check it out personally."

"So much for a low profile."

"I need to go to the garage and get my car. Will you be alright until I get back?"

Reynolds was still standing close by. "I'll stay with her until you get here. Take one of the officers with you, just in case."

Jon grimaced and headed for the car. Like he really needed the protection.

He made her sit down again and snagged a passing medic to tighten the dressing. The bleeding had slowed down to a slight trickle. It felt good to have him by her side. He would be the kind who would stay with you and love you through the hard times. Don't ask her how she knew that. It just resonated in her bones.

She shouldn't have felt that way considering Reynolds thought she had committed a crime. Must be the loss of blood that was causing her to be light-headed and have hallucinations. That or the lack of sleep was causing her to feel something that wasn't there. By the time Jon got back, she was leaning against Detective Reynolds' shoulder and dozing off.

8

"The Good Lord never gives you more than you can handle... Unless you die of something." Guinidon cartoon caption.

THE TRIP to the hospital was uneventful. Since she knew the staff, they were upset about what happened. They also oohed over her ring and Jon. He had wandered off while the doctor sutured her arm. Some boyfriend he was, didn't even offer to hold her hand. See if she got him a card for Valentine's Day. Her tetanus shot was up to date, no worries there. Rachael knew Jon was off talking to Wilson about the attack. She got her instructions for care and when to come back and get the sutures out.

The charge nurse told her to take the next shift off. Since she would have been due to be on duty in less than three hours, that was a relief. She would have had to arrange the time off to go to the police station, so that was a plus. The charge nurse already had it covered. One worry off her plate.

Then she hunted Jon down and they arrived at the townhouse around dawn. At least this time it was uneventful.

Jon helped her put sheets on the sofa bed and found some extra pillows. He even loaned her a t-shirt to wear as pajamas. For once, he was quiet and didn't make any remarks about sleeping together. Her head hit the pillow, she was gone.

Rachael woke up to a quiet apartment. There was a nagging pain in the front of her head which meant she had probably dreamed. Hoped she hadn't cried out. Jon had left earlier, but she just dozed back off. The smell of coffee drew her to the kitchen. A note was propped up against a cup telling her he would be back in time to take her to the police station. Also, that there were bagels and cream cheese in the refrigerator. After fixing her breakfast, she read the paper he had left on the table.

Moody's death was front page news. It was filled with speculation on the shooter, and noted the police were questioning persons of interest, but no suspects.

She snorted at that comment. Person of interest her ass. Reynolds suspected her for it. If he had a shred of proof she'd be in jail in a hot minute even if he had let her lean on his shoulder last night. He probably took his shirt in for trace evidence. Wouldn't have put it past him to have gathered up the piece of Jon's bloody shirt the EMT's had cut off to test for DNA.

The rest of the news extolled Moody's service to his country and how great a family man he was. Rachael knew how great a family man he was, he beat his wife and had molested both daughters. The only reason it hadn't been reported was the fact his wife kept quiet was due to political pressure and the girls were too young to say anything. If it had been her, he would have been dead or at least badly beaten the first time he had touched one of them or her for that matter. Men who abused their children or mate were nothing more than scum of the earth as far as she was concerned. They were a blemish on mankind.

Moody had enough bad stuff in his personal column to ease any qualms she might have had about shooting him. His wife probably had a secret desire to send her a thank you note with a box of candy and flowers.

Add in the details of the secrets he had sold and how many soldiers had died due to his betrayal, he deserved killing. There were no plans documented in the news about his funeral. The powers that be were dragging their heels on a state funeral if she had to make a guess. If the news only knew the truth about how he had betrayed his country and family, the uproar might have been a little less full of righteous anger.

Rachael finished off the crossword puzzle and the comics. It was time to get ready for her big interview at police central with Reynolds and company. She found some plastic wrap to cover her arm and keep her sutures dry in the shower. As she stood in the shower and let some of her aches and pains ooze away, she thought about the detective.

It was a shame really. Reynolds was someone she really could have liked if things were different. For some reason he touched a chord in her. Odd how she felt drawn to him even when she was ticked off. She wasn't the type of person who usually obsessed about someone when she first met them. Was it because he reminded her of someone? She just couldn't put her finger on who for some reason. He was at least honest and somewhat open. Which was more than she could say about most people she knew.

No dressing up today. She wore jeans, boots and a black turtleneck. A leather jacket would be enough in this weather. Leather bands on her wrist and she was ready. No make-up, and her hair braided into one plaint. Haute couture are us. No weapons. She wouldn't get them past the security at the police station. Plus, she didn't feel like answering questions as to why she felt the need to carry. Even when you had a license for concealed, the police were still antsy about it. They just didn't have a sense of humor about some things. Washington, D.C. police were worse than most.

She checked her phone, which she had turned off during the night. Just too tired to put up with phone calls. Figured if Wilson couldn't get her, he'd call Jon. Jon was tethered to his phone twenty-four-seven. A message from her director at the hospital asking her to stop by sometime today if she had a chance. One from the First Lady's assistant asking her to call. Since she didn't feel like talking at the moment, she'd get back to them later.

Jon could drop her off at the hospital, and she'd walk home. The apartment was walking distance from there, which had made it convenient. The exercise would do her good since she hadn't been able to work in her daily run in the last couple of days. Except for a slight throbbing in her arm, she felt okay.

Jon picked her up right on time. Parking in D.C. was a nightmare. He usually made use of the limo whenever he could. Mass transit type didn't fit his style. Today he drove his own car. It was a red sporty thing. She thought it was a Porsche. Identifying car models were not something in her wheelhouse. Let her look at a horse and that was a different story.

Since Jon didn't have much to say, the ride to the police station was quiet. They were apparently going to tell the truth for a change, so there were no special instructions from the boss. It was refreshing not to have to make up a story since, for once, she was the victim.

Jon cleared his throat slightly and glanced at her across the seat. "You must have had some bad dreams last night."

Rachael stiffened slightly and grimaced. "What makes you say that?"

"You were restless and you cried out a couple of times."

"Sorry, didn't mean to wake you up. Must have been the hamburger."

"Rachael, you have a stomach of steel. What's bothering you?"

"It's not anything that affects my job. Besides if you want a strong stomach you need one like a buzzard. Steel can rust."

"You're changing the subject...buzzard?"

"Ha! I knew you couldn't resist." She settled deeper in the seat. It was such a hoot to drive Jon crazy. And so easy sometimes. "The buzzard's digestive tract can neutralize all kinds of bacteria, including botulism and all types of plague. Someone really ought to fund a study to see if they can come up with an antidote to a lot of nasty bugs based on their ability to neutralize a majority of the nasty critters in the world."

He just shook his head and plowed ahead to the

subject at hand. "If something is bad enough to make you cry, then it's important to your performance."

"Back off. I told you it's nothing to do with the job. I've had nightmares since I was in Iraq. I try not to remember them anymore."

"Rachael, if you need to talk..."

"Shut it, Jon. I don't want to talk about it." She spent the rest of the trip staring out the window until they reached the police station. Knew she had been rude. There were some things she wasn't willing to talk about. They found a place to park that was marked for official use only. Jon put his placard in the window and off they went.

She sighed to herself. "I'm sorry I snapped. I just don't like to talk about it." He left it alone as they walked out of the parking garage. He had learned not to pry when she didn't want to talk. He'd even learned not to open doors for her unless it was a social engagement. Sometimes he proved he was a smart man.

They were taken to a conference room and offered coffee or a soft drink. So, they were going to be treated as witnesses, not criminals. She wondered how much longer that would last, at least in her case.

Although Rachael would normally drink coffee any time she could, the horror tales about how bad the coffee was at police stations kept her from accepting. Every emergency room she worked in had police officers coming in at all hours who always drank their coffee. Since hospital coffee was right up there in the top five worst in the world, she shuddered to think what police department coffee was like.

The fact they were being treated as witnesses rather than suspects, Rachael figured the offer for beverages was a ploy to catch them off guard. Apparently, Jon had come to the same conclusion. He grimaced and rolled his eyes at her and mouthed for her to behave. Since she was always the model for diplomacy, she couldn't imagine why he thought she needed to be reminded to watch her behavior. She grinned to herself at what Jon's answer to that statement would be. Really, she could behave if she had to.

Rachael didn't see any reason to change her approach. Even if she knew she was guilty, they didn't have any proof and shouldn't be harassing her this way. So, attitude was what they were going to get.

Reynolds and Watts strolled in carrying files. Reynolds handed her a cup of coffee. "Cream and sugar, right?"

"Going to take more than that to make up for the mess you made."

"But all you mentioned was the coffee. Truce?"

"Bite me."

Both the detectives snorted back a laugh and Jon reproached her with a mild, "Rachael."

"The detectives sat down and straightened out their files. The files were way too thick to just apply to their little mugging. They were trying to play head games and make them think there had more than they did. She couldn't read much off of Reynolds, but the younger detective was trying to hide his excitement.

"Will you please go over what you did yesterday afternoon, Ms. Cade, just so we're clear."

Rachael just rolled her eyes at Reynolds and answered flatly, "I got off work late and ran home. Literally, I live close enough to the hospital that I walk to work. I didn't meet or see anyone in the lobby or the hallway. I got to my apartment and took a shower. You all were knocking on my door when I got out. Is that clear enough? I can draw a picture using stick figures or write out a form with bullet points if that helps."

Reynolds didn't answer her, and rolled on with his questioning. "You previously stated it was seven-thirty when you got there?"

"Yes, I told you the nurse who was supposed to relieve me was late. I looked at my watch as I came through the lobby. Since we have a security system, I'm sure you have the discs so you know exactly when I got there."

"Yes, but only the lobby is monitored. The roof cam is out due to construction. Have you seen any strangers? Anyone hanging around the building that looked suspicious?"

"Nope, nary a soul."

"The attack on you and Mr. Masters this morning, did you recognize any of the men?"

"No, I didn't. I could describe them for you, but since you have them in custody that seems a moot point."

"How about you Mr. Masters? Did you recognize any of them?

"No. I did look them up this morning. They seem to have a long enough rap sheet though."

"Yeah, they've been around the block a few times. In fact, this will be the third strike for two of them. They'll be doing jail time as soon as they get out of the hospital. One of them had surgery last night. I didn't realize an elbow was so hard to fix. Something about nerves and muscle attachments." Rachael saw Watts break a small smile that he quickly hid. "Mr. Masters would you mind going with Detective Watts to sign a copy of your report?"

Jon looked at him quizzically, "What about Rach here? She was there too."

"I have her copy from yesterday evening. I just need to ask a few more questions."

Jon looked like he was going to balk but changed his mind and went with the other detective.

"Ms. Cade, may I call you Rachael?"

"No, we're not friends." It was a shame really. He did have the Sam Elliot look going for him. It was one she preferred to Jon's handsomeness.

She caught the hint of a smile at her answer. "No, we're not. I don't know why, you bother me, Ms. Cade. I can't find anything to prove you did this, but my gut says you did."

"Must be the lousy coffee you have around here. It would upset anyone's intestinal tract. In fact," she crossed her arms on the table as she took a deep breathe, and leaned forward, "Jon and I were discussing buzzards on the way in."

"Buzzards?"

"Why do people give me strange looks? I read, look it up. Buzzards have a phenomenal digestive tract, so they don't get upset stomachs."

He grunted in response to her remark. It looked like he was trying not to be amused. It was hard to dislike someone who made you laugh. Like Jon, he decided the better part of valor was to return to his original line of questioning. It didn't work for him either. When she didn't want to talk, she didn't.

"I have to let you go. Just remember you're still in the mix. I'll come after you when I find anything."

"I'm sure you will. You strike me as a stubborn SOB."

"That I am, Ms. Cade. You can take that to the bank. Good luck on your wedding plans. I hear Mrs. Blair plans to help you with them."

Rachael grimaced. "Everyone seems to want to get me married off. This isn't the Dark Ages where if you're not married by fourteen, you're an old maid. I just haven't had time to get ready for it. So, I'm free to go?"

"Yes, you're free to go. For now, anyway." He pulled out a packet and handed it to her, "Happily your pistol came back clean and your paperwork checked out."

"I'm so happy you're happy."

"I didn't say I was happy. Just don't use it in a crime, it's in the system now. Maybe now you'll have the time to plan the happy occasion." From her expression, Reynolds didn't think she was as anxious to get married as everyone thought.

"It's registered, so it's already in the system. Quit trying to bullshit me."

He reached out and touched her arm as she started to rise up from the chair. She had pushed up her sleeves because it was warm in the room. He touched her on the bare skin between the leather cuff and her sleeve. They both froze as they felt the heat that traveled up both their arms from the touch. He watched as her pupils dilated and mouth parted at the feeling and wondered if she saw the same thing in his face. He moved his hand and cleared his throat. "Well, that's never happened before."

Rachael didn't answer. She simply gazed at him for a long second, pulled her sleeve down, and then put some distance between them. "Goodbye, Detective. Take care. Being able to know the truth isn't always as wonderful as it would seem. You should have learned that by now."

He watched as she left the room. Then he noticed he was rubbing his hand against his sleeve to hold on to the warmth from her touch. He thought wryly to himself, what the fuck just happened?

9

hat we usually ask of God is that 2+ 2 does not equal 4." Unknown

RACHAEL MET Jon at the front lobby. He took one look at her face and asked what was wrong.

Rachael's arm still tingled from Reynolds' touch. "He's like me."

Jon grabbed her arm to make her face him. "Who's like you? What are you talking about?"

"Reynolds. He has the same ability I have to tell if people are lying or not. I don't know how strong he is. Now I know why he's been after me. My shields are too strong for him to tell if I'm lying or not but his gut is telling him I'm guilty. He won't let go of it until he can prove I did it."

"If he's like you, why can't he tell?"

"When you have a talent like this, you learn to build up shields so no one can read you. If you don't shield, everything gets in. It would be like living in bedlam with total chaos beating at you constantly. At first you have to work at molding your wall and shoring it up. Then it just becomes a natural part of you. Unless someone is phenomenally strong, they can't get around your defenses.

Or, once in a while, for whatever reason, a person may really get to you and slip in between the cracks. The last person who could do that to me was my mother. Of course, mothers have strange and awesome powers anyway.

"Then we need to go to Wilson. They want you with the First Lady and that won't happen if you're in jail for murder."

"Not to mention what it would do to my social life. I'm not too fussy how you keep him from investigating as long as they don't do anything to him personally."

"What do you mean?"

"I know everything we do isn't always the right way to solve a problem, only the most advantageous. I won't have him removed or his reputation damaged because he may cause problems for the company."

"I don't guess you can change his mind?"

In the past, if she thought hard enough at someone, they would forget about seeing her or members of the team. She could cloud their minds enough that they would forget about the moving shadows they saw in the night.

It wasn't a complete erasure. More of a blurring. The mind didn't recognize it, so it dropped it out of its memory bank. She had used it to save their lives, but she didn't like it. It wasn't so bad when it was just blurring their presence, but to actually try to change memories felt wrong.

The act left a dark sludge in her brain that was hard to shake. It also made her queasy, with a tremendous headache afterwards. She had only practiced the erasure part in the lab at Wilson's insistence. It revolted her and she refused to do it anymore.

Blurring someone's mind was bad enough, but screwing with a hardwired memory just to mess with someone's head for her own benefit was wrong. It wasn't justifiable, even if it meant going to jail. "I wouldn't do it even if I thought it would work. Which I doubt it would. I'm pretty much immune, so he probably is too. You were there when I told Wilson I wouldn't use my talent that way."

"You definitely have too many morals for this job."

"I will compromise them for some things or the greater good. This isn't negotiable."

"I'll talk to Wilson and see what he wants to do."

"Just remember, if anything happens to Reynolds, I will hunt you all down. You all gave me the training. You know it's not an idle threat."

"Don't make statements like that. There's no reason to piss your life away for a man you barely know. One who, up to now, has done nothing but cause you grief."

"The man you're talking about is doing his job. He also happens to be honest. I may not be able to read him as clearly as most people, but I can tell that much." And for some reason, she really cared about what happened to him.

"I'll talk to Wilson." He held his hand up to stop her from commenting. "Minus the threat of retaliation. I will let him know how you feel. Maybe he can send the hound on another scent."

"Take me home please. I have an apartment to clean. Wait a second, I forgot. Drop me off at the hospital. The director wanted to talk to me. I can walk home from there. And for the record, the detective is not a hound." You hold that title, she thought to herself.

10

"I'm so busy I don't know if I found my rope or lost my horse." Texas Bix Bender

THE MEETING with the director was not what she suspected. She asked how her arm was and then told her she didn't need come back to work. The director assured her there wasn't anything wrong with her performance. The nursing agency she worked for had requested that she be allowed to opt out of the last two weeks of the contract. They would cover any cost for extra coverage. Rachael would be welcome back any time in the future to work there again. It appeared Rachael had no say in the matter. She was pissed. She always finished her contracts.

There was no need to even go to her locker. The director just handed her a box with her things in it. The police had probably been through it. Luckily, they hadn't considered a stethoscope, hemostat and bandage scissors weapons of mass destruction, so they were still there. They were lucky. They didn't know how attached nurses were to the tools of their trade. The director concluded their meeting with congratulations on her upcoming wedding.

Rachael was seething by the time she got home. The walk hadn't helped and facing the wreck of her apartment wasn't getting her in a better mood. She knew who was behind the request at the hospital and realized that guarding the First Lady was higher on the food chain than her job in the emergency room, but they could have asked.

Deciding that cleaning house wouldn't change her state of mind, she got ready to go for a run. It may not improve her attitude, but at least she wouldn't have the energy to bitch as much.

The C&O Canal Towpath was her route of choice. It was eighty-nine miles long, so she could vary the length of her run to fit her schedule. Since it was mostly gravel and dirt, it wasn't so hard on the knees. One big bonus, the scenery was fantastic. She decided to run the route from north of the Key Bridge at Georgetown to the Boat House at Fletcher's Cove. It was a nice four-mile run.

"Maybe sometime soon she could schedule in a

longer run. As far as she knew she didn't have another twenty-mile desert trek in her near future, but it didn't hurt to be prepared. Then, when she had the time, she could take the longer path to the Great Falls and back around. It was mostly cyclists who did the full thirteen miles past the locks and canal, but there was no law against running it. There and back was about twenty-six miles. Add in a cool down run, and she'd have over her twenty plus miles. The path had hills and bumps so it also helped to train for changes in terrain.

This was one of the nicer locales she had been assigned to for great places to exercise. The scenery helped to alleviate the drudgery of running at times. It wasn't that she disliked running, but when you were tired it could be a chore. Having something interesting to look at made it easier.

There was also the fact that it helped to be in shape to run from some fights. Admittedly, she was a bad ass in the hand-to-hand department but she was female and on the small side. When your opponent was bigger and untrained, training gave you an edge. Unfortunately, in her world, her opponents were almost always bigger and often well versed in martial arts or at the very least street fighting. When skills were even, unless you got awfully lucky, size wins. That's when running came in handy. Her size made it easy to hide. Never, ever underestimate the power of being sneaky.

Running actually helped to even out her state of

mind. It even amused her that she had picked up three tails during the process. She would have to tell Reynolds that they needed to work on their physical fitness requirements. At one point, she thought she might have to turn around and do CPR on one poor guy.

The door to her apartment was slightly ajar when she got back. Now what? She heard someone giggle in answer to a low comment. Since most people with breaking and entering on their mind didn't usually giggle, she pushed the door open. A young girl in a uniform from a local cleaning agency looked up.

"Oh dear. We were supposed to be done so it would be a surprise."

"Oh, it's a surprise. Who asked you to clean the place?"

The girl looked in her notebook, "A Mr. Masters. He said there had been a break-in and the police had left a mess. You were so upset, he wanted to surprise you with a clean apartment. We're almost done. He'll be so disappointed."

"He'll get over it. Thank you. It looks wonderful. It really was a nice thought. Cleaning isn't one of my favorite things."

"Give us about fifteen minutes, and we'll be out of your way."

Rachael went into the kitchen and got a drink of water. She leaned back against the counter. There seemed to be a conspiracy that she didn't get to be alone. The only time she had been without people around was during her walk home. On her run, she'd had her "shadows." She wasn't worried about them taking any action while she was in such a public place, but that didn't keep her from being alert.

It was the main thing she disliked about her job. She really could never let go and not worry about her surroundings. Keeping on a high level of alert at all times got old.

The cleaning people left, and she headed for the shower. The phone rang before she reached the bedroom door. It was Wilson.

"I hear we had a problem today."

"You've talked to Jon."

"He's not happy with you."

"Like that's unusual. Can we break up now?"

"No, in fact you need to pack up your things. You're moving into the White House this evening. I'm sure it'll be a room someone important slept in."

"The thought chills me to the bone. I hope they changed the sheets." She thought she heard Wilson start to laugh as he covered the audio on his phone. "I guess that will put a crimp in my police tail. You need to let Reynolds know his men need to shape up for their next physical fitness test. I thought I was going to get to practice my CPR skills."

"What tail?"

"I counted at least three on my run."

"There are no police tailing you. Reynolds has been told to step down. The FBI is taking over the case."

"I was definitely being followed."

"I'll look into it. You get packed. Take what you need for your stay and I'll have the rest picked up and put in storage. The Secret Service is sending a man for you at nineteen-hundred."

"Will he have a rose in his lapel or a special handshake?"

"Quit being an ass, Rachael. I wouldn't have you do this if it wasn't important or there was another option."

"I know. I'd hate for anything to happen to Mrs. Blair. You do realize that Reynolds is not the type to back off without a fight?"

"He's a good detective. It's a shame he caught the case. He wasn't supposed to. Are you going to behave?"

"Aye, aye sir." So, the almighty agency did have its plans screw up once in a while.

"Like I said, a smart ass. There better have been a salute with that remark," he hung up the phone before she could answer him back. She made a face at the phone and disconnected on her end. Salute...it'd be a cold day in hell.

Rachael decided to pack first and then get her shower. There really wasn't much to do. The maid service had taken care of the household cleaning chores. She left the unperishable food for the next tenant and dumped the stuff that would spoil in the trash. Retrieved her suitcases from the storage area and packed her clothes. The scrubs and books went into boxes. Except for a few books to take with her, she wouldn't need them at the White House. She always had her e-reader for when she ran out.

If she had to go to any formal functions, she'd have to get some clothes. The agency usually supplied her with any special clothing she needed and then it went back to them. The few personal items went in her suitcase. She always carried a few pictures of her parents and home when she traveled. It was all the family she had. And now she was going to stay at the White House. Wouldn't her mother be proud? When she got old, she could stand around at a cocktail party and brag how she had slept in the same room as Queen Haughty-Totty.. or not. It was enough to make you gag. She should be glad there wasn't a purple room to put her in. Of course, then again, there was a good chance there was one.

There was a knock on her door at 1850, the Secret Service guy was early. He was general service issue. Tall, neat haircut, black suit, right credentials, square jaw, but the wrong shoes. Secret Service agents couldn't afford Gucci loafers. Bad guys always got the shoes wrong. She motioned him into the apartment, and as she pointed him to her luggage, she "accidently" bumped his arm. Definitely wrong. He was nervous and had a sense of urgency that wasn't necessary for this kind of duty.

Rachael jumped back as he brought up the syringe he planned to use to knock her out. She batted his arm to one side and lashed out at his knee. This one wasn't like the untrained thugs last night. He knew how to fight.

"Come on, little girl. Don't make this hard on yourself."

"I'm not your little girl," she snarled back. "I don't think I'd care to wake up where ever it is you want to take me."

He answered with a nasty grin, "You got that right, girly."

They circled each other warily. Rachael had the advantage of knowing how the apartment was arranged, so she could concentrate on her opponent. He had to keep up with the décor. As he glanced down at a chair, she picked up a lamp and hit him in the side of the head. He staggered, but didn't go down. The act of bringing his arm up to protect his face, did make him drop the syringe.

Now it was all out battle. He blocked her punches. She ducked and weaved to miss his. The man had reach and weight on her. That meant in the long run, unless she got lucky, he would win. Since running wasn't an option, she moved in closer. Most fighters don't know what to do with someone who gets up close and personal. Men are used to keeping some distance between them and their opponent. Males are so picky about their personal space. She hit him in the nose and spun a low kick at his leg.

He flinched back from the nose blow, but avoided the kick. Suddenly, he broke and ran for the window as the real Secret Service agent burst into the room with his gun drawn. She yelled at him to stop. There wasn't a fire escape. He never slowed down. He broke the window and out he flew.

The agent and she both raced to the window and looked out. Apparently wings or parachutes were not general issue for kidnappers this year. The pavement didn't make for a padded landing. He wasn't moving and blood was starting to seep around his head as a van pulled up. Two men jumped out and pulled the body into the vehicle and sped away.

The real agent was calling on his radio and going into protection mode. These guys really had a nanny complex. He pulled her away from the window and blocked her from the door. He apparently was waiting for the ravening hordes to come in and attack her. She peeked around him, didn't see nary a horde in sight. Men!

It didn't take long for the police and everyone else to get there. Jon was with the first wave. Reynolds with the second. Life just couldn't get any better.

Jon was growling under his breathe. “Can't leave you alone for a second, and you're in trouble.”

“Hey, I didn't ask for the Secret Service escort. I could have gotten there all by myself, and this wouldn't have happened. Better yet, I could just commute and have a place of my own.”

“Did you get a good look at the guy?”

“Well, I know he has a broken nose, and I would imagine quite a few other shattered bones since he took a header out the window.”

“You seem to attract the strangest men. I see you're as cooperative with everyone as you are to the police department,” Reynolds observed mildly. He seemed amused. “Your arm's bleeding again.”

“You're, here aren't you?” she looked down at her arm, “Shit, I probably pulled the stitches. What do you want from me? I answered the door, and the guy tried to send me to la-la land. Look around. The syringe is here somewhere. He dropped it when I hit him with the lamp.

He was about six-two, approximately two-hundred-ten pounds. He had a military haircut, brown hair, light brown eyes with a scar over his left eyebrow. Nose was long and narrow before I broke it. He had thin lips over the prerequisite square jaw. Well-muscled with a flat butt. He was wearing way too much cologne, which I found odd in an agent. I didn't recognize the scent, but it had a lot of musk in it.

He was dressed in a black suit, and he had a Glock-nine in his shoulder holster. Except for the gun and shoes, he was standard issue agent. Has had some hand-to-hand training but not in a formal martial arts class. Is that an adequate description? I might have more to add if I hadn't been trying to rearrange his face in self- defense. He was over confident and wasn't wearing gloves, so you might get some prints off the syringe."

"What about the vehicle and the guys that picked him up?"

"When he hit the ground, a generic white van pulled up. It was nondescript and didn't have plates. I don't do cars so I can't tell you the make but it looked well used. It had a dent in the left rear panel. No side windows. Two men got out of the van, they slid the side doors open and grabbed the guy and pulled him into the vehicle. They were both dressed in white coveralls, dirty white tennis shoes and had blue baseball caps pulled down low on their faces. The hair that showed was dark.

They were both white, but with olive skin and dark beards. One of them had salt and pepper coloring in his facial hair. They were both about five-ten or eleven in height. One of them glanced up to look at the window, and he had on a pair of wire rimmed glasses with the funny round lenses. I didn't get a look at the driver. Apparently, they are environmentally conscious, since they picked up their trash. The agent saw them, he might know the make of the van."

Reynolds looked startled, "Getting a little out of sorts, are we? Where's that sunny disposition we all know and love? Are you always this observant?"

"I'm tired, I hate parties, you wrecked my apartment. I got mugged and then had to go to the hospital and the police station. I think my disposition is just fine considering the crap that's happened in the last twenty-four hours. As for my description, I have an eidetic memory and an eye for detail. What can I say?"

"You always include a description of their butt?"

"One must take their fun where they can get it. I notice that sort of thing. Kind of like a leg or boob man. The guys from the van wore their jumpsuits too loose to tell anything about theirs."

Reynolds coughed back a laugh. "I guess that would sum it up."

Wilson entered the room. He pointed at Rachael, "You need to leave now. My agents will drive you." He addressed Reynolds and the other agents. "I will see to it personally that you all get a report and description of the kidnappers. If any prints can be lifted from the syringe, you'll get them. If not, maybe Ms. Cade can pick him out of our suspect book. We'll send you his identification as soon as we have it."

Jon took her arm and led her from the room. She heard Wilson bark at another agent, "I want to know what's in that syringe. Get surveillance from the lobby. Someone check to see if any of the street cams picked up anything."

His voice faded as they went down the hall. "Boy, Wilson sure is in overdrive. I need to talk to him about cutting down on his caffeine usage. I guess it would be too much to ask to stop and get something to eat?"

The look from the other agent and the grunt from Jon was her answer. Sometimes her sense of humor was sorely unappreciated.

11

"Don't take life too seriously, no one gets out alive." Unknown

RACHAEL DID REMEMBER to thank Jon for getting the cleaning crew. Now it would have to be done over again, but it was the thought that counted. Good thing the company covered the damage deposit. Of course, the company probably owned the whole building. If that were the case, the whole thing was on tape anyway. The agent had mercy on her and made a swing through a drive thru to get something for her to eat.

It probably wouldn't be kosher to be caught rummaging through the White House kitchen for something to eat before she was introduced and it was way past dinner time. She had heard that someone was always available for the first family if they needed a snack, but she wasn't in the loop yet. She needed to get a decent meal. A meal that contained some other food group besides fast would be nice.

There were fresh flowers and a note from Mrs. Blair waiting for her. The First Lady had also included a basket of fresh fruit, which was really nice of her. The agent showed her the layout and informed her that Robert Johnson, the head of the White House's security wanted a word with her in the morning. Goody, more rules.

Jon had left her at the door with the agent. No good-night kisses at the White House. She wondered what Wilson had come up with on her attacker. It wouldn't take him long to find out all there was to know. He may look unobtrusive, but he was efficient as hell.

Rachael redressed her wound. The stitches had pulled enough to bleed, but were still intact. After another hot shower, she got ready for bed. Cuddling up in a big wing-backed chair she tried to read, but her mind kept drifting away from the plot. After reading the same page for the third time she gave up and went to bed.

Then stared at the ceiling. It had been a while since she had the nightmares that made her cry out for help in her sleep. Just wished that it hadn't happened when Jon could hear her.

Rachael had been traumatized as a child. It was like the millions of other kids that suffered the same indignity from people who were supposed to protect them. The trauma had triggered her ability to read other's emotions and some of their thoughts. It was the only good thing that had come out of it. Her uncle was the abuser. He started slow, just being overly friendly and touchy-feely.

When he offered to take her to the zoo her parents didn't see any reason why not. Since he was her mother's brother, he must have had some ability to block because her Mom didn't suspect him of anything. After the zoo, he had stopped at a hotel that was on the outskirts of town.

Rachael wasn't old enough at the time to know what was going on but even then, her bullshit meter was pretty good. She may not have known exactly what he had in mind, but knew she wouldn't like it. Before they could get to a room she bolted from the car. He caught her and dragged her into a room. She fought, but he was older and bigger. He won.

When he was finished, he started to drink and finally fell into a stupor. He had tied her to a post on the bed to keep her from running. Rachael was hurting and she could feel blood running down her legs. She may not have been big enough to fight him off but she wasn't a quitter. Her dad had taught her how to tie knots. Also, how to get them lose. Rachael managed to get free. Her wrists and arms were cut and bleeding but it was worth the pain.

Afraid to use the phone to call for help. Scared it would wake her uncle up. She quietly pulled her clothes back on and snuck out of the room. Her luck ended there. He woke up, but she was young and fast. He was old and drunk. She dashed across the parking lot into the woods that surrounded the motel.

As it got darker, her panic escalated as she ran through the woods. The sound of her uncle stumbling in pursuit made the fear worse. If he caught her, he would hurt her again. Just when she thought she couldn't run anymore she tripped and fell into a hole in the forest floor. It must have been an old well, and the bottom was full of water. Her uncle ran past. Too terrified to know what to do, she held as still as she could and stay afloat. When she could no longer hear him, she tried to find a way out.

The water was cold, but it did help with the pain in her lower belly and the gorged wounds on her wrists from fighting with the ropes. The temperature was dropping. Wondered what her uncle would tell her parents. If they would even look for her here. Paddling around the circumference of the well, she looked for a way to climb out.

The walls were rough and roots had broken through in some places. Maybe if she had been taller or stronger, she could have scaled the wall. As it was, the cold and fatigue were increasing.

Her father had taught her about being in the woods. He had told her what to do if she ever got lost. How to use leaves and such to stay warm. Unfortunately, that hadn't included falling in a hole full of water. Staying in one place wasn't an issue, but staying warm was. There was one root within her reach. Pulling her belt off, she looped it around the root and hooked her arm through it. That held her in place and kept her head out of the water when she dozed off.

Rachael knew she was going to die from being too cold. Her father had taught her too well. Her teeth had stopped chattering. She knew it wouldn't be long before she fell asleep and didn't wake up. It was supposed to be an easy way to slip out of this life into the next according to her Dad. But she wasn't ready, she had too much to do with her life, hadn't even grown up yet.

Rachael's mother always knew when she was in trouble. Sometimes it didn't feel like a good thing, especially when she was doing something she shouldn't. Maybe if she thought hard enough her mom would find her.

She tried to remember the way she had come in the woods, name of the hotel that her uncle had stopped at. Anything to help find her. She tried so hard and was so tired. Her arm slipped out of the loop she had made, and as her head went under, she gave way to the terror that she had been trying so hard not to buckle under.

The dam in her head finally broke, and she could hear her mother's voice calling for her. Fighting her way back to the belt, she again anchored herself to the wall. Cried out for her mother again and again. When she couldn't call any more, she started to doze off. The sound of the dogs and the rescuers yelling her name broke through her stupor, but her voice was hoarse and her throat hurt. She could hear one of the dogs snuffling at the edge of the well. He started baying and the lights of the handler found her in the dark.

It was her father who rappelled down the wall and brought her up to safety. She spent days in the hospital recovering first from hypothermia and then pneumonia. Her mother never left her side. She didn't know that she would often scream in her sleep and cry about the pain, the cold and the dark. It was her mother's soothing thoughts that would quiet her and allow her to sleep.

The police had been suspicious when her uncle had reported her missing. He said that she had wandered at the zoo. Unfortunately for him, the surveillance cameras at the zoo had shown them leaving together. From there they managed to piece together the rest of the story. The desk clerk at the hotel saw the Amber alert, and recognized her uncle. He called the police. It gave them a place to start the search.

Her Mother's talent for finding her, gave them a direction to look. Rachael often had nightmares about falling asleep and being lost to the cold and dark. Lucky, she had escaped before her uncle got to finish what he wanted to do. He had planned on holding her for a while for his amusement and then killing her.

The police were finally able to solve some old missing children cases after they went through his room at his parent's house. For some reason, she never could shake her fear of dark, wet, closed in spaces and the total loss of control over her options.

She still had the scars from the ropes like a brand around both wrists. That's why she always covered them. It was easier to just say the wide bracelets were a fashion statement rather than explain how she had gotten the scars. When stressed she would dream about it and transpose her frustration into being back in that well. It was easier to think about that than the rape.

The incident had caused a lot of distress and dissension in the family as a whole. No one wanted to believe that the only son was capable of such a terrible thing. Even with the proof of witnesses who placed him at the hotel, and other cousins coming forward about their experiences with him would convince her grandparents that he was guilty.

Her parents had even showed them the hospital records that had recorded the rape and abuse. They believed to the day they died that Rachael had made the whole thing up or brought it on herself. Even the police investigation and the evidence presented at the trial didn't convince them. They're heads were in the sand and it was a huge conspiracy to blame their son.

Her mother was distressed that she hadn't known about their brother. She had been sent to boarding schools and often spent holidays with school friends or other relatives. Rachael's grandparents apparently wanted to spend all their time and energy on their only son. His sister distracted them from that focus. Therefore, her relationship with her brother wasn't close. The fact that he wanted to get to know his sister and her family despite that had made her mother happy as their parents had remained cold and distant.

Rachael's father's parents had both died young. He never talked about them but had encouraged her mom to get to know her brother because he felt family was important. She was never really sure how her mom had talked him out of killing her uncle. Although he never talked about what he did in the military, she knew instinctively he was capable of it.

Her parents had believed her. So did the police who more importantly had built a case and her uncle was convicted. Her parents moved away. No effort was made by either side to try to heal the breach. When her uncle died in prison, the rift was set in granite. Rachael still hated being anywhere that was wet, close in and dark. She forced herself to endure those conditions so she would no longer be afraid. It was easy when awake to psych herself up for it, but in her sleep, she had no defense. She was a small girl again calling for help, and terrified of being abandoned.

When her unit was attacked in Iraq, she had felt no remorse about killing the men who had attacked them. They had tried to kill the soldiers who were protecting the medical team and kill or capture the ones who were injured.

She turned down an option to return to the states before her tour was complete. No one was going to be able to call her a quitter. The soldiers treated her with respect. The medical team with horror. As a nurse, it shouldn't be in her make up to take a life, even to save herself or others.

Even she had a hard time at first, dealing with the ease with which she had killed. Telling herself that it was them or her team wasn't a good enough reason for the lack of remorse. Sometimes she thought the time she had spent in the well thinking she would die had broken something in her.

The medal came as a surprise. It and the report of her actions was what brought her to the attention of Wilson and the agency. When she was approached by Wilson, she thought long and hard on the conflict between killing and healing. They trained her, and she found she could kill again and do it well.

An excellent assassin was born. It was almost scary.

The opposite side of the coin was that she was a superb nurse. Due to her gift, she could sense what was really going on with the patient and deal with it. Nursing was her repayment if she was doing anything wrong. It was the white to the black of her actions. Rachael herself always felt she was the gray. One of her favorite characters as a child was a story about a paladin. The pictures always showed him dressed in grey or shining silver in his armor. Needless to say, she had an ambiguous relationship with her God.

The lack of remorse had sent her to a priest who couldn't give her any answers. He had forgiven her in God's name. That was one problem she had with her religion. How could a man know what God wanted? She stared at the ceiling for a long time before settling into bed and finally drifting off to sleep.

12

ever miss a good chance to shut-up." Texas Bix Bender

THE PHONE RANG EARLY with a request for her to join the family at breakfast. Both the President and Mrs. Blair were concerned about the attacks. She was assured that the President's doctor would be more than happy to check her arm and take out the sutures when the time came. The breakfast included a lovely buffet, so she piled up her plate with goodies and intended to eat it all. Real food at last.

Rachael sipped on her coffee when she was finished and listened to Mrs. Blair's assistant go over her appointments for the day. Unfortunately, she had left three hours open for Rachael and the First Lady to go over and outline her wedding needs. The assistant sounded as excited as Mrs. Blair. What was it with these people and weddings?

An agent came to take her to the meeting with Johnson. Johnson was in his forties, still in good shape, dark hair and the tell-tale streak of white. He had a no nonsense look in his chocolate brown eyes. Rachael had decided long ago that someone must suck out any sense of humor the Secret Service agents had before they graduated. Then injected a dose of surly to take its place.

He shook her hand, and Rachael was at least relieved that he was in the good guy column. "I'm going to be blunt with you, Ms. Cade. I'm not thrilled about you being here. In the last few days, you seem to be drawing a lot of attention to yourself."

"Not my idea. I was happy with my job and life."

"I realize this is Mrs. Blair's brainstorm and not yours. I honestly think she gets bored with all the diplomatic crap she has to put up with. The only time she looks happy is when she does her charity work. But back to the subject at hand, she does get hold of an idea and won't let go." That remark was said fondly. "I just don't want her to get hurt because someone has it in for you. Do you have any idea why there have been two attacks on you in less than twenty-four hours? No irate boyfriends or enemies at work?"

"No old boyfriends. Or new ones for that matter. I work with medical people. They're more inclined to poison you or use drugs then resort to violence. Besides, I only stay up to three months in any one place. If they don't like me, they just have to wait for my contract to be up and I'm gone."

"The only thing I can think of is someone thinks I know something about Moody's murder. It's when everything started. I didn't see anyone in the building. As far as I can remember no suspicious looking characters have been hanging around." She shrugged her shoulders, "Maybe they think I know something that I haven't thought of."

"We will do our best to make your stay here pleasant because that's what Mrs. Blair wants. But, to be clear, her safety is our priority. If any bad shit goes down, you're on your own because my people will only have her safety in mind. Is that clear?"

"Crystal."

"Good, then we understand each other. You have an outstanding military record and up until now a clean slate. Hopefully this will blow over. The FBI thinks the killer is still in the D.C. area and hope to finally catch up with him. Let's hope they succeed."

Or hopefully not, Rachael thought to herself.

Rachael spent the rest of her free time settling in and reading. One of the things she had asked for and received clearance was the freedom to go through the

Congressional Library. Not the stuff anyone could see, but the information only available to the President and the Chiefs of Staff. It showed how much faith the President and Wilson had in her.

A couple of hours researching the architectural plans of the White House and some of the previous president's private papers with emphasis on the early presidents who had resided in the present White House took up some of her time. As an afterthought, she also looked through some of the plans from the Park and Forestry Service for any information on the surrounding parks. Finished, she stretched and returned the material to the cart as requested. Since she still had some time, she decided she would get some exercise.

She had asked one of the agents where she could run and if she was allowed to use their weight room. The answer came back yes, so she would find out if Mrs. Blair's schedule was still the same and plan her own.

She had also had a map of the White House and surrounding grounds. It was the same one given to the public and newly elected officials. Later, when she got to the agency, she'd go over the real blueprints that the public wasn't allowed to see.

The good luck fairy just wasn't in her corner again today. The First Lady had plans. Lots of them. The living area for the first family was actually quite cozy. Mrs. Blair had added personal touches to make the place look homey and lived in. Lots of earth tone colors with bright splashes of red and yellow. It was in sharp contrast to the formality of the rest of the place. The table in the dining area was covered in bridal magazines and brochures for reception halls and other goodies. Rachael thought about running away. The idea of someone wanting to kidnap her was almost cheering.

Maybe she should have let herself be captured last night, then she wouldn't be facing two women who were in seventh heaven about planning a wedding. Could life get any worse? She thought for a second. Unfortunately, yeah it could.

She decided the only way to get through this was to pretend it was for someone else or as an operation. They could plan the whole thing. Then she could find a way to give it away. Maybe auction it off for charity. That would work.

Having decided on an acceptable course of action, she pasted a smile on her face. Listened to Mrs. Blair and Ida, her assistant, as they outlined their ideas for the perfect wedding. She may have appreciated it more, if only she had the perfect groom.

ACROSS THE CITY, Don Wilson was thinking some of the same thoughts. If only. He knocked on Reynold's office door, and his heart sank a little at the look on his brother's face.

"What do you want?

"No, how have you been, long time no see?" Wilson answered back.

"Time works both ways."

"I know. I'm sorry, no excuses. May I come in?"

"Why not? You're here. Least I can do is find out what you want from me so I can tell you no. Wait a minute, let me change that to hell no."

Wilson sat down and aimlessly straightened his tie while he gazed at his brother's books and pictures on the shelf behind him. He knew his brother had a significant number of citations and awards for bravery and duty, but none of those were displayed. They may not communicate, but he kept up with what his brother was doing. Wilson was rarely uncomfortable in any situation, but he wasn't doing well when the predicament was of a personal nature. Families were almost always hard.

"You didn't come to critique my choice of decoration in my office. What do you want?"

"I could just be here to see how you are."

"We both know that's not the case. Is there some big bad terrorist you need me to touch to see if he's telling the truth?

"That was a long time ago. Besides don't try to tell

me you don't use your gift to find out who's guilty or not."

"Not long enough. As for my 'gift,' I use it as I see fit, not because someone is telling me what to use it for. I told you that then and it still stands. I won't work for you."

"I know that. But I promised Mom I'd take care of you and that was one way I could control how much danger you were in." He held up his hand before his brother blew up. "I'm not playing the Mom card. I have a reason to be here that is work related. But I do miss you despite what you think."

"Yeah, your cards and letters have overwhelmed me."

"As you say, it goes both ways."

"Got me there."

"I need you to back off the Moody case."

"I've already gotten the memo. Since all the alphabet agencies want this killer, it's hands off."

"Then why are you still having Cade tailed?"

"I never put a tail on her."

"She's being followed. She picked up three of them when she was out running. Actually, she said to tell you to get your guys in shape. She almost had to turn around and do CPR on one of them."

Reynolds tried not to grin. That sounded like something Cade would say. The woman definitely didn't have a muzzle on that mouth of hers. "Wasn't us. You need to check with the rest of your cohorts."

"No one claims responsibility."

"Then if Cade isn't guilty, which I doubt. Someone thinks she knows something. She does have a photogenic memory. Maybe she just doesn't realize what she knows."

Wilson grimaced. His brother had picked up on that little fact. "But you have backed off?"

"For now. Why this interest in Ms. Cade?"

"She works for me."

"I didn't know you had a need for nurses in your psychotic group."

"We are not psychotic. Not all of us anyway. I know you don't agree with some of our methods, but we do what we do to protect our country."

"So, what does she do for you? I'm curious. With her mouth and attitude, I can't see her taking orders."

"She provides cover for Masters. The man needs to see his fiancé once in a while, no matter where she is. It gives him a reason to be in certain places. We have a unique working relationship. She has an unusual talent. I allow her a little more autonomy then most of my other agents."

"Then her engagement is a cover, not the real deal?" Reynolds wondered why the knowledge the engagement was a sham made his heart skip for a second. She was a suspect for God's sake.

"On her part, yeah. We actually thought they might make a real thing out of it." Wilson sighed, "But Rachael definitely thinks out of the box."

"I noticed."

"I'm going to tell you something that is not general knowledge. There's been a threat made against the First Lady. We need Rachael to be close to her. She is really good at assessing threats, and we feel she is our best bet at keeping Mrs. Blair safe. That's why I need you to back off."

"She's good at assessing threats because she has the same skill set you wanted to use me for."

"It's along the same lines. But she is lethal when it comes to protecting someone."

"I saw what she did to those guys who attacked them."

"Close in there's no one better. She really is something special."

"See, brother, that's where we part ways. She is not a thing. Rachael Cade is a person. I may believe she's a killer, but above everything else, she is a human being. You treat the people who work for you like pieces on a chess board. What happens if someone does go after the First Lady? Is Cade collateral damage?"

"Sometimes to protect and keep this country safe, some people get hurt. That's one of the things we disagree on. I believe the end result sometimes justifies the cost. Even if the cost is high. You don't."

"I never said that all things don't come with a price. We need to think of how high the sacrifice. Don't worry, I'm off the case. Plus considering all the pros and cons, your girl is safe for now. At least from me." He watched his brother's face. Wilson had the world's best poker face, but he could see a flicker behind his eyes that gave him away. "She's not just a pawn to you, is she? You actually care about her." He just leaned back in his chair and stared at his brother in shock.

"Whether you believe it or not, I care about all the people who work for me." Wilson cursed to himself, they knew each other too well. No one could know his feelings for Rachael. It would be a major disaster. He decided to cover it up with by reversing the tables on him. He had seen how Eric had looked at Cade when he didn't think anyone was watching.

"It's a shame really. You and Rachael would make a good pair. You both have the same moral compass. You know what she asked me when they awarded her a medal for her actions in Iraq? She asked why she got a medal for killing people when she hardly ever got a thank you for keeping them alive."

"How did you answer her?"

"I told her that I guess the reason is that when you stop an imminent threat, you can count the number of people saved. Usually, the action is flashy and observable. When saving, or helping one person at a time there is no way to quantify what you've accomplished."

"And her answer to that?"

"She came to work for me. Just remember one thing Eric. You don't know how much some things or people mean to me. Don't judge until you know all the facts. Keep in touch."

With that, Wilson was gone. Reynolds sat and looked at the door. Wilson was his older brother. When their parents died, he had looked to him for everything. His brother hadn't failed him. He watched out for him until he was on his own. When he still tried to keep him safe.

Wilson wanted Reynolds to work for him so he could continue to baby-sit him. Reynolds had tried for a while, but his code of ethics and his brothers didn't always run the same course. It had horrified his younger self, the things his brother was willing to do. Willing to sacrifice in the name of keeping the country safe.

Now he could see that his brother wasn't all steel and ice. There were cracks in the wall after all. And one of those cracks was named Rachael Cade.

Don had him change his last name so no one would know they were related. He did it to protect his younger brother. Through the years, they had fallen apart. Reynolds saw his knack for telling if someone was being untruthful a gift. His brother felt it was a tool. He refused to be a tool for anyone. He left and became a cop. Though he missed his brother, he didn't know his brother had missed him too. Unfortunately, it still didn't solve the problem of Rachael Cade.

Everything he found out about her said she couldn't be a sniper with thirteen known kills to her name. But then again, nothing proved her innocent either. There were too many mixed signals about her abilities. On one hand, she was a possible assassin. The other showed a woman who worked to save lives. Even at the risk of her own. Wasn't the converse true? If you knew how to heal, didn't you also know how to kill? She may have a strong moral compass, but which way did it really point?

13

"Few people can be happy unless they hate some other person, nation or creed." Bertrand Russell

RACHAEL'S next few days soon turned into routine. Breakfast with Mrs. Blair and her assistant. Sometimes, the President was there. The First Lady's schedule was reviewed and time set aside for planning. She would go with her to the different meetings and try to be as unobtrusive as possible. Mostly she watched and evaluated the people around her as to their threat potential. So far, no one rang any bells. Sometimes she wondered what Reynolds was up to. He didn't strike her as the kind to give up because he had orders to. She also wondered why he was on her mind at all. There was something about him that still bothered her. They had never met before this mess, so why did he look so familiar?

Wednesday afternoons were scheduled for the First Family to have some together time. Rachael thought this was something original to the Blairs. Some first couples seemed to be happier apart than together.

Since the free time was available, it was time to go take care of her weapon. The people at the armory were used to seeing her. She always checked out her equipment before and after she used them. Taking her rifle down from the rack felt like saying hello to an old friend. It had been built especially for her. Based on the Barrett 50 caliber, it broke down easily and had great firepower. The gunsmiths had made it in a smaller more compact version due to her size. The fact that in her line of work, it wasn't a good idea to take parts off of anyone standing close to the target. Its daddy, the Barrett, had a shock wave that could literally shear off someone's arm if they were standing close enough to the intended target. The company employed many skilled gunsmiths who used their talents to make weapons geared to the needs of the agents. But hers was unique. If any of the agencies chasing her got a hold of it, then she was toast.

They had discussed changing up her weapon so no one could get a ballistic match. It didn't matter to Rachael which rifle she used as far as accuracy went.

But her rifle was modified to overcome the different topographies and ranges from which she had to take her shots. It was easy to break down and carry. Although based on the Barrett, it wasn't as heavy.

Rachael trained to run long miles to reach extraction points away from any hot zones so that it couldn't be construed that the government had anything to do with the kills. Unfortunately, she wasn't built to carry as much poundage as a fit male of the species. No matter how much she trained, Mother Nature would win in the end. Most women could not build up the same amount of upper body strength as a man. So, the one rifle it was.

The weapon had been cleaned. No one who knew anything about weapons would put one away dirty. But she still needed to do it herself to make sure it was done right. She pulled out a weapon cleaning kit. It had all the components needed to do the job, from the cleaning brush to the t-handled obstruction remover.

Rachael sat down at a cleaning bench, checked to make sure it wasn't loaded, and began to disassemble the gun. First, she removed the rear locking and mid-lock pin. Next she pulled the charging handle to the rear until it cleared the barrel extension. Holding the charging handle to the rear, she lifted the back end of the upper receiver until it cleared the bolt. Her hands moved smoothly, and the familiar practice settled her nerves. It was almost a Zen thing to clean her gun. It was calming. A mechanical chore. One she could perform with her eyes shut or in the dark, if needed. Plus, she was alone. The last few days she had very little of alone time.

She pulled the bolt carrier rearward and inserted the rear lock pin into the top of the ball carrier. After she disengaged the front hood of the upper receiver from the hook pin of the lower receiver, she lifted it clear. Then withdrew the barrel key from the slot in the barrel and slid the barrel rearward into the upper receiver. Now she was ready to clean the parts.

Picking up the panoply patches and cleaning patch tool, she started to clean her baby. Everything was there: the extension rod, the cleaning eye patch rod, cleaning cable bronze bore and chamber brush and a couple of ounces of Break Free. What more could a girl ask for? Some people knitted. She cleaned guns. A familiar process that let her hands work and her mind roam. It also helped to clear out the cobwebs, all the wedding plans where spinning.

Ralph Simon entered the room. He was the gunsmith that had modified the rifle for her. It was as much his baby as hers, but she was its caregiver.

"I see you haven't lost your touch."

"I had a good teacher."

"Benny cleaned it. I checked."

"I know, but I needed to make sure."

"Wish I had more like you. Most of these mopes just

bring the weapon back and expect us to take care of it. Watch the tension on the barrel spring."

The tension on the spring was about seventy pounds. If you released the spring suddenly, you could lose a finger. "What did Benny injure this time?"

Ralph grinned, "The boy's getting faster. You gotta give him credit. It nicked his wrist on the way by. I checked the spring before he finished getting it reassembled. The spring's in good shape. No damage except to Benny's ego. That and the air around here. I think he turned it blue with his foul language. We really need to get that boy to church. No harm, no foul."

"I'm not sure we should punish any denomination by foisting him off on them. Thanks for looking after me though. I won't be much longer."

"No hurry. We're checking inventory this week, so I don't need the space."

Rachael kept her head bent working on the parts. She felt Ralph watching her. "Something on your mind?"

"You. How long do you plan to do this job?"

"I don't know. Haven't really thought about it. I'm getting so much press right now I may be worthless as an agent."

"I wouldn't count on it. You're too valuable an asset to let you come in from the cold."

Rachael didn't say anything, only raised her head so she could keep eye contact. Ralph wanted to talk. Since he was usually taciturn, she was interested in what he had to say. She didn't need to see to clean and put her gun together.

"It's like this, girl. You're young, and I have to admit the best I've ever seen with a weapon. I know my babies are taken care of when you have them. But some day you're going to want a life outside of this madness."

"Then I'll leave."

He snorted, "You don't leave until they say you can. If you're lucky, you get to go on your own terms and get a pension. It also depends on whether or not you go down in the line of duty first. They don't want you out and you insist, well there's plenty of ways to shut you up."

Rachael knew he was talking about 'accidents." They were hits made to look like a natural event. "I've never been given that kind of assignment."

"Of course not. You're the golden girl right now. Don't want to scare you off. You'll last awhile or at least as long as your cover holds. We humans aren't hard-wired to believe someone who looks and acts like you is a killer. Even when you're older, you'll do okay."

"Why are you telling me this?"

"Because I like you and don't want to see you get hurt. Or worse, get cold like most of the bastards around here. You deserve better. Think about it. I gotta get back to work. See you around.

I doubt it, she thought to herself. Fifteen minutes

later, it was done. She stretched and then stood to replace the reassembled rifle to the rack and locked it in place. Looked up at the camera hidden in the light fixture. Rachael grimaced and wiggled her finger in the direction of the ceiling. The people monitoring the feeds would know, she knew what just went down and take care of it.

Next was a stop to the restroom to wash up. The next visit with the First Lady wasn't for another couple of hours. She had already had her run. She had done the four and a half miles around the Mall this time and worked out with weights.

Locating the room where the Agency kept their maps and data on Washington, D.C, and the surrounding universe, she was searching the blueprint of the White House and finding things like hidden staircases that weren't on the public map or even the one's in the Congressional library. The air pressure changed and looked up to see Wilson in the doorway.

"Can't take that with you. It's classified."

"Well darn, I was going to see if I could have it framed and hang it on my office wall. That's not what you came in to tell me."

"You don't have an office. I talked to Reynolds. He still thinks you're his shooter. He's backed off officially, but he'll continue to dig."

"You don't know that. Could have added one since

you've had my house blueprinted. Any way I figured as much about Reynolds. He's like a dog with a bone."

"Anything on the threat?"

"Nope. I'm wondering if it's a red herring. So far everyone close to Mrs. Blair actually likes and respects her. I can't get any negative vibes. Not even a feeling of remorse because someone's being coerced into something. The only one was Cody, and he's hanging on to the President's coattails. You sure about this?"

"Intel is golden. They need to strike soon. The thing they don't want the President to do is getting close."

"I don't suppose I can know what that is?"

"Sorry, above your pay grade."

"So, I just muddle along and hope someone decides to do something violent and stupid?"

"Then you take them out. The Secret Service will protect the body. You get the attacker."

"You know that it'll just be a hired hand? We need the planner. You do realize it will only prove to Reynolds that I have the capability to be the shooter. So far anyone I've done damage to was the attacker. It was all hand-to-hand, and I was defending myself."

"Working on it. Your heads up on Cody has brought some interesting things out. But he's not the brains. We're leaving him in place for the time being. See where it goes."

"I could have told you that. He has no control. Whoever's in charge is cold. Remember, even a small cog can cause a lot of damage if left in the place where it can do harm."

"I know, we need a lead and we're not getting one. I gave the President a heads up. He'll be on guard. Believe it or not, he can take care of himself. If anyone came at him hand-to-hand, they'd be in for a surprise. Whoever is running this is good. Their cover is solid."

"Maybe it's a mole. I didn't think these new terrorist groups had been around long enough to be able to entrench one that deep. Actually, I wouldn't have thought they had the patience for something like that. I think Cold War when I think of moles. Oh, well, that's not my department. You said you had another job for me. Not to be quarrelsome, but I don't like working in the States. They take death and destruction so personally."

"Since you never complain or say how you feel, I'll take your feelings under advisement."

"When pigs fly. What is going on?"

"When the President took office, everything was a mess. The preceding President hadn't helped the situation, if anything, he made it worse. He was openly hostile to anything that wasn't PC or would affect his poll ratings. Why he wanted to be President when he didn't even seem to like this country is beyond me. Not to mention how hard he made our job with his animosity toward anything covert. If it hadn't been for some of the Chiefs' going behind his back, we never would have accomplished anything."

"So, go on."

"Iraq has been a disaster from the get go. Our reasons for attacking were the right ones on the surface. The terrorist threat was real, and the fact that there were weapons of mass destruction available wasn't something made up. Hell, we're the ones that provided some of them. They just didn't always end up in the intended person's hands. Messing with that kind of stuff can be a crap shoot if it's not done right. It was all the undercover stuff that caused us to get screwed."

"We needed the oil or at least thought we did. The current regime wasn't going to let us in on their new oil fields. So, some people started routing around for a reason to dispose of Saddam. He was a bastard and he deserved what he got. But, and there's always a but, the country ran fairly well for the most part. The women had more freedom, and health and education were improving. In fact, the health care was some of the best in the Arab nations."

"The utilities worked, and unless you turned up on the party's hit list the common man was doing okay. Not great, but getting by. Saddam was a paranoid SOB, so he didn't allow any religion to dictate to him. We went in and destroyed all that. Not only Saddam's regime, but we knocked out the whole infrastructure. The people we sent in to pick up the pieces made more problems.

They were only interested in sowing more confusion and lining their own pockets. The ones that wanted to do a good job were swimming upstream."

"After all this time, the people in Iraq still don't have the basics. Electric power is erratic. There is no decent, safe water. Unemployment is horrific. We fired all the trained police and militia, so most of them went to the other side. You and I both know that the common rank and file is usually not corrupt. They obey orders. We could have weeded out the bad eggs and kept a trained force of soldiers and police that knew the people. Instead, we just kicked them all to the curb. We really know "how to sort of win wars and not win over the population." I doubt we ever would have been loved but we had the opportunity to be respected.

Rachael knew what he was talking about. Now the militants and fanatics had filled in the void.

Wilson continued, "Religious factions are getting the upper hand, and women are back to being oppressed. Since health care and education aren't high on anyone's list who are trying to subjugate the country, it's gone too. Their philosophy is if you want to take over a country it pays to keep the populace ignorant.

Everyone we try to help get in power is just another thug feathering their own nest. We need someone who actually has the best interest of the country at heart. Someone who doesn't allow religion dictate to the care and feeding of the people. There's a reason our forefathers wanted a separation of church and state. It wasn't to keep God out of the picture, but to keep any one religion from running things. And to be honest, we need someone who will deal honestly with, and be friendly to, our government.

Rachael knew in her heart, that Americans find it hard to understand that not everyone thinks we have the solution. There are some people who do not prosper without structure and rules. They do not like or flourish with our type of freedoms. They don't really understand them. There was a real need to find a person who was from the region who knew and understood his people. Would do the right thing for them.

Wilson broke in on her train of thought. "I'm tired of working my ass off to put thug after thug in power only to find he's stabbing us in the back. Just milking the coffers dry for his own benefit. Or even worse, have an agenda that goes back to the dark ages and punishes anyone who isn't toeing their line or not male. To be honest, I'm not sure what we can do to solve this mess. At least this President wants what is best for the general population."

"Can we do anything about how things are done in an Arab state? I don't know. I do know you can't reason with fanatics. It's even more suicidal to be dependent on them for fuel or peace for that matter. But the people would rather deal with their zealots than with us. We need to change or at least modify that. We need to be a country these people can at least trust to try to do the right thing. Even if they don't understand us and we don't understand them. I do know that I don't like being on the side of the fence that's sending these people back to the Stone Age. They deserve better."

"The easiest thing we should be able to do is rebuild their infrastructure. That would at least show that our priorities and heart is in the right place. We need to send people over there that will do the job and not try to steal monies that don't belong to them. Yes, we will have insurgents who will try to disrupt the process, but we need to go forward. This whole country is smaller than some of our states. We should be able to get the power turned on again."

"We found a man who seems to want the same things we do. He's willing to reorganize and work to rebuild what has been torn down. No, he's not in our pocket, but most importantly he's not in any one religion's pocket. He may not want all the things we wish for, but at least we are on the same playing field. We can live with that."

"We have a Public Health Service Commissioned Corp that can set up a stable health and sanitation system that the people can take over and work with. The up side is they're used to working with different cultural groups since they do the health care for the Native Americans, Alaskan Natives and various other cultures. They wear a uniform but they're not soldiers, therefore not a threat. They have a built-in system of trying to get those populations into jobs within the system."

"Our Corp of Engineers is trained to reinstate power and get the country up and running if we can get the road blocks out of their way. If basic needs are met, then education and health care will follow. This man has studied our plan and is willing to run with it."

"Our job is to allow him to do it. We need to give him the support to present these plans to the people and allow them to work on the projects. We don't need to import labor. It's there, and they want to work. Maybe if they build it themselves, they won't help anyone else tear it down. It gives them ownership. This plan allows one of their own to run things and use the resources available to bring about change."

"Will they love us for it? No. Is it pie-in-the sky thinking? I hope not. But maybe, just maybe, they will concede that we're okay to work with and be at peace with. They'll have to decide which tenet of their religion they will believe in. The one that preaches peace and that murder is a deadly sin or the one that says everyone else must be converted or destroyed."

"The ones that don't want change, that want the looting to continue are the ones after the First Lady." Rachael had latched on to his line of reasoning.

"You got it. There are always bad apples. No country or government is immune. Those who don't want to lose power or money will fight to maintain the golden goose they have. They want the status quo. Confusion and a chaotic government give them the cover they need to get away with crap. That includes people who supposedly work for us. If we don't get our man in place and allow him to do this, we may lose this war. We may lose it anyway, but at least we'll be able to say with honesty that we tried to do the right thing and win justly."

"Jihad can only take place if they have fighters to bring it on. The Arab world needs to see that they can co-exist and prosper in this world without killing off the infidels. I don't care who or what you are, but a world that consists of tearing everything good apart is not the way to live or survive."

Rachael was quiet for a few seconds. "I would like to agree with you. It sounds wonderful. Unfortunately, we don't have a good track record trying to work with cultures that have a different mindset than we do. I think and truly believe that most people mean well. They just want it done their way and cannot fathom any other choice."

"I've read the Qur'an. When you started sending me to that part of the world, I wanted to learn about it. I read what the scholars say. I looked at opinions, both right and left. I also read translations of their history."

"I don't know how people of goodwill fit in this belief. I know there has to be those who do not want to this to be the way things are. But it is the voice of the fanatics that is heard loud and clear. I'm not a theologian or a scholar, but all I see is the teaching of hatred. Even the moderates have trouble explaining things to us. I hate to see anybody targeted because of what they believe. But we also need to be realistic and know they are painting a target on us for what we believe in."

Wilson sighed and answered her, "So true. Like I said, we don't know if this will work. Our man is having trouble with those within his own party. It may fall down like a house of cards. But the effort needs be made. If the President hesitates or backs out," he hesitated slightly, "we may never have another chance at this. Blair knows this may cause his political death and maybe his physical one if he pisses off enough people. He's willing to take the chance."

"This world needs some rest from being threatened with destruction all the time. We finally got the cloud of nuclear war with the Cold War countries off from over our head. Now we have fanatics with nuclear weapons and dirty bombs who want to blow us up again. The rules have changed. We didn't even get a chance to take a deep breath. The earth is still the only planet we know of that can sustain life. We need to do a better job of protecting her and the life she supports. On the whole, we're not very good tenants."

"But, back to our original discussion. I have come to understand the President will do whatever it takes, but his foundation is his wife. If we pull that out from under him, he may falter. We know it, and his enemies know it. That's why it is so important for you to keep her safe. I can honestly say I have never worked for a President that I respect and like more than this one. For me, that is saying a lot when I know all their dirty little secrets. He feels that if a good man is not willing to rise or fall on his principles then we will never make any headway."

"I will do my best."

"I know that. If it comes down to not knowing who to go to for help, I want you to know you can call on Detective Reynolds. He may want to put you in jail, but he can be trusted with anything you need him for."

"That's a big promise. Can he keep it?"

"I would stake my life on it."

"If it comes down to calling in outside help, I may be staking mine and Mrs. Blair's life on it. I hope he's everything you think he is."

"He truly is. You need to get back."

"I'm on my way."

BUT SHE WAS STILL RESTLESS, and despite what Wilson said she still had some time to kill. She thought she'd see if John Bull was at the gym. She hadn't had a good sparring round in a while. It was important to have a bout where she could work on technique without worrying if someone was trying to kill her. Since lately it seemed like someone really wanted to stop her clock, she needed to see if there was a way to have an edge. Maybe that would settle her jitteriness.

Bull fit his name. He was at least six five and weighed in at three hundred pounds. The bad news for anyone facing him was that it was all muscle. He had black curly hair like a bison. She wouldn't have been surprised to find horns budding up along his scalp. For someone who projected bad ass to the ninth degree, he was a pussycat and hated to hurt anyone or thing.

When she first joined the agency, he was supposed to teach her how to spar and box. She knew martial arts, but sometimes it was necessary to just get flat-footed and duke it out. Street fighting at its dirtiest had its place. One must never underestimate being treacherous and sneaky, especially in a fight.

Bull taught her all he could by using the bag and how to move. But when it came down to getting in the ring and actually going one on one with her, he couldn't do it. There was no way he would take a swing at anyone as tiny as she was and a woman to boot.

She still went to the gym sometimes and worked out with a bag to get pointers, thought she'd see if he was in. There were two people in the ring and everyone had gathered to watch. One of the boxers was around six-one and one-eighty. The other was a new female recruit. She was around five-six and weighed in at one-thirty. Bull wasn't there or he would have stopped the fight.

It wasn't so much a training experience as a knock down. She saw the uncomfortable looks on some of the trainee's faces but no one had the wherewith all to interfere. The girl had her guard up and was trying to get some blows in, but her opponent just kept hitting her and talking trash.

"See, this is why women shouldn't try to get into a man's job. You're not cut out for it. Come on, lady, I'm standing wide open and you can't touch me." He demonstrated by stepping out of her reach and opening up his arms. He was a real showman. "You need to go back to your desk job and marry a big bad agent and have his kids. That's how you can make a contribution."

Rachael had heard enough. She swung up into the ring and pulled the woman behind her. "Why don't you pick on someone your own size? Think you're the big man because you can push a beginner around?"

"I'd fight someone my size, but I don't see anyone who fits the description," he sneered back.

"Where were you when they gave the sexual harassment class?" She snapped her fingers, "I know. You were in your cave grunting over how women don't know their place. Why don't you see if you can take me down? I seem to fit the class you like to run over. Or are you afraid of little old me?"

A larger crowd was starting to form and Bull was

barreling through them. "Cade, you can't take him on, he is so out of your league."

"Sorry Johnny, he's a bully and he needs to learn a lesson."

"Ah, hell, at least put some gloves on first." He grabbed a pair as he passed a table and threw them up to her. "I'll go call the paramedics. Crocker's going to need them by the time you get through."

"I don't plan on hurting him that bad." She laced the gloves on to keep Bull happy.

Crocker had been listening to the conversation. She could see the wheels turning slowly in his head, "You're Rachael Cade?"

"That's what my Momma named me."

"I pictured you as lot bigger."

"Yeah, it disappoints me too. You ready to fight?"

"I don't want to hurt you."

"It didn't seem to bother you with the other agent. You better give it all you got or it's not going to be pretty."

Rachael rose up on her toes and dropped into a horse stance for balance. This wasn't formal boxing, and she would use every fighting technique she knew to get the job done.

Crocker looked around to see if he was getting any help from Bull or the crowd. Then it dawned on him, he was on his own. He charged her across the mat. Rachael held her position, and then weaved to one side, bringing up her fist, caught him under his jaw. She danced out of range.

She let him beat himself. He hadn't learned that for every motion there is an opposite and equal force that can be used against you. He depended on his size to instill fear. She simply let him do all the brute work and leveraged it back at him. In under three minutes, Crocker had two black eyes, a sore and bloody nose, three loose teeth and his lip was bleeding. He had hit the mat at least three times and there wasn't a mark on her.

He was laid in the middle of the ring on his back, moaning. She looked down at him. "Never underestimate your opponent because they happen to be small. When you decide to get that chip off your shoulder, I'd be more than willing to work with you. Until then, as far as I'm concerned, you're nothing but a bully and a blowhard. You use your size to intimidate.

You'll never make a good agent because you'll piss someone off. They won't fight you, they'll just shoot you. If I can do this to you, think how much damage someone your size will do. You might want to get your attitude adjustment in place really fast. Because the first person I plan to start training is the agent you just tried to embarrass."

"How did you learn to do that?"

"I worked at it. I had more incentive than you."

"Why is that?"

"I'm always going to be the little guy."

She threw him a towel and walked over to the ropes. She ducked under them, but before she could jump to the ground, Bull picked her up in a big bear hug.

She laughed, "It's been a while. I do believe you've gotten even uglier."

Bull's voice was a deep bass rumble, "And you're just as wise-assed as ever. You've even gotten more beautiful. How you been, little girl? We just hear rumors now and then. Though I have to admit if the rumors be true, you've been one busy young lady."

"Only believe half of what you hear and wonder about the other half."

They started toward the door to the locker room. Rachael knew she was starting to run late. "I hear you're planning a wedding and staying with the First Lady."

"There go those rumors again. I really need to go. It was good to see you again. Do me a favor and start training that new girl like you did me."

"I'll take care of her for you. If they want you around the White House, it means something big. Watch that skinny back of yours, girl."

She stood on tip-toes and kissed him on the cheek. "I'm always careful. Give my love to your family. I really miss Amy's chess pie. No one makes it like her."

A rushed shower followed, and she was out of there. Bull was keeping the female trainee busy, so she slipped out without being inundated with thank yous.

She missed Wilson's meeting with Ralph Simon. Probably because it was also above her pay grade. Rachael knew he had heard the conversation in the armory and would draw the same conclusion she did. Ralph had crossed the line and was working for someone outside the agency.

14

"Scientists say the universe is made up of protons, neutrons, and electrons, they forgot to mention morons." Tee shirt

Rachael was correct about her conversation with Ralph being reviewed by Wilson. He now stood in front of Wilson's desk and smiled. Ralph didn't know what this meeting was about, but since Rachael was on a special assignment, he figured she needed some special toys.

"Sit down. Let me finish this up, I'll be just a second."

Ralph sat down and looked around the office. For the head of the unit, it was unimpressive. Stacks of files, books, and maps covered every hard surface. No personal pictures or awards were in evidence. Wilson was a hard man to get to know.

"So, Ralph, how long have they had you in their pocket?"

When he had decided to make a little extra money and maybe get, what he felt was his rightful recognition, getting caught wasn't something he planned on. Ralph jerked and started to sweat. Wilson didn't go in for small talk. If he was being questioned, Wilson knew. Stall tactics were his only choice. "Sir?"

"Don't play coy. It's not your style. You've sold out. What was that little song and dance with Rachael Cade about? Did they ask you to try to get her second guessing her assignment or maybe try to undermine her confidence? She likes and trusts you. Maybe you thought she would listen to your brand of cool-aid?"

"I was just talking to the girl. I like her, but she's a little intense about the job. I thought I'd try to give her some perspective so she'd lighten up a little. Did she report me or something? I didn't do anything inappropriate."

"Since you still have all your teeth. We know that part for sure. We've been watching you.Rachael didn't say anything. She didn't have to. Besides it's not her style. You said it all. I'm just curious. What did they offer you to make you betray your country and your oath?"

Screw it anyway. If Wilson knew what questions to

ask, the game was up anyway. He wouldn't be in his office if they didn't have the proof. "A place in management that has never been offered here along with a salary that I deserve with my talents."

"Ahh, sour grapes. That salary would have included a bullet to the head when your usefulness was over. Now it's a retirement to a cell."

"You can't do this. I have a right to a trial."

Ralph sighed. "No, you don't. When we screw up, it's a prison sentence or death. You were told that when you signed on the dotted line."

"Cade will notice I'm gone. What I said will take root. When she notices I'm not here to dream up a fancy new weapon for her, she'll ask what happened to me. You'll end up losing her in the long run. So, I win." He sat back in his chair with a smug look on his face.

"If I lose her, it won't be because of what you said. She knew you were lying. She just didn't understand why."

Jon and two agents entered the room. "Take him away and do the usual sweeps of his home and office."

Ralph just walked out quietly. At least, he had enough character not to have to be dragged out yelling. Wilson sighed. He had been a good man.

"He's not the only one. There's someone higher up." Jon commented.

"I know. The stuff leaked was above his need to

know. I doubt they even told him to talk to Rachael. He was just trying to mess with her mind."

"She would know he was putting her on."

"That's why she didn't react. Ralph doesn't know she can read a lie from a mile away."

"So, what now?"

"One down and who knows how many to go."

15

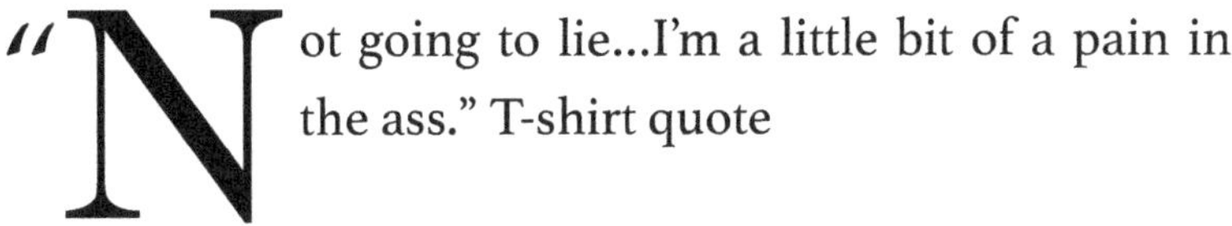

"Not going to lie...I'm a little bit of a pain in the ass." T-shirt quote

"My doctor asked me if anyone in my family suffers from mental illness. I said, "No we all seem to enjoy it." T-shirt quote

As Racheal left the agency, she mulled over both Wilson's lecture and Ralph's words. Wilson was speaking from the heart. Dumping information wasn't his style. He was strictly a need-to-know kind of guy. He had truly believed in what he said. Which meant he was very good for telling her.

Ralph on the other hand was lying through his teeth. He was trying to get inside her head. Wilson had the place wired, so she didn't have to play tattle-tale. There was a good chance Ralph wouldn't be there when she went back. There were parts of her job she really hated.

She was hungry. She was near the greasy spoon that she and Jon had stopped in the night of the bash. It was on the shadier side of U Street, but since it was daylight, no worries. Normally she tried to eat healthy. Never underestimate the power of greasy fries and chocolate to lift your spirits. Plus, no need to get anal about it.

Racheal ordered and noticed a table in the back. Headed there when she got her order. It was close to an exit door and where she could see the front entrance. The back entrance to the kitchen was down the small hallway leading to the outer door.

The first bite of the burger was pure heaven. The taste of meat mingled with ketchup and a hint of mayo, lettuce, tomato and, of course, provolone cheese. She leaned back to savor it. Add thin cut French fries covered in salt with grease oozing out onto the paper liner, what more could you ask for? Maybe someone to share it with? What's the old saying? Be careful what you wish for.

Reynolds walked through the door. He turned slightly to hold the door open for the person behind him. Manners usually not found in D.C. Momma must have trained him right. Now that she could watch him unobserved, there was something so familiar about the way he moved. She knew someone else who had that same compact rhythm. Sooner or later, she'd figure it out.

He had to be a little bit special. Wilson had never spoken so highly of anyone in her presence before today. Since most federal agencies usually had a snobbish distain for local law enforcement, it was really odd. As she took another bite of her burger and wondered how long it would take him to see her.

It didn't take long. He was casing the room as soon as he came the rest of the way through the door. His eyebrows rose as he saw her. She smiled slightly and raised her chocolate milkshake in his direction. The people at the diner must have known him. They greeted him before he identified himself. The guy at the counter, grinned and handed him a bag and a drink.

After paying, he strolled in her direction. He weaved his way through the tables with their red tops, salt and pepper shakers in shiny holders. The grill was a mixture of the early 1950's and Route '66 diners. He looked down at her when he reached her table.

"I wouldn't have thought this would be your kind of place. Thought you medical types were all about health food and such. Would figure if you wanted to stray into junk food, you'd go for something like the Chili Bowl."

"You ever eat hospital food? The dietician doesn't

get within two floors of the cafeteria. Besides, isn't grease a food group? Guess I need to go back and check my textbooks. I thought it was up there with chocolate and desserts. I live for the days I get to go to ACKC Coca Gallery or Leonidas Fresh Belgian Chocolates on Wisconsin Avenue. Just taking a deep breath will cause you to gain weight. I don't care much for hot dogs or chili though."

"You mind?" He indicated the empty seat at her table.

"Sure. It's a free country."

"How's the wedding plans going?"

Rachael shrugged her shoulders. "Everyone seems to be freaking delirious about them. So fine I guess."

"For someone who is engaged to one of D.C.'s most eligible bachelors, you don't seem too thrilled."

"Maybe if my mother was still alive, I might enjoy the insanity more. She had a way of making things fun. Besides, you know what I am. How long would you stay with someone who couldn't lie to you without you knowing? How does having sex go? Knowing every little thought or feeling they have while doing the dance. Dealing with someone in your life. Always there, always needing. They don't have a clue about how you feel or what you need. Even worse, they can't hide when they quit caring and don't really give a flip anymore. They just haven't figured out a way to tell you yet. Those are things I wanted my mother to tell me. She never got the chance. So, there you go."

"How would you deal with it? Do you have anyone you can talk to? Someone who won't get paranoid when they find out what you can do? You're the first person I've met who's anything like me. There must be a way to deal or we couldn't reproduce."

Reynolds rocked back in his chair. This definitively wasn't the conversation he normally would have with a murder suspect. He almost wished they could go back to the commentary on buzzards.

Rachael waved her hand in the air, "Never mind. I shouldn't have asked. It's just temporary insanity from all the people around me who think planning a wedding is such a big, freaking joyful deal." She picked up a French fry and pointed it at him, "They say that someone lies to you every five minutes. How do you put up with it? In your line of work, it's more like three times that. How do you cope? I don't need an answer, I'm just venting. What are you doing here? Is this an accident or are you still following me?"

"Do you often have these flights of ideas? If you do, that would explain a lot. I think they actually have medicine for it though." He answered the last question, "An accident. We're off the case. I eat here at least once a week, usually on Wednesday. They make the best burgers around."

"Well, at least we agree on one thing."

"Why do you stay with Masters if it's such a problem?"

"Because he's tolerable. He's practically a null. I don't always pick up on his emotions. That can be peaceful sometimes. Besides, the powers that be think it's good for business. I know it's just a political thing with him. And," she added a little wistfully, "sometimes it beats being alone."

"Other times?"

"I prefer to be alone."

"So, what are you going to do?"

"Right this moment, I don't know. They told me they have a surprise for me tomorrow. That should be hilarious. Go ahead. Eat your food before it gets cold."

As he unwrapped his burger, he wondered what to say to Rachael. Though he still thought she was good for the shoot, she fascinated him. Somehow, she didn't seem the type to kill off anyone without a good reason. But she worked for his brother so that was a problem. He decided maybe he could try a neutral subject. "Are those really cowboy boots or just a fashion statement?"

"They're the real deal. I actually train and ride horses occasionally. You'd probably find honest to goodness horse manure on them if you looked hard enough."

"I'll pass." So much for fashion. "You're a pilot too."

"Guess you found my plane. She's a sweet Cessna 182 RG."

"RG?"

"Retractable gear. Helps with gas mileage. There's less drag when you don't have the wheels hanging down."

"Makes sense. So why do you have a plane?"

"I use it to go home when I have a long weekend. I miss my horses. This way I don't have to worry about airline schedules. Nurse's schedules are never carved in stone. If someone gets sick or has a family emergency, the unit needs coverage. There's not a large airport close to where my farm is. That adds on land travel time. I have a small strip and hanger built on my land."

"And your places in Maine and Colorado?"

"My, you have been a busy boy. I fly into small airports there. They have FBOs where I can tie my plane down."

"FBOs?"

"Fixed base operators. Think of a mixture of a gas station, rest area, and parking spot for planes. Sort of like a shop and rob. If you like, I'd be happy to take you up for a ride sometime. D.C. is a restricted fly zone, but I could take you over Virginia. Richmond has some great restaurants. I also fly to stay current."

"I'd like that if things between us were different."

"Well, there you go. Guess it doesn't look good for a cop to be seen with someone he suspects of a crime. The offer is out there if you ever change your mind."

They ate in silence. He noticed she enjoyed her food

and wasn't shy about eating something besides a salad. Must have the metabolism of the energizer bunny on crack with her size.

She licked her fingers clean and started on her fries, "So what mess do they have you working on now since I'm off limits?"

"A few murders. We've had a couple of women turn up dead in the Arlington Cemetery area. Close, but not in the cemetery."

"Any links? Signatures?"

"You know I can't answer that."

"What did the women do for a living?"

"They were call girls."

"What age?"

"Early twenties."

"Can you tell me if they were similar in appearance? Were they sexually assaulted?"

"I guess I can tell you they sort of looked alike."

"Hmm, take that as a no, on the assault issue." He watched her look off into the distance as if she was pulling a memory out of the air.

"You might want to look at women who have been deployed and just made it home recently. Someone who might suspect her husband of cheating while she was out serving her country. If you really were intrigued, you might also want to get in touch with the police in Berlin. They had the same problem when I was there two years ago. They never found out who did it. The women were found close to military cemeteries. It might give you a clue."

"What makes you think the killer is a woman? Was it you?"

"They weren't sexually molested in any way, were they? Besides, I wouldn't kill a woman for screwing around with my husband. I'd kill him."

"For someone who's talking to a homicide cop and is still a person of interest as far as I'm concerned, in a murder, you use the word 'kill' easily."

"I also use freaking and some other words frequently. Use the information or not. I just remember the story from when I was there. I doubt it made it to our news reports."

"I'll do that."

"Well, I better run. Things to do, places to be. Goodbye, Lieutenant. Oh, by the way, is Wilson any relation to you? I'd guess brother, even with the different last names. You move exactly alike."

Reynolds choked on his drink.

"I take that as a yes." She flipped him a careless wave as she left the table.

He watched her as she dumped her trash in the garbage and started to stroll out of the diner. She was indifferent to the admiring glances that followed her. He felt the atmosphere in the restaurant change. It was never something he could explain to anyone. It was a vibe or feeling. Apparently, Cade caught the same vibe he did. She turned on her heel and came back to their table.

Smiling, she bent and reached down under the table like she had forgotten something. "Two men in line. One's third from the front. The other one moved to the second line. They're both carrying. They're not here for the money. They want to kill as many people as they can."

"How do you know that?"

"Same way you know which way a crowd is going to turn. I'll go in through the kitchen and try to get their attention. You come in from the back. They haven't pegged you as a cop yet."

"You aren't armed."

"You take care of your end. I'll do mine."

"I'll call for backup."

"You do that, but you better be moving because they're getting antsy." She was gone before he stood up. The door to the kitchen swaying slightly from her passing.

He took out his cell, and walked toward the front exit. Passed the man in the line closest to him when the second man stepped up to order. The second the cashier looked up, he pulled out his weapon to threaten her.

Rachael stepped out from the back and snagged one of the heavy ceramic coffee cups that were on the shelf. Her "hey you!" drew the shooter's attention to her, and she winged the coffee cup at his head while pulling the clerk down to the floor. He went down without a whimper. She kept the girl sheltered with her body in case someone got a shot off.

His partner had his gun out but froze as he felt Wilson's automatic press into the back of his head. "I'd drop that if I were you. You'll be dead before you can pull the trigger."

The man set the gun down on the counter and laced his hands behind his neck. "I see you've done this before. Get on your knees." The gunman did as he was told. When Reynolds glanced at Cade, she had hopped over the counter and was checking the other gunman's pulse. Gotta to admit, the girl had one hell of a pitching arm.

"He's just down for the count. Pulse is strong. You got another one of those restraint thingies?He's going to be way pissed when he wakes up. I need to get some of these cups. It didn't even chip." She checked the unconscious man for weapons and found another automatic pistol and an urban assault rifle hanging under his coat. Then added a hunting knife and a couple of magazines to the pile and placed them on the table next to Reynolds.

Reynolds tossed her the zip tie and did the honors on his captive while he read him his rights. The sirens were getting close.

Rachael restrained the dazed man's wrists and turned him on his side for safety's sake.

The patrons of the diner were starting to talk and moved around restlessly now that the danger was over. It was sheer nerves and stress. Cade jumped back up on the counter and waved her arms to get their attention. "Everyone stay calm. You really have been super. No one's hurt. The police have it under control. Enjoy your lunch while we're waiting. Free fries for everyone. Don't leave before the officers get your statements. Let us know if it'll cause problems. We'll write the principal a note." That comment drew a few laughs. "We appreciate your cooperation and bravery under such stressful circumstances."

She jumped back to the floor, this time on the serving side of the counter. "Come on, guys, let's get some fries out there to settle these people down. The cops will get to us soon enough. Who's the manager?"

An older man wearing a stained, but clean, apron approached her. The girl at the counter had jumped up and ran to the older man. She had her arms around him and he was stroking her back. "I'm the owner and manager. My name's Thomas Ginovia." He put his hand out to shake hers, "Thank you for what you did."

"Rachael Cade. No problem. Just glad I could help. Sorry about the free fries' thing. It's the first thing that came to mind to calm everyone down. I'll cover the cost since it was my idea. You make great fries and burgers by the way."

"Thank you again, and you are always welcome here as my guest. You and your friend. I owe you more than you know." He looked down at the girl, "This is my youngest daughter. I don't think things would have ended well if you hadn't been here. The fries are no problem. A small price to pay to keep my customers happy. I'll get them started. We're not set up for waiting on tables though." Rachael smiled at all the hand gestures that went along with the conversation. Mr. Ginovia lived up to his last name.

"I'll help. Looks like I'm here for the duration."

Reynolds watched Cade work the room as she got everyone settled and started helping the kids that worked there deliver fries and drinks to the customers. He even saw a few laughs and smiles as the people started to relax. The scene was under control, and the statements were being taken. He saw people starting to trickle out as they were finished with the processing. Watts walked up to him.

"And what just happened? Thought you were just getting some lunch. How did our main suspect help you take down what looks like two spree killers?"

"Right time, wrong place. I've got to say, the lady does have guts and can think on her feet. She never hesitated to go up against an armed man with nothing but a coffee cup. I've never seen anyone throw china quite like she does. I hope she's not the type to throw dishes when she's mad. With an arm like that, she'd be deadly."

"Why were you both here?"

"I came in for lunch, and she was sitting in the back eating a burger. We talked. She started to leave and then came back. Gave me the heads up about the guys with guns. Didn't even give me time to argue. Told me what she was going to do and did it. I'd love to see that throw again. Man, she nailed him right between the eyes. She'd be a hell of a baseball player." He saw Watts' mouth twitch as if biting back a grin. "She's behind me, isn't she?" Watts just nodded.

He swung around, and there she was.

She dropped him a pretty curtsy. "Thank you, kind sir. I played shortstop in high school. No petty remarks about my stature, thank you very much. I'm not short, just built low to the ground for speed and accuracy. I think everyone is settled and getting sorted out."

"May I give my statement and get out of here? I'm sort of running behind schedule. I called but it's not good form to keep the First Lady waiting. Anyway, I would like to know what they were up to. They gave up too easily. Spree killers usually want to die along with their victims."

"Thanks for your help. If you don't mind giving your statement to Detective Watts, you can go. I guess we know where to find you."

"Guess the big white house is hard to miss around here. Ready, Detective? This shouldn't take long since you already have more information on me than you'll ever need. How's Sherriff Randy by the way? I haven't talked to him in a while."

Reynolds shook his head and walked away. Rachael Cade definitely fell in the incorrigible category. He hoped Watts didn't ask her about the banjos.

16

"I meant to behave but there were too many other options." T-shirt quote

The robbery had felt random or at least a spur of the moment thing. Rachael wasn't egotistical enough to think it was all about her. But why pick the time she was in the eatery? Had she, for some unknown reason to her, made someone nervous? What did they think she was, a one-woman army? Unless it had to do with the ambush in Iraq. Was this an issue with her being with the First Lady or was it about her job with the agency? There was just something weird about the whole thing. If it wasn't a cosmic coincidence, were there two different groups at work?

She called Wilson and let him know about the latest escapade. After explaining her theory, she went on to tell him, "They didn't appear to be aiming directly at me. They acted like they meant to take out everyone. Maybe I'm paranoid, but three weird things in a row isn't is off. I don't believe in these many coincidences. The great cosmos doesn't really give that big of a whoop to want me dead this bad. But my gut says someone is after me. Has Hinkley found anything yet?"

"I'll look at the police report and question the two shooters. You're right. It does look like someone wants you either out of the way or dead. Hinkley hasn't had enough time to find anything yet. He did say that at least three of your neighbors who are usually home during the day got calls offering them a special deal at a new restaurant. The catch was, they had to go at that specific time. It was for a new, high-end restaurant, so they couldn't resist. Don't worry, we'll get to the bottom of this."

"I'm at the House, so I'll talk to you later."

"Glad you're okay."

"You and me both."

When Rachael returned to her rooms and found a message to call Ida, the First Lady's assistant, immediately. She was now in the middle of a gaggle of women who wanted to go pick out a wedding dress. Her wails of "We don't even have a date yet!" went completely unnoticed and unheeded. Mrs. Blair's comment that dresses didn't spoil wasn't a help.

The parade left for the bridal salon. They were going after hours so that the Secret Service could secure the store and provide protection for Mrs. Blair. The agents where probably clueless why apparently perfectly sane women were acting like they were totally possessed. She agreed with the agents.

Now they were surrounded by yards of orgasmic white in all shapes and materials. The place literally rained pearls, beads, and sequins. Rachael sat next to Mrs. Blair while they were served floral teas, which she hated, and pastries which weren't half bad, while the salesperson brought out dress after dress.

Rachael had discovered Ida was engaged and her fiancé was out of the country. They planned on marrying when he returned. She watched Ida's reactions to the gowns. Jodi, "with an i", their bridal consultant, had just shown them a particularly beautiful gown. The bodice was sown with seed pearls and beads in a floral pattern. It was heavily embroidered, a full train and way too much for Rachael. But Ida was in love. She couldn't put it away, but placed it beside her and patted it as if it was alive. Rachael got her to try it on.

It was a gown Ida would do justice to. She was tall and lanky so the extra padding of the beads and pearls softened her angles. On Rachael, it would make her look like a sequined float lumbering down the aisle. Ida would simply look like she was gliding. The way her eyes changed when she talked about her man was amazing. They went from muddy brown to dark and dreamy. Her hair was her crowning glory, all red gold curls that were absolutely gorgeous. She would make a beautiful bride because she was in love with her groom.

There was no way Rachael was going through with this wedding, why not do something good with it? Ida's family couldn't afford the plans the First Lady was making. The invitations and personalized stuff couldn't be transferred, but the rest of the plans would work for anyone. Wilson would reimburse the default fees on anything, if needed. Rachael could afford it for that matter. But the dress would be a done deal. Rachael was stuck with whatever she chose. There was nothing to stop her from getting Ida the one she liked.

Rachael wasn't hard up for money. Her parents had left her comfortably set. She had hardly touched her inheritance. The planes and horses were her only ongoing weaknesses. The condo for skiing had been a one-time splurge, but it made money during the rest of the year. It basically paid for itself. Normally, she lived on what she made. It was nowhere near the money Jon had, but hey, she didn't need enough for world dominance. Enough to have a cushion was fine with her.

She would just re-arrange the scheduling to fit in with Ida's wedding. It was a win-win situation. Ida would have the wedding of her dreams. The vendors wouldn't lose any money. She relaxed. The dilemma of what to do about this farce that would make everyone happy was solved.

"Rachael, you need to try something on. This is so much fun." Mrs. Blair was enjoying herself.

Gads, poke me in the eye with a stick. "Okay, that one there." Rachael pointed to a slip of a dress with a fitted bodice that flared out into a slight train. It was plain white silk with a faint silver pattern embroidered into the train. It caught the light and shimmered like mother-of-pearl when the material moved. If she was picking out a wedding dress, this would be it. The one Ida favored was beautiful, but too much of the pearls and glitter for her taste.

After going into the dressing area to change, Rachael paraded in front of everyone. Mrs. Blair had tears in her eyes. "You have a great eye for fashion. That suits you perfectly. I'm disappointed in a way. I thought we would get to shop around. It's perfect and I don't think you could do any better." She sat back in her chair and sighed, "You'll make a lovely bride.'

Jodi bustled forward. "Shoes are easy. We have the silk heels that match our dresses. What do you want to do about a veil? We have all kinds or we could make one. Let me get you some examples and the catalogues, and we can have a look. Then we can talk about brides-maid dresses." She set about bringing gossamer collections of netting and lace made into nests that fit on top of your head.

In desperation, Rachael looked at the First Lady and Ida. "What do you think? Do I need to put something on my head?" She hesitated. In for a penny, in for a pound, "If I was having it in a church, I would need a head covering. This wedding will be informal. A High Mass in the Rose Garden would be awkward." Not to mention the grass stains from kneeling.

They both laughed and came up to stand by her. Mrs. Blair repositioned the train and stood back. "I have to admit, I don't know if you need anything else to complete the picture. A veil is traditional, but it is up to you."

People had been going and coming since they had arrived. The teams of agents making rounds and forming the protection around the First Lady had been a steady flow, so when the door opened, Rachael only noticed it peripherally. She looked up simply because she had to. Her training wouldn't let it pass. And looked into the startled eyes of Detective Reynolds.

17

"In my defense I was left unsupervised." T-shirt quote

"Whatever makes you weird is probably your greatest asset." Joss Whedon

He imagined he looked like he had been hit with a two by four. By everything he held holy, she was beautiful. Since he had overheard Mrs. Blair's remark, he cleared his throat and commented, "I wouldn't change anything."

"Didn't realize you had experience as a wedding advisor. What are you doing here?" Rachael asked with a surly twist in her voice. The man was impossible. He turned up everywhere.

"We were informed the First Lady was here. We had upped patrols. There's a group of demonstrators who have apparently gotten wind of her presence. I'm here to offer the agents any assistance they need to get her out of here safely."

"What are they demonstrating about?"

"Women's rights."

Mrs. Blair looked puzzled. "I've been an open supporter of women's rights. What are they protesting?"

"You're either not a strong enough supporter or they want more. Or it could be some people are never satisfied. They don't appear to be violent for the most part. I'm just here as another body to assist."

Rachael was stripping out of the gown on the way to the dressing room. She knew why they had sent Reynolds. His bosses might not know how he did it, but they were aware that he could read people accurately. They were using him to gauge the crowd's temper. He wouldn't have bothered to come in the salon if there wasn't a problem. If he said it was time to leave, she wasn't going to question it. She was mostly dressed and out in under forty seconds. She buttoned her blouse as she talked to Reynolds, "What are you feeling?

Reynolds didn't even blink. "I think the majority of the people are law abiding and passive. I feel an aggressive undercurrent."

"Get the First Lady home."

One of the agents started to sputter something about Rachael wasn't in charge. It was too late. Rachael had already launched herself to cover Mrs. Blair as the grenade came through the window. She snagged the fancy sofa to provide cover. There was a dull thud, and the window exploded but no flash and bang. Someone in the room didn't want to be disorientated. That or it had malfunctioned. Two agents piled on top of her to protect the President's wife. Rachael pushed them off of her and pulled the lady to her feet. "We need to get out of here!"

The agents tried to get them to the limousine they came in. Rachael was holding Mrs. Blair back. "No, that's what they expect." She whipped around and looking for her not so favorite detective. Found him moving toward them. "Reynolds."

He was dirty but okay, "What?"

"Your car. Where is it?"

He pointed to the curb. It was a little dented, but still serviceable.

"Go get it. Drive it through the window. Then get her out of here!"

The agents were still trying to get Mrs. Blair to the limo but the First Lady was following Rachael's lead. They wouldn't listen when Rachael yelled "It's a trap. Don't do what's expected!"

Reynolds had sprinted to the car. He had left it

running, and he gunned it over the debris. Although Cade was difficult for him to read, he picked up on her vibe that something was wrong with this picture. He agreed. He managed to maneuver the vehicle between the limo and the First Lady so the agents were forced to stop their push to the car. Had the passenger door opened as he slid to a stop. The First Lady had hesitated just enough for Rachael to get her way. She shoved her in the car, and the agents had no choice but to follow. "Go! Get her safe!" And they were gone.

Two other agents ran for the black SUV and two that she didn't recognize jumped in the limo. Rachael screamed at the agents in the SUV to stop as the first one slid over and started the car. Grabbing Ida and Jodi who were both still huddled on the floor, she dove behind some of the rubble from the first blast. The SUV exploded, sending out flames and debris. She ran toward the car, but there wasn't anything left to save.

Ida was past crying. Just sat with her hand over her mouth, rocking back and forth. She was going into shock. Jodi just stared straight ahead. They were both going into meltdown but there was nothing Rachael could do about it right now. She had to watch the limo drive off with the two unidentified agents. It was a trap.

She pulled Ida and Jodi out of the mess and made them sit against a car on the sidewalk, away from the burning building. The demonstrators had scattered. Then went back in to see if there were any survivors still inside. Three agents were down. She couldn't feel a pulse in two of them, but she pulled them clear. Either she was missing a wound or the blast had killed them. The fire from the shattered SUV was spreading and she didn't want to add burns to their injuries if there was any chance they were still alive. She couldn't immobilize their spines, but the fire was spreading too fast to wait for help.

As soon as she had them clear, she set to work on the one with a pulse. Triage at its finest. You saved the one you could. He only had what appeared to be a minor head wound. His pulse was rapid and thready. Starting at the head she worked her way down his body, cataloguing injuries as she went. When she slid her hands under his torso, she finally found the bleeding. Used her jacket, she applied pressure by packing it under him and using his own body weight for pressure. She tried to move him as little as possible.

The sound of the fire engines was growing louder as they rounded the corner. Thirty seconds later, she was surrounded by cops, agents, and her boss. Da ja vu all over again. The shop was encased in flames. It was one hell of a way to shop for a wedding dress.

18

"You know that thing inside your head that keeps you from (saying or doing) things you shouldn't '? –yeah, I don't have one of those." T-shirt quote

JOHNSON WAS SCREAMING AT HER. "What the fuck happened? I have four dead agents and others injured. I want to know what's going on."

Rachael ignored him. She got one of the cops to get her a jump kit from an ambulance. The medical personnel weren't allowed on the scene until it was cleared as safe. Between the fire and the explosions, that was taking some time. She did talk them into escorting Jodi and Ida to where the ambulances were waiting. They were in shock and the noise and chaos of the scene was adding to it. Removing them from the immediate area was the best she could do.

She got two lines started in the agent and with the help of two of the TEMS (tactical EMS) that had shown up with the SWAT team. They had logrolled the agent to his side and got the wound dressed. The bleeding was down to a slow trickle. The fluids were bringing his blood pressure up. She had started him on oxygen from the small tank in the pack. They finally cleared the scene enough to let the EMS through.

Sadly, the paramedics had agreed with her original assessment. The two agents were dead at the scene. They had found the bullet holes she'd missed. Someone had taken them down during the noise and confusion. The EMS personnel recognized her from the emergency room. They listened to her assessment and didn't give her a hard time about the care she had given the agent. She helped them get him packaged for transport. He was waking up by the time they moved him to the ambulance. Luckily, he was moving his extremities and could answer questions, so that was a good thing.

Johnson was still on his tirade and kept trying to get in her face. She was about ready to clock him one when Wilson got between them. Before he could carry his rant any further, Wilson was in his face. "If it wasn't for Cade here, they would have the First Lady and all your agents would be dead."

"What do you mean?"

"They would have followed procedure and put her in the limo. The bastards would have had her. Due to Cade thinking outside the box and sending her out of here in another car, their plans were disrupted. She saved Mrs. Blair's life and did her best to save your agents. So. Back. Down."

"Reynolds got her to the White House? Is everyone else okay?" Rachael finally got a word in edgewise.

"She's safe. The others have some minor injuries and they're being taken care of. What happened?"

"I tried to stop the agents in the SUV. They wouldn't listen or couldn't hear me over all the noise." Somehow, she needed to get Johnson to understand that she had tried to save his agents.

"Reynolds came in to tell us the demonstrators were getting ugly. We were getting ready to leave. Then this explosive device came through the window. I thought it was a flash bang at first, but it just blew up. Reynolds was still on his feet, and I sent him for his car. The whole thing was a little too pat. It was purely a set-up to cause confusion. I didn't recognize the agents who came through the door as he left."

"He drove the car into the store, and I shoved Mrs. Blair into the car with the two agents I knew. The other two agents ran for the SUV to back them up, but the agents I didn't recognize went for the limo. That's when I figured the SUV was rigged to blow. Real agents would have left the limo and gone with the agents in the SUV or would have stayed to work the scene."

Johnson growled, "How did Reynolds know the crowd would get ugly? Why wasn't anyone disoriented from the flash bang."

"Whatever it was, it made a lot of noise, and blew out the window, but didn't cause any disorientation." Rachael hesitated on how to explain Reynolds, trying to think of a way to explain what he did. She knew how he had assessed the crowd's temperament, but, didn't want to give him away. Wilson saved her from answering.

"Eric's always had a good feel for crowd control. He's always right on the money on which way a crowd will swing."

Wilson must have been more upset than he let on. He used his brother's first name without thinking about how it would sound.

Johnson faced her again, he shook his finger at her as if she was a first grader. She was tempted to break it for him. "I'm not through with you. As far as I'm concerned, you're not welcome back to the House, persona non-grata. We'll pack your stuff and send it where ever you want."

Wilson pulled him back around. "It's not your call. The President and his wife want her there. She pulled your ass out of a sling today. She kept the First Lady from being kidnapped and saved your agent's life, so don't take your frustration out on her. Talk to your men before you think to blame Cade for this fiasco."

Johnson stalked off. He got in his car, and Rachael could see him talking on his phone.

"Do you think he's calling in some favors to get me out of his hair?"

"Probably, but it won't do him any good. It wouldn't have helped things if you had broken his finger. The President already knows what happened, and he's thankful you were here. I don't think he can win this round."

Wilson knew her way too well. "He's right though. This wouldn't have happened if we hadn't been here."

"It would have gone down somewhere else. Somewhere you may not have been able to get her out. It would have been touch and go if Eric hadn't been here and you know it. This wasn't your fault and the agents' death aren't on you. They were following procedure, and it cost them their lives. The reason you're here is because no one ever knows what you're going to do and they can't plan for it."

"I'm not that unpredictable."

Wilson sighed and his shoulders slumped slightly. He was tired. "You're the only agent I have, that if I sent you out after a tiger, would catch him by calling 'here kitty, kitty' or offering him catnip. Don't get me wrong. Most of the time it's a good thing."

They were interrupted by Jon arriving on scene. He swooped in like the concerned fiancé and started to fuss over her in front of everyone.

“Stop it right now.” Her voice was frigid.

“What? I’m not supposed to be concerned?”

“Concerned, yes, mother hen, no. I’m fine, just tired and dirty. I want a shower and some down time with some hot chocolate and a good book to help decompress. I don’t need to be clucked over.”

“I’ll take you back to the White House.”

“Ask Wilson first if they’re going to let me in.”

“What’s going on?”

“Johnson is requesting that my invitation be rescinded.” She sat down on a piece of curb that was clear of debris, out of the way of the firefighters. She waved her hand in the air. “Go. See what the boss says.” Seemed like she was spending a lot of her time lately on curbs, staring at concrete. Her head hurt. She must have been hit with some debris and it hadn’t registered at the time. Of course, having three-hundred plus pounds of Secret Service agents on top of you wasn’t good for your health either.

Wilson walked back over with Jon. “You’re still a guest in good standing. The EMTs need to check you out first. You’ve got blood all over you. Then let Jon take you back. Get some rest. Just a thought, what do you get off of Johnson?”

"The blood's not mine. I think I've had a couple of donors today." This had been one of those times where no matter what you did, you wouldn't be able to protect yourself from other people's blood. You just hoped for the best and that all the victims were clean. It was either that or you let them die. Johnson's fine. Genuinely concerned about the safety of the First Lady. I didn't get any bad vibes. He didn't roll out the welcome mat, but he wasn't hostile. Not until today anyway. Maybc you need to read him into the program. It might help to get his co-operation."

"I guess we need to do that now. It's pretty obvious that you're here for more than planning a wedding. This whole op is turning into a cluster fuck. Why is it never easy?" He left to get in his car without waiting for her answer and headed out for the debriefing awaiting him. The fun never stopped.

The news people hung around the edges of the scene like sharks. The police kept them back. She could hear the cameras whirring and knew her picture would be in there somewhere. The thought occurred to her that this might be her last assignment. Her face would be known. That wasn't a good thing for an assassin. She also wondered if she really cared.

After climbing into Jon's car, she laid her head back. Wondered about her reception back at the White House. Maybe Jon did care about her a little or he was preoccupied. He hadn't spread out a tarp to protect his precious car seats.

At least this time it was definitely the First Lady who was the target. Maybe now that they showed their hand, we might get a break in finding out who they were. One could only hope.

19

"There are two theories to arguing with a woman. Neither one works." Texas Bix Bender

THE SECURITY around the White House was intense. Wilson was right. She was still on the guest list. She had to endure a search which she figured Johnson did out of petty meanness, but nothing more was said to her about leaving. After the search was completed, the guard handed her a message. The President wished to see her in his quarters. She did take the time to wash the blood off her hands and arms.

Rachael knocked lightly on the First Family's door. She was ushered in by Ida's assistant. She'd been around a lot and seemed to enjoy the insanity of planning a wedding. Her name was Sara Beth. "How's Ida?

She whispered back, "They said she was fine. She wasn't injured, just shook up. Mrs. Blair told her to go home and rest. She said she'd be back tomorrow morning." It appeared that one had to have some intestinal fortitude to put up with all the politics surrounding the First Lady, no matter how nice she was.

The President and Mrs. Blair were sitting, cuddled together, on the couch holding hands when she came into the room. It was obvious they truly cared about each other. This wasn't a political marriage, but the real deal.

Blair looked up, and patted his wife on the arm, and stood up. He had to clear his throat before he could speak. "I understand I have you to thank for my wife's safe return."

"No, Sir. The agents did their job. I was just closer and saw things they didn't."

"That doesn't change the fact that you acted on what you saw and kept my wife from not only being injured, but potentially being kidnapped."

"I don't think they wanted to hurt her, Sir."

"Not then, no. But we both know how it could have ended if she had been taken."

Rachael started to argue and then stopped. Sometimes when someone believed you had saved them from something, it was better to wait until they either changed their perspective or had filed it away. "It was my pleasure and duty to do whatever is needed to keep Mrs. Blair safe."

Mrs. Blair's eyes narrowed slightly, and she patted the couch next to her, "Come here and sit a minute, dear."

Rachael realized at the same time as the President that a light bulb had gone off in her head. They were both in for it.

"Let's talk about this duty."

"It's just a figure of speech, ma'am. A holdover from when I was in the service."

"Don't try to sweet talk me, young lady. You're here to guard me. The wedding was a ploy."

Rachael, know she was in deep water with alligators creeping, no swimming fast, in her direction. She glanced at the President for help, but his face clearly showed she was on her own. He was secure navigating the land mines of politics, but when it came to his wife, she knew who had the winning hand. Rachael was on her own.

"The President has had some concerns about your safety, and he knew I could help protect you. He knew you always wanted to plan a wedding so thought this would be a good way to ease his mind about your safety and let you do something to make you happy." She was stuck. Mrs. Blair motioned for her to go on and the President murmured something about getting some coffee as he made his escape. Coward. See if she voted for him again.

His wife smiled. It wasn't a pretty thing, "Don't worry, I'll get to him later. You need to continue."

Taking a deep breath and trying to stay out of even hotter water, Rachael plowed on. "I do some work with Mr. Wilson. He suggested that maybe I could help relieve some of the President's concern if I was with you. I could help with your protection detail. I don't see things the same way the Secret Service agents do. Sometimes fresh eyes can head off problems. I'm sorry you were in danger today. You were there because of me, and I feel responsible." There, use the guilt card. Maybe she would fall for it.

"Honey, you can't use guilt to get out of this. Is the engagement real?"

Okay, total fail. Rachael wondered if Mrs. Blair was a tad sensitive. It would make sense. You needed to be able to read people accurately when you were the President's wife. "The engagement was set up a long time ago. It had nothing to do with this. Jon needed the cover to travel to certain places without suspicion. I really am a trauma nurse. My job with the traveling nurse's agency is real. They simply cooperate with making my assignments."

"Do you love him?"

"No. I've told everyone concerned that I will not

marry him. Not for the agency, God, or country. I won't marry someone I don't love."

"Good girl. So, what were you going to do about all this planning?"

"Ida plans on getting married when her soldier comes back in country. I've been talking with her. Most of her salary goes into living here and helping her family pay for her brother and sister's education. I thought when this is over, we could agree to give my wedding to her. It's everything she's ever wanted. I saw which dress she wanted today. Hopefully, they can get another one like it. I just planned to order it when they ordered mine."

"You have a good heart. My husband and I will discuss why he decided to keep this from me. Since he's apparently so concerned about my safety, we will continue this charade to keep him from going bat shit crazy over worrying about me." She smiled at the look on Rachael's face at her comment. "I had four brothers. I didn't always have to watch my language. Now. I think we have gotten to know each other well enough for you to call me Mary."

"I never wished to deceive you in any way. But it was necessary because whoever it is, who wants to hurt you, has someone feeding them information. Someone who should be trying their utmost to protect you."

"I know, dear. I'm sorry you had to find that out in

your life too. How early did someone you love betray you?"

Mary was definitely a sensitive. "When I was seven. No, I don't want talk about it. I learned then to go into my mind to make it go away. He was stopped. The person who did it is dead. Not by my hand, but through illness. He suffered a long and horrible time. Sometimes God does mete out his punishment to those who cause harm so their victims can see it happen."

"And if he hadn't?"

"I ask God and myself that question a lot. I still don't know the answer."

"The fact that you asked God to help you or even question whether the action is right or wrong is all the answer you need, child. Now go. Clean up and get some rest. We still have a wedding to plan. Ida's young man comes home in two months and that's not hardly long enough to plan a decent wedding. That and I have a husband I need to have a discussion with. It would probably be better if you're not here for that."

Escape option. Rachael took it.

20

"Happily, never after." Unknown

RACHAEL DESERTED THE PRESIDENT. He was on his own in handling this problem. The bastard hadn't helped her out. He ran like a dog. Left her to explain things to his wife. If she wasn't so tired, she would have loved to be a fly on the wall to that conversation. The First Lady definitely had a mind of her own.

The shower felt great. She brushed her teeth to get the grit out of her mouth. The pounding in her head was down to a dull roar. There were some over the counter-pain- killers in her bag. She took a couple of those. Her side was hurting. She must have pulled the muscles again. If she kept listing her woes, she'd never get out of bed.

Her phone rang as she walked back into her room. It was Jon. She really didn't want to talk to him. Then again, maybe he had some information on the attack.

"Hey, I told you I was fine." She stopped herself for a second, it wasn't Jon's fault she was in a bad mood. It was rude to snap at him before he could even speak. "I'm sorry I snarled at you. It wasn't your fault. If it hadn't been for Wilson, I think I'd have punched Johnson out."

"That is something I would have liked to see. I know. We've all had a bad day. But we do need to spend some time together. You're supposed to want to see the person you plan to marry."

"I'm just tired." She sounded whiney, even to herself.

His voice softened slightly. "I imagine you are. First you take down a bully in the ring. Then save the First Lady. I'm going to have to buy you a cape."

"Can't keep anything from you, can I?" Rachael had to cover a laugh. Jon had his moments.

"Rachael, he only outweighed you by eighty plus pounds. What were you thinking?"

"He needed an attitude adjustment and learn a lesson. There are enough bullies in this world without nurturing one in our midst."

"I think he got the message. If he didn't Bull explained it."

"I thought he'd put in his two cents worth. You and Wilson will keep an eye on him?"

"We will. Bull's opinion carries a lot of weight. Look, there's a parlor for guests to use. Why don't I come to see you for say, half an hour? I really do want to make sure you're okay. Then you can get some rest."

"Okay, see you then. I need you to bring me something."

"I should have known you wouldn't have given in so easily if you didn't want something."

"Just so we understand each other." She rattled off the list of things she wanted.

"No, I don't understand you, but I 'll be there. You seem to have a lot of faith in me to get this stuff past security." He hung up before she could say anything else.

21

"I can explain it to you, but I can't understand it for you." Unknown

"HE WHO CAN SPEAK WELL, can also lie well." Proverb

THE PHONE RANG AGAIN. It must be her night for phone calls. She didn't recognize the number but answered anyway. Reynolds was on the other end, and she could tell he wasn't a happy camper.

"Cade, I was put through the wringer due to your stunt today."

"Nice to know you're unhurt too. Except for the

wringer part. I hear they can really flatten you out. That was a nasty piece of equipment. We really don't give our ancestors all the credit they deserve. I didn't realize you were old enough to know what one was."

"Cute, real cute. Do you always go off on tangents like that? Please take your medicine or at least get diagnosed. The Secret Service was not happy with yours or my actions today."

"Funny, ha-ha. I can't see what they're going ape-shit over. Our actions saved the First Lady from being kidnapped. They should be grateful. Where's the love?"

"You apparently haven't learned yet that agencies like this do not like people who think differently than they do. Protocols are made to be followed, not broken."

"That's a narrow-minded attitude. See what it got the two agents who did the right thing? They got blown up, or shot for their trouble. Is that better than succeeding in the primary directive which is to keep the package safe?"

"I don't know her very well, but I don't think the First Lady will go along with being called a package. What the hell happened today?"

"I don't know, I think she'd get a hoot out of it. The threat against the First Lady is what happened. I know you think I'm rotten to the core, but my assignment is to guard the President's wife. That's what I was doing. I'm sorry you were the method I used to get her out of danger. I knew I could trust you to do the right thing and argue later. The agents would have hesitated."

"I don't think you're rotten. I think you're misled by Wilson. He can talk you into things that you wouldn't normally do and make you think it's all part of your patriotic duty."

"I don't have time to debate this with you. I have one hell of a headache and you have brother issues."

"Have a date? I saw your honey outside the interrogation room. He seemed to find my questioning amusing."

"So now we've gone from discussing my working conditions to my personal commitments. I don't need or want your input. Since you consider me a murderer anyway, what's your problem?"

"I don't know what my problem is! You frustrate the hell out of me, Rachael Cade! I don't like it."

"Back at you."

"We caught the killer."

"Sorry, I just lost you. You just made a snide comment about me having flight of ideas. Pot calling the kettle black, here?"

"God, my brother deserves you! You must drive him bat shit crazy! I was referring to the case we discussed. You were right, the tip you gave me panned out. It was a female soldier whose husband cheated on her while she was deployed. The killings took place when she came back from her assignments. We went back a couple of years and found some more unsolved murders in other places she had been stationed. She would find out who he had been with and hunt them down and kill them. I guess the cemetery thing was so that someone would recognize that they were sacrificed on the altar of revenge or some such psycho-babble. Said they deserved it because they betrayed someone who was doing her duty."

"I still say I would have gone after the husband. And for your information I don't drive your brother crazy. He thinks I'm wonderful and the most cooperative and buttoned up agent he has."

"Remind me never to marry you. You are definitely delusional if you truly think that's what my brother thinks. I almost feel sorry for him...Nope, you deserve each other."

"I didn't think you cared."

"I think this conversation has strayed into no-man's land. I'm hanging up now."

"Coward." There was a knock at her door. "I have to go. I am sorry about the rest of it, but not using you to get Mrs. Blair out." She disconnected before he could say anything else. Eric Reynolds was a problem for another day. The problem for today was at her door.

Jon handed her a box lovingly wrapped with a bow. “Here’s the stuff you asked for. I don’t know how you plan to get in and out of here without getting caught.”

“Easy. I’m with the First Lady and she doesn’t get frisked. Besides I need it to make a last stand for when the bad guys attack the White House.”

“They could still force you through the checkpoint. You are not on their list of favorite people right now. Besides, no one would be stupid enough to try to take her in here.”

“I saved their butts today. I can’t believe they’re that petty.”

“You should know being made to look incompetent is not a way to win friends and influence people.”

“Next time I have people lobbing grenades at me and trying to kidnap my charge, I’ll hold out my time out card and discuss the appropriate actions with them. Not.”

“Rachael, you did the right thing. Just give them time to put their spin on it so they don’t look like they have dirt on their face. They lost some of their own today. That hurts. They don’t like owing the D.C. police or anyone else a favor.”

“I know. I just hate politics. It’s one of the reasons I prefer to work alone.”

“I asked if we could have some coffee sent to the parlor. Come, sit and relax for a little while. Try to act like a normal engaged female for a change.”

Rachael followed him down the hall. The sitting room was small but comfortable. It was done in shades of green and pink. The color scheme should have been sissy, but it worked. The furniture was somewhat formal but easy to relax in. One of the staff members was setting a tray down on the table as they walked in. Rachael had seen the woman when they had refreshments at one of the meetings she attended with Mrs. Blair.

"You're having a late night, Beth."

"Yes. ma'am. There's lots of comings and goings due to the incident. I offered to stay over and help."

"Thank you. The tray looks lovely."

"I saved some of the chocolate cookies you liked when they said they needed a tray sent up here. I'm off after this. I work tomorrow so I need to get home."

Rachael touched her shoulder and smiled, "Thank you for remembering. Be careful going home."

"I will Miss. They always walk us out to our cars at night or down to the station to catch the Metro. I don't live that far from here, only two stops down. I'll see you tomorrow then. Good night." She hastened out of the room while wiping her hands on her apron.

Jon poured the coffee and set everything out on the table. He had started to take a bite of one of the cookies when she stopped him. Wrapping it up with a napkin, she slipped it into his pocket.

"Get it checked when you leave here."

"You are paranoid."

"She was never in the room when I ate or drank anything. Someone had to tell her about the cookies. I think she was trying to warn me. Anxiety was coming off of her in waves. I would bet you one of these lovely cookies that she was told that her family would get hurt if she didn't do what they asked."

He looked down at the pastries and sighed. "You're sure? They look good, and I'm starving."

"I would think everything else is fine if you want to chance it. She was warning me about what was bad. You think you could put someone on her and her family, just in case?"

"Not worth it taking a chance. I'll see about getting someone to watch them for a while." He poured his coffee into the nearest flower pot.

"I wonder how often they have to replace those plants."

"Only you would think of something like that."

"Just an idle thought."

"I did scan for bugs so we can talk."

"They probably have one of those microphones that you just have to point at a room and you can hear everything anyway. The Secret Service don't need no stinking bugs. They can go high tech."

"Believe me. Their budget isn't that great. They're probably still using lip readers. How are the wedding plans going?"

"Shows how important we think the President's safety is. Don't budget the Secret Service for the toys they need and then blame them when they can't do their job. The wedding stuff is going fine. I did find a dress today. It really was gorgeous. The invitations are designed. The printers are waiting on the date. Tomorrow we we're supposed to go to a cake and food tasting. I guess they'll move it here. I can't see them letting the First Lady out so soon after a threat. After that it's flowers. There was also some mention of brides-maid's dresses. I don't know enough people to have a bridal party that large. Apparently, it's easier to plan a war than it is a wedding. It's a sad commentary on our society."

Jon as usual decided to ignore most of her rant. "I'm surprised the bakers here aren't making the cake." He gave another mournful look at the cookies.

"The reason we can't use the bakers here is free enterprise. You can't utilize the White House staff for private parties. Since I'm not a relation, we have to go outside of the bakers here. Democracy in progress. We have to give everyone a chance. I understand they are great though. If their cookies are any indication, they are wonderful. What explanation have the powers that be come up with to explain today. The press is ranting but not saying much about the agents that died. I just think it's a shame that the media glosses over the sacrifice of the people who risk their lives to keep the President and his family safe."

"Let's not talk about food. I haven't eaten since lunch. You know the President and First Lady aren't like that. They'll do something for those men's families. They're grieving along with them. The powers that be have come up with an explanation for what happened. They're blaming it on a gas leak. The story is a protester lobbed a dud grenade in, it sparked, setting off the explosion. Looking for the usual subjects, the First Lady is shaken up, but fine. They expressed their condolences about the agents. Arrangements will be announced for the funerals as soon as they are finalized. The President and First Lady plan to attend. The usual empty platitudes."

"I know. I'm simply feeling like I failed somehow." She tossed him a power bar. "Here, take this to hold you until you get something. Take a couple of the cookies. Maybe they aren't all tainted, and you can taste one. Can't have you fading away from hunger."

"You're such a comfort to me."

"I know. I'm such a snuggle bunny. Is the time up? I'm tired. It will be a long day tomorrow."

"A real lover. Yes, it's been enough time. Do you think you could at least give me a hug and kiss like you mean it?"

She moved into his arms, "I try, Jon. I'm sorry, but I don't love you."

"If not love, a little affection or even lust wouldn't hurt."

Rachael hugged him. She leaned into him for a few seconds and with a soft kiss whispered, "I'm sorry."

He watched as she walked down the hall to her room. He had tried. He had really, really tried.

22

"A purple heart just proves you were smart enough to think of a plan, stupid enough to try it, and lucky enough to survive." Unknown

"You prepare for the details of every single possible thing that might come your way in the future, because the future is uncertain." Auliq Ice

Rachael finally got to sleep. It was a restless night. The First Lady's question had brought up old memories. She could keep the trauma that she went through as a child in a box. Bad things happened to most everybody. There was no reason to allow it to rule her life.

Unfortunately, her mind had other ideas. Her sleep was interrupted by fits and starts as she dreamed of things she wanted to forget. The phone's ring jerked her up in bed. Guess she was awake now.

It was Jon. "You were right. The cookies were doctored so you would become ill. Nothing dangerous, but enough that you wouldn't be interested in getting out of the bathroom for a while."

"How much longer do we have before the President does his thing?"

"Twenty-four hours and counting down."

"It'll be today then."

"Wilson has upped security as much as he can without causing any more of a stir. It looks like it's going to be up to you."

"Isn't that a great back up plan? What can I do to keep her safe? There should be no way anyone could take her here."

"You know as well as I do that you could come up with at least three, if not more, ways to do it. Whoever it is has access and feels confident they can pull it off. You make them nervous, but not enough to stop them. You need to be careful. They'll plan on taking you down first."

"Yeah, but I don't think like a man. Why me? I haven't even had my coffee yet."

"Because you're good at what you do. Watch what you eat and drink today. They may try again."

"They touch my coffee, and they're dead meat anyway. Will I see you later?"

"I'm sure Wilson will find some reason for me to see you today."

"Guess I better get moving then. Take care."

"You too. And Rachael..."

"What?"

"Nothing. I'll see you later."

Rachael rolled the rest of the way out of bed and got dressed. She chose jeans. A dark tank for a top and a long-sleeved shirt over it to hide the knives she hid in sheaths on her arms. A loose-fitting jacket hid the gun at her back. She would have preferred a shoulder holster, but that was too hard to hide. She hid another gun and knife, one in each boot. Cowboy boots were great for a lot of things. Her watch was on a bulky leather strap and she put a plain leather cuff on her other wrist. She would try to reason with the agents and see if she could get permission to wear a legal gun. If not, what she had would be a surprise.

When she got to the breakfast table, Ida was back. Mary was eating her breakfast. The agents looked jittery. She couldn't blame them. They had lost some of their own yesterday and almost lost the First Lady.

"Good morning, dear. You look tired."

"Didn't sleep too well. Must have been something I ate."

Mary's eyes narrowed for a split second and then

she smiled, "Have some coffee. We need to finish this pot off before it gets cold."

The First Lady caught on fast. She was letting her know what was safe. Rachael got some coffee and settled for cereal. Hopefully that would be too hard to screw with. Mary had already eaten, so she couldn't follow her lead. It was a shame. The food was really exceptional.

Ida started outlining the day for everyone. The President and Mary had spoken with the fallen agents' families last night. The funeral arrangements hadn't been made yet. As soon as those plans were finalized, the schedule would be rearranged to accommodate them. There were a couple of meetings to finish up some details on Christmas decorations and food. Apparently, these things had to be done way ahead of time. Christmas was still months away.

A speech was scheduled at one of the women's clubs at the First Lady's favorite charity. They were coming to the White House. It had been rescheduled to take place in the Rose Garden. Then they were cleared to go to the caterers to sample food for the wedding reception and dinner. Now, there was one activity Rachael could get enthusiastic about. Johnson came in as they were finishing up.

Mary looked up and smiled at the big man. "I know you want me to stay here and not go anywhere today. I can't let some lunatics keep me running scared. I have you all to keep me safe, and I won't hide."

It was almost funny to see Johnson look like a small boy being chastised by his mother.

"I understand, ma'am. I really do, but maybe just for one day," he cajoled. "You had a scare yesterday and we can't be sure if they will try again."

Rachael moved slightly, drawing Mary's gaze, "I agree with Agent Johnson. We can do the wedding stuff later. Staying home today might not be a bad idea."

"My husband and I discussed this last night. I will not allow anyone to stop me from doing the things I need to do in this job. Especially ones I really get to enjoy doing. We cannot be bullied into hiding. I need people to see that it is business as usual."

Johnson rolled his shoulders in resignation. "If you go today the guards will be doubled."

"That's fine. I know it'll make you feel better. I want you to give Ms. Cade a gun. I know she is fully capable of using one. She proved yesterday that she knows what she's doing."

Johnson looked nonplussed.

"I told you my husband and I talked about this last night. I know who she is and why she's here. The wedding planning is real, just cleverly arranged to give her a cover story. Let me have the fun of doing this and make her job easier."

Rachael held Johnson's eyes for a second. "I didn't

put her up to it. I was going to follow you and ask. She just beat me to it." She also noticed the First Lady hadn't given away the fact that the wedding wasn't for Rachael.

He turned abruptly toward the door to leave. Johnson resentfully added over his shoulder, "Come with me and I'll set you up."

Rachael got up, looked longingly at her coffee cup. The First Lady laughed and told her to take it with her. She cradled it in her hand and grinned back, and then followed Johnson back to his den...ah, office.

Johnson began speaking as the door closed behind them. "I'm still not happy about this. I talked to the men. They said you never hesitated in protecting Mrs. Blair. I also spoke with the President. He said you were here because they think we have a leak and you're the one to plug it. He thinks highly of you. I hope their faith in you is justified. I lost four of my men yesterday. It would have been worse if you hadn't done what you did."

Rachael figured that was as close as she was going to get to an apology. She followed him the rest of the way to his office.

He didn't give her a chance to say a word. "I don't like loose cannons. That's what you are. You don't obey procedures or orders. It's what saved you yesterday. I understand the train of thought. We follow procedures, you don't. Therefore no one can anticipate how you'll respond. But because you do the unexpected, you put my men at a disadvantage and at risk."

"There is a reason for training the way we do and it works the majority of the time. Our job is to keep Mrs. Blair safe, and at least we have that in common. Since the President has insisted, I'll issue you a weapon. I'm also pretty sure you already have one, but we'll try to keep it legal. It is also mandatory for you to attend a disaster class and take a marksman test."

Rachael grimaced as she accepted the weapon. "You're just flexing your muscle on that. Actually, that's just plain mean."

"You may be right. The protocol is if you want to be part of the protection detail, you need the training. There's a class in ten minutes in Room 3A in the basement. I'm teaching it, so I'll escort you down. The holster straps are adjustable so you should be able to get them to fit. I hope you're as good as they say you are."

"I hope so too. You don't trust me not to go to class?"

"Damn straight."

Rachael took the gun out of the holster. It was a nine mil, Sig Sauer. Not her favorite handgun, but she could use it. She dropped the clip and checked the ammo and slid it back in place. Then pulled the slide back and chambered a round. "You have any extra clips?"

He slid two more across the desk. “You really think one in the chamber is necessary?”

“Your men are good and they follow orders. They try to fight fair and follow rules. The bad guys will be locked and loaded. If we’re not, we lose. The good guys don’t always win, Johnson. Your men played by the rules yesterday and lost. I’m not rubbing it in. The simple fact is we try to play by the rules, they don’t. It gives them an advantage.”

“You may be all they say about you. Good luck and keep her safe.”

“I’ll do everything I can. Believe it or not, I care about her.”

“Then we’re off to class.”

The class was a refresher for the backup agents now on duty. They all had e-pads out to take notes. Rachael sat down behind the largest agent and pulled out her e-reader. She might as well do something constructive while she was wasting time. Jim Butcher was much more entertaining than Johnson.

She glanced up when everyone turned and looked at her. Johnson has asked her a question.

“Do we bore you, Ms. Cade?”

“Actually, yes, you do.”

“Why is that? You don’t think planning is important?”

“I believe planning is extremely important. It’s

memorizing the same contingency plans that I find tedious."

"Please enlighten us from your viewpoint then."

"Hellfire, you need to learn the basics. It's a well-known teaching fact that the way you learn something the first time is what you'll fall back on in an emergency. We see that in nursing every time they try to change how you do CPR. It happens with police officers when they try to save their brass during a shootout because that's what they were taught during training. But having a set plan is suicide. You don't think that every terrorist or whack job that's serious about taking out professional responders hasn't memorized the plan?"

"So, what is your opinion?"

"We all should have a Plan A. But we should all realize that it will be fucked up in less than thirty seconds on any op. Actually, that's being optimistic. Always have a Plan B, C and D, because you'll need them. The more original and unexpected those plans are, the better your chances are of coming out of it alive, with your package safe. If you're zigging instead of doing the expected zag, you may stay ahead of the lead they're slinging at you. I know you don't agree with me, but that's the way I see it."

"So, you think everyone should just do his own thing?"

Rachael sighed as she sat up straighter in her seat. "I

usually work alone. When you work with a team, you follow the team leader. As a team, you should make your plans contingent on the operation. It should be for that op only, and every op should be handled differently to throw your adversary off. Sometimes it's the little things that bite you in the ass or save your life. You also have to be aware of the fact that the leader can be taken out at any time, and you better have your next plan ready. Remember one of the golden rules of combat that if you ever find yourself in a fair fight, you didn't plan correctly."

"Any other words of wisdom you wish to impart?"

"Ever wonder if illiterate people get the full benefit of alphabet soup?" She gave him a wicked grin and settled back in her chair. Sometimes she just couldn't resist pulling someone's rope or is it yanking someone's chain? Get a sense of humor for heaven's sake, life can be grim enough. Even in a serious profession one needed to lighten up sometimes. Of course, medical people had their own warped sense of humor. She heard a few smothered snorts of laughter, quickly hidden. Well at least all was not lost, some of them had kept a shred of humanity despite the training to drain it out of them.

"Thank you for your input." Johnson had given her a measured look and gone back to teaching the class. Rachael swore she saw his mouth twitch. She went back to her book. Everyone had their own thing. Routine wasn't hers. Rachael ignored the sidelong looks she got from the rest of the class.

The next stop was the range. She had made a stop at the restroom to put on the shoulder holster that Johnson had given her. She didn't want to blow any headway she had made with him seeing the weapons she had already added. Even if he already suspected she had them, no sense in giving him a swelled head by proving him right.

The range master was chuckling when he pulled her target back and it only had one hole. Rachael had put her gun down and waited until he had really examined her target. "Well, I'll be damned. Every bullet in the same place. I've never seen anyone do that before. Even our team shooters have some variation."

"Something I've always had a knack for. Whatever I aim for, I hit." She shrugged slightly. "My Dad blindfolded me once then pointed me at the target. I still hit it. He took me to some professors who were studying spatial orientation. They said I had perfect pattern pathways. Once I aim, my mind sets up the pattern. I don't miss."

"Can you do it again?"

"One more time and then I need to get back to work."

The target was an exact match of the first one. "Would you like to try out for our shooting team?"

Rachael could see the excitement in the man's eyes.

Dreams of trophies that could be won. Rivals vanquished. She almost hated to break his bubble. "I'm not an agent. Just a pesky guest and a pain in Johnson's ass for the time being. I wouldn't qualify."

He looked at Johnson. "Can't you work something out?"

Johnson just shook his head. "Sorry, Bubba. Some things aren't meant to be."

Rachael reloaded and settled the gun back in the holster. "I need to get back. I don't like leaving Mary this long."

"I'll take you. She's back in their apartments." She did notice there was some respect in his eyes that hadn't been there before. Sometimes mountains did move.

23

e must have pie. Stress cannot exist in the presence of a pie." David Manet

"I AM NOT a glutton-I am an explorer of food." Erma Brombeck

MARY AND IDA were going over menus and brochures as she entered the family quarters. Rachael didn't know what magic the First Lady had wrought, but Ida was relaxed and appeared to be enjoying herself.

"There you are. We were just about to give up on you." Mary sent a questioning look at Johnson. "Did she pass all her tests with flying colors?"

He smiled back. "Almost lost her to the range master. He wants her on the shooting team. Broke his heart she wasn't military. I guess we could get the President to put in a good word about reactivating her commission."

"You wouldn't dare. We have plans made."

"Don't worry," Rachael came back, "It would take major clout to get my MOS changed. Shooters are a dime a dozen. Trauma nurses are scarcer than hen's teeth."

"I'm sure the President would qualify as having major clout."

"Why, Agent Johnson, you almost make me think you've changed your mind about keeping me around."

"You're right. The team will just have to take its chances without you. I have enough gray hair as it is." With that statement, he said his goodbyes and left.

"You seem to have hit a nerve with the agent, Rachael," Mary said moderately. There was a twitch to her mouth that looked like she was trying to hide a grin.

"I sometimes have that effect on people. He doesn't appreciate minions who think for themselves."

"That's a little harsh, don't you think?"

"You're right. Bless his heart, he's just doing his job. I don't fit into his box, so he doesn't know what to do with me. He'll be so happy when the wedding takes place, he'll probably offer to give away the bride."

Her comment caused both Ida and Mary to laugh.

"I've been to the south enough to know that comment is a two-edged sword. I had to give the agents our schedule last night so they could set up surveillance." Mary sighed, "I really hate the loss of freedom to be spontaneous. I'd give anything if Will and I could just decide to go to a movie or go out to get coffee. The fact that we have to have guards who are willing to risk their lives for us is gratifying and frightening all in one."

"Sometimes we give up things we treasure for the life we choose. I guess the deciding factor is if it's worth what we sacrifice."

"You are so right, my dear. I would guess you of all people would know what you're talking about. There really isn't a reason to whine. There are perks. Like no dishes or doing the wash. So, let's get back to the delicious subject of food. I hope you're hungry. We get to try everything today." Since Rachael hadn't had time to finish breakfast, that wasn't an issue. She hadn't missed this many meals when she was in the desert.

It still took another half hour to get the cars and everyone in their place so they could leave. Rachael was in agreement with Johnson. They should just sit on the First Lady until the deal was done.

One good thing was all the caterers were to be in one location. It was set up like a job fair. They would go table to table to sample the food and then try to come up with a menu. They even had a clipboard with a score sheet for every vender. Rachael had no idea how she was going to determine what was safe to eat and what had been tampered with. There were too many variables. That fact alone might work in her favor. They couldn't poison everyone. Or know what she would or wouldn't eat. They wanted the First Lady alive. At least that kept total death and destruction was out of the question. At least she didn't have to worry about explosive devices. The Secret Service had probably already checked for those anyway.

The affair went off without a hitch. Dream Cakes was the hands down winner in the wedding cake department. Their smaller confections weren't half bad either. The chocolate truffle cake was to die for. The dinner menu for the rehearsal meal was a little harder. One competitor had a great main course, but not so much on the dessert. Since Rachael considered dessert a major food group it was an important issue. Even if it wasn't for her, she couldn't allow Ida to suffer through a bad dessert. Besides maybe she'd score an invitation to the wedding.

She had no interest in all this wedding planning stuff. It was just a cover and all that. But this was food. She could really get into this part of the process. Rachael was aware she was one of those hateful, disgusting people who didn't gain weight easily. Eating was a vice she enjoyed. Rachael didn't smoke at all. She drank on rare occasions and then sparingly. Sex was a moot point since it was almost impossible with her "gift." So, she really., really could get into eating.

It was also one of the reasons she was such an adrenaline junkie. Her excellent metabolism might not last forever, so she might as well get in the habit of exercise and being active. The added bonus was that food made her feel good and didn't diminish her senses. She hadn't missed the faint smile on Mary's face as she watched Ida and her wrangle over the appetizers. The First Lady knew instinctively that Rachael didn't have much opportunity to enjoy female company or one on one time.

The agents were getting antsy at the delay in their time schedule. Rachael actually held out longer on the menu decisions so they wouldn't be on the correct time table. It threw the enemy off. They were usually as anal as the good guys as far as time schedules went. Ida and she were still amicably discussing the menu as Mary led them to the car.

The whole afternoon ended up being a pleasant experience. Something Rachael didn't have often. Lack of close friends or a social life to speak of, due to both of her work schedules. The people she had been close to in the service had scattered and life happened. Most had families, and they drifted apart. Ida had confided in her that she was taking notes for her wedding and wanted it to be as close to this one as she could manage. Sometimes the magic worked.

As soon as they got back to the White House they separated. The President was waiting for his wife. They greeted each other with a hug and kiss and walked off to their quarters with their arms around each other. Rachael watched them walk away and sighed to herself. Would she ever find someone?

Her musing was cut short when Wilson stepped out of the shadows. "Come and walk with me for a few minutes." He offered her his arm, and they headed to the Rose Garden.

24

hen love and skill work together, expect a masterpiece." John Ruskin

WILSON WAS quiet until they passed the perimeter of agents and guards. "How was your day?"

"Uneventful. Johnson actually cooperated on the gun thing."

"I heard a rumor that there was a certain range officer who was practically salivating at the thought of you being on his pistol team. It might behoove you to miss sometimes."

"Believe me, I've tried. It's just hardwired in. Even when I want to miss, it hits the target."

"Don't let any of those professors get a hold of you.

They'll want to dissect that brain of yours. I'm surprised the Army didn't try."

"I'm a nurse. They weren't interested in whether I could shoot or not."

"Good thing for us. Bad for them."

"You didn't bring me out here to discuss my shooting ability. I'm sure you have a report of every target I've hit. Person or paper. So, what's up?"

"I can't be interested in you as a person?"

"I wish. But no. Because then you wouldn't be able to use me as a weapon. You can't be sentimental about someone you send out to get shot at."

"You really are pragmatic, aren't you?"

"I have to be. When you already know how people feel all the time, it's hard to stay warm and fuzzy. Loving someone isn't something you can fight, it just happens."

"I'm curious, what do you get off of me?"

"You have a natural shield. It probably comes from the same genes that gave your brother his talent. You're more sensitive than the norm, but you were given a strong shield to buffer it. It's also why you don't freak out about what I do. If you didn't have some kind of defense, it would have been hell to deal with a parent and younger brother who always knew what you were up to. It's also why you let me have more of a leash then you do anyone else. You hope I'll find things out for you."

"So, you figured Eric and me out? I wondered how long it would take."

"The resemblance is there if you look for it. You move alike. That was the first thing I noticed. That and you both have the same flavor when you hit my shields." She held up her hand when he started to ask another question. "I can't explain it. Plus, if you're as sensitive as I think you are, you understand what I'm talking about. After that it was easy. I just took an educated guess on the parent part."

"I need you to do something for me."

"Well, that was a quick switch. I guess discussing our feelings is over. Is this the job you were talking about?"

"No, we put that on the back burner for now. If it becomes urgent, I'll assign another agent. This is personal. You have the right to say no if you don't want to do it."

"You've never asked me to do anything for just you. It's always about the safety of the country."

"It's my job to keep this country safe and one I take seriously. Eric sees it differently. I try to weigh the consequences of my actions with the resulting outcomes. I get tired, just like everyone else. When I first started this job, I tried to get Eric to work for me. It was a way to keep my promise to our mother to watch out for him." He hesitated a second. "But I was also new to my position. and I was willing to use his talent to get results. He resented it. We argued. We've been estranged for over five years now. We live a few miles apart, yet this is the first time I've spoken to him in all that time.

"You brought us back together. Because of the Moody shooting, we had to see each other again. I find that I missed him more than I thought. I always kept track of him and knew how his life was going, but I didn't interfere. Maybe what I saw in you is because of my brother. I kept the issue of us being apart on the back burner. It was something I always planned on doing but just never got to. My request is, I need you to carry a message for me."

"You know I'll do whatever you need me to."

"The President has a job for me. I'm going to be the point person on this op. It may not end well. I may have to call a strike down on my own head to eliminate this threat."

"Can't someone else do it? To lose you would destroy the agency. You're the glue that keeps it functioning." Not to mention what it would do to her.

"No. I know what you're thinking and you can't do this for me. It's not your ability that's an issue. It's your gender. These people would not work with a woman at any price. As for assigning someone else to do this, I couldn't do it with a clear conscience. If it was something I couldn't do or someone who could do it better, that would be a different story. I have never sent any of you on a suicide mission. I knew I could lose you in the course of the op, but there was always an escape plan. I would never ask one of my people to go into a situation with no way out."

"If you won't let me take your place, what can I do?"

"I have a will. I can't talk to Eric. He has my complete trust. But, he doesn't have the security clearance for me to tell him what I'm doing. There's also the fact that if I'm being watched, they'll wonder why I needed to talk to him. I won't put him in that kind of danger. If anything happens to me, I need you to tell him I'm sorry about what happened before and I love him."

"Why can't you tell him yourself? Hell, write him a letter. It would mean a lot more. Your brother thinks I'm a murdering assassin. He would throw me in jail without a twinge of regret. Why would he listen to me?"

"Because you two are alike. He may think or even know what you've done. Eric also knows you wouldn't lie to him about something like this."

"He thinks I'm already lying."

"Has he ever flat out asked you if you killed Moody?"

Rachael had to think for a second. "Actually, no. We've danced around the subject, but he never asked me directly."

"Because he really, in his heart of hearts doesn't want to know. Not at this point anyway. I think it would hurt my brother more than you think to lock you away. He's involved off and on with a very difficult, volatile woman. I know he wants out, but doesn't know how. I'm not sure if what he feels for you is real or what to him would be an honorable way out of his situation."

"I respect you immensely. I think you are brilliant at what you do. To be honest, even though I know it's not in the cards, I'm in love with you. But I think you just lost it on this one."

He looked startled for a microsecond and then patted her on her arm. "We just discussed why that isn't a feasible option. I wish things could be different. You'll have to trust me on this one. I know my brother."

"You do have the right to be happy. I think you would do your job better if you had someone you could really depend on. Someone who would take care of you for a change. A person who wouldn't put up with your bullshit. If you're going to get yourself blown up you need to know how I feel. I've loved you since the day you walked through my door. The way your brother sparks my shields is because he is so much like you. I can't use him as a substitute for you. It wouldn't be fair to either of us."

"What about Jon?"

"You know my feelings in that department. I don't love him. I won't marry him. Is he going with you?"

"No, he needs to stay behind. He offered to do it. I need someone I can trust at the helm until I get back or

I am replaced. The First Lady is still your priority. There's still time for them to take her and use her as leverage against the President. We haven't found the leak, yet."

"She'll be alone tonight?"

"Yes, the President will be monitoring this mission from a safe location. We can't allow anything to stop this from happening at the precise time that's set. Anything that disrupts it will be a disaster."

"Do I ever get to know what's going on?"

"When I get back, I'll take you and Jon to dinner and tell you about it. If I don't make it." He shrugged his shoulders and watched her face. "You'll know about it from the blow back. Will you promise to do as I asked?"

"I promise. But if anything happens to you, I will hunt down who did it and they will pay. I will also find you and kill you over again for causing me so much grief. And one other thing. When you come back, you promise to have a heart-to-heart talk with Eric."

"You do know you could be held on insubordination with talk like that?"

"That's the main reason you love me and keep me around. You know I'll always tell you what I think."

"Much to my chagrin, I have found that to be true. If I ever have a child, it would be a blessing and a curse to have one just like you. Be careful. You're in as much danger as I am. At least in my case I know who the bad guys are."

"Is Jon my go to guy?"

"No, he is in lock down. Only voice communications until this operation is over. No field work allowed. He can only direct. He was rather upset when he left my office. Wanted to talk to you first. I told him I'd let you know what was going on."

"So, what about your promise to me? I'll even facilitate or referee as needed."

"That would be like sending in a wolf to decide how to split up the sheep."

"You're avoiding answering my question."

"I promise. When I get back, I will have a '*Come to Jesus*' meeting with my brother."

"One of the agents was signaling to Wilson. "I need to go."

Rachael stood on tiptoes and kissed his cheek. "Go with God. Be careful and come back. You would be missed by those who love and care for you." Pulling him closer to her, she pulled his earbud out. She stood on tiptoes and whispered a message in his ear.

He looked down at her and cupped her cheek. "I don't think God listens to me anymore, but it goes double for you. I guess you're positive about that." She nodded her head as he leaned over to kiss her forehead, he whispered his answer back. He walked back to the waiting cars as the agents studiously turned their heads. Ah, the rumors that would fly.

25

"Life is hard, then you die. Then they throw dirt in your face. Then the worms eat you. Be grateful it happens in that order." David Gerrold

"No one is going to feel sorry for you, so you have to go out there and be fierce." Gabby Douglas

"Everyone will have a night of years." Unknown

Rachael went straight to the family apartments. Mary was looking out the window. She had that blank look in her eyes that said she wasn't really in D.C. anymore. Rachael went into the kitchen and started fixing coffee to give Mary time to collect herself.

"When do you think, they'll come?"

"Tonight. They'll think we're asleep. That gives them time to get things in motion because no one will expect to see us until it's time for the morning routine. It will also allow them to disrupt the plans and not give the President enough time to reconfigure his game plan. It's what I would do if I was planning this."

"So, what do we do?"

"Where is everyone?"

"I sent the staff home early. I told them I thought they needed a breather after yesterday's events. That I needed a break. I let on that with Will gone, I could get some girl stuff done. Except for Ida, they're all married so they understand. I didn't want anyone else to get hurt."

"I have a plan. It's on the vague side. Open to a lot of readjustment as needed."

"Those usually work for the best, dear. No plan ever goes as expected. Being fluid is the only way to survive." She laughed at the surprised look on Rachael's face. "I grew up in a military home. You don't think I didn't hear about battle strategy and how to plan a campaign? Add that to living with a politician for all these years, if I wasn't flexible, I'd be crazy."

Rachael changed the direction of the discussion. "You look tired."

"I am a bit. It's been a long couple of months. Will can't always tell me what's going on due to all the security issues. I know when something is bothering him. This week has been more so than usual. Not the wedding. That's been a wonderful break."

"I've always known that there were those out there who think that killing the President would be the cure for everything that's wrong. Even if the reason is only for the attention or confusion it would generate. That type of danger I can understand. I never gave any thought to anyone wanting to hurt me personally because it might influence my husband. It never really crossed my mind. It should have. There is a reason I have my own security team. I just accepted it, but didn't think why I needed one."

"I knew they would come at me with words, not actions. I understand the concept of your life being in danger. I've never had to deal with it as a reality. It's always been an intellectual exercise. I can't grasp how you deal with it on a day-to-day basis."

"I guess I don't think of it that way. It's like a game. Yes, the stakes are high, but you don't think of the future. Only real time. Yeah, there's an adrenaline rush, but if that's all you did it for, you wouldn't last very long. The other side would get you or your own would take you out because you are a danger to the whole team. Maybe it's a form of attention deficit disorder. I get bored if I don't have something to keep me engaged."

"Or maybe you live in the moment because the future is only speculation. I guess in some ways I have a split personality. Some days I want to be more like Jesus, others like Jesse James. I think the James brother wins the majority of the time."

"What about the people who care for you?"

"There isn't anyone who truly cares for me. My guardians do their best, but I'm not their child. I have work friends and casual relationships. I am willing to protect and die for my team when I have one. Maybe when I find someone who wants me for who and what I am, warts and all, I'll feel differently." Odd how Wilson entered her mind when she made that statement.

"What about Jon? I know it's like an arranged marriage sort of thing, but he does seem to actually care for you."

"I think Jon thinks he loves me. Don't get me wrong. We make a good team. But that's all it is. He's thrown out hints at times that he'd like it to be more. Probably it's because I'm the first woman that hasn't wanted him. It's the thrill of the chase. The fact I can say no to him is what interests him. It makes me unique. If I told him I loved him, we'd have a honeymoon period and then it would end. There's nothing enduring in our relationship. He has too many irons in the fire to make love his first priority."

"Aren't you sad?"

"Sad? No. I get lonesome sometimes. But more in the way of I want someone I can talk to and share an experience with. It would be nice to have someone to go out to eat with or go to a movie. I do get down about sometimes. In some ways, I'm practical and in others a romantic. There's a lot of work in a good relationship. I feel there has to be something there to put that much time and effort into it."

"Someday I'll find someone who is worth the trouble or finds me worth the trouble. Then I'll go for it. But that someone has to be the one who will love me all my life and I'll return the favor. I want to be that something to someone. I know if I loved a man, he would be everything to me. I'm selfish enough to want him to feel the same way. My parents had that kind of love. Until then, my life works for me. Besides, unless I find someone with the same security clearance as me, I'd have to lie a lot. I can't live that way."

"Don't sell yourself short. I think you have a lot to give the right person. Actually, I get the feeling you already have someone you feel that way about. Of course, I'm an old-fashioned mom so I try to get everyone married off."

"You're a great lady. When I first met you, I knew you were exactly the woman you presented. No pretense. Your Secret Service detail would die for you even if you weren't the First Lady. Most bodyguards aren't suicidal. They want to live and keep their charge alive. The agents that guard you are essentially bodyguards. They plan so that everyone lives. If they have to die for someone, it's nice if it's a person they feel is worth it. That says more about you than you can ever imagine."

"Those men we lost, if they still had a voice, would tell you they were just doing their job. A lot of the time they shield people they don't care for or respect. You are someone they feel is worth giving up their life for. They would be proud to know that the bad guys lost and you were safe. Don't tarnish their lives with regret. Celebrate it, knowing they were thankful that if they had to give up their life for someone worthwhile. Not all of us are able to think that."

They were quiet while Rachael poured the coffee and set out some cookies for a snack. She continued with the plan for the evening, "I think what we need to do is have a quiet time together. It needs to appear as if we're just doing a girl thing. I need to bring someone in to help us. Someone I can trust. I need you to act like I'm here with you. I'll go to the meet and sneak him into the apartment."

"How do you plan to do that? There are security cameras everywhere, not to mention the guards and agents."

"I spent a few hours at the library. You'd be amazed what people write in their personal journals. Such as, how they snuck out of here to meet with a lover without anyone knowing about it. Or had a secret meeting with people they didn't want to be seen with. It's all Nancy Drew-ish with secret passages and tunnels."

"Wouldn't any secret tunnels and such be common knowledge by now?"

"No one wants to give up all their secrets. We've gone through so many presidents and curators that a lot has been lost or forgotten. I compared maps and blueprints. Some of them don't jive. Walls are too short. No door where there should be one. I took it upon myself to find the ones I needed. That's how I worked out an escape plan in case it became necessary."

Mary started to grin. "Nancy Drew was my hero when I was a kid. Is there a secret passage in our apartments?"

"You don't think that all the past presidents were totally trusting of their guards, did you? To be president you have to have a devious mindset or you would never survive. Actually, if you didn't have a ruthless streak you would probably make a horrible president. We need a person who has the backbone to lead. You can't make hard decisions if you are too kind or weak."

"All of us are a blend of good, bad, and indifferent. We need all our attributes to survive. It would be a lovely world if we didn't need the steel to stand up to our enemies. Sometimes that's even our friends and loved ones. I don't think we will ever be fully at peace. My favorite author, Robert Heinlein said that 'By the data to date, there is only one animal in the Galaxy dangerous to man-man himself. So, he must supply his own indispensable competition. He has no enemy to help him.'"

"It just isn't in us. There will always be some human who is not content. Someone who thinks they have all the answers and wants to run things their way. Whoever it is, they will upset the apple cart and cause dissension. Even the angels argued with God. Where else did the concept of Lucifer come from? He was a fallen angel."

"Does that include my husband?"

"Do I think he's a fallen angel?" She quirked a grin back at Mary's head shake. "No. I think he's a good president. I voted for him. I would vote for him again. I think he can make the hard choices. I hope that he will always err on the side of good."

"He can be strong when he needs to be. So, let's get back to our discussion about secret passages. Is there a way out of here?"

"Of course, there's a way out of here. Do you think I would have chosen to stay here if I didn't have a bolt hole? You always need a backdoor. A passageway that I don't think anyone's aware of anymore. There hasn't been any traffic in the ones I've searched out. It only stands to reason. We not only had philandering husbands. We did have some presidents who were unmarried while they were in office. Although they didn't have the problem with the press we do today, they still liked to keep their private life private. Therefore, it was necessary to have a way to sneak around."

"Sometimes you are so cynical. What's the plan?"

"I need to get out to meet someone. Detective Reynolds."

"I have to admit that surprises me a little. I thought he wanted to throw you in jail and lose the key."

"He still does. But I'm sure he can hold off on that lovely moment if it means saving your life."

"I liked him. He was kind the other day."

"Yeah, well, except for the part about wanting to throw me in jail, he's a pretty decent guy. Okay. Here's what we're going to do."

26

"The problems we have cannot be solved by the same level of thinking that create them." Unknown

"EVEN SILVER HAS GREY IN IT." Unknown

RACHAEL MADE her phone call to Reynolds.

"Why do you want to see me?"

"I don't particularly want to see you. I have a problem, and I need your help."

"Oh burn. Again, why me? You work for an agency that can get you whatever you need, legal or not."

"This isn't about your brother or me. I really need you to help. I'm trying to keep the First Lady from getting hurt or worse. I don't have anyone else I can trust."

"My brother has nothing to do with my feelings. I still think you're a murderer and need to be in jail." Despite the fact that he would really hate to have to do it.

"Can we put aside our philosophical differences for one night and work together?"

"What do you need?" he huffed. It made her smile. The fact that she could irritate him that much indicated she meant something to him. Even if it was just a pain in his ass.

Rachael rattled off a list of things she needed to make her plan work.

"You honestly need this?"

"Yes, if I'm to keep the First Lady safe through the night. I'm assuming the Director told you."

"If he hadn't, yesterday would have given it away."

"Is sarcasm another service you provide?"

"Are we going to fight or do this?"

"Then you're in?"

"Gee whiz, why not? I was just telling myself, 'Self, you lead such a humdrum life. You need to do something exciting. I don't know, let's go out and help a killer protect the First Lady from some kidnappers. Then I can be in danger from I don't know who and how many. It just makes my evening so much clearer and easier to plan. Here I thought I'd have to settle for a book and a beer."

"You actually drink that stuff? I'm really not all that bad. I go to church and everything. What book are you reading?"

"You still kill people for a living. You'd also be great in a group that was into flight of ideas. It's a John Berry book."

"I also work very hard at trying to save their lives. Your reading material says a lot about you. Like the fact you'd really like to be a secret agent."

"So, you're admitting you do both. And never in a million years."

Rachael decided it was better not to answer the implied question. "Meet me at these coordinates in two hours. Will that give you enough time?"

"I don't know why, but I'll be there. What about my partner? He's a good man to have at your back."

"If he's willing to work with a presumed killer. Why not? The more the merrier."

REYNOLDS SAT in his car for a few seconds thinking. How had he let himself get roped into this rodeo? He knew Cade was guarding the President's wife. Apparently she didn't trust anyone she worked with. Plus, she was willing to trust him about his partner on his say so.

Bottom line, why did that thought send a thrill through him that he couldn't explain?

"You have totally lost it, Eric Reynolds. If you live through tonight, you will regret ever having anything to do with Rachael Cade." Yet he knew he would also deeply regret it even more if he didn't.

Amazingly, Watts hadn't said a word when he explained the situation except to ask what he needed to do. Now they were huddled under a copse of trees at the GPS coordinates Cade had given him. The coordinates had landed them in Meridian Park.

The park had a varied history. When they had both started as rookies, it had fallen into ill repute and was used for drug deals. A place for the homeless to bed down and other things better not mentioned. It had been cleaned up. Had major renovations, mostly completed in 2010. Now it was a tourist attraction and its own security guards. They both started when she appeared, seemingly out of the ground a few feet from them.

"Let me show you where the car is hidden." She moved so they could look between the trees. "See that apartment across the street? It's the brown van that's parked in the last spot. The keys are hidden in the front driver's side wheel well. If I'm not right behind you, do me a favor. Please wheel the bike out so I have transport. You all will head toward Rock Creek Park. Just follow the GPS in the van. The coordinates are set. I'll provide interference. The van wasn't built for speed, but endurance.

You need to keep an eye out for the people in the apartment across the street. They appear to have erratic hours. Later you might want to pass that on to your narcotics unit. I've moved the surveillance camera's so you won't be seen. Let's go before anyone notices us."

"Hold on a minute, I thought we were going to guard the First Lady. Just what are you planning?"

"We're taking her out of the White House and hiding her until morning. If all goes as planned, she'll be safe."

"Yeah, like everything with you goes as planned. That book and beer are looking better and better."

"Quit being such a whiner." She thought she heard Watts smother a laugh. "This part is so cool. You 'all won't believe it." They followed her to the front east corner of the park, behind a tree bent with age. The holly bushes behind the Buchanan Monument hid the opening. She reached down and removed a plug of grass and revealed a pull to a hidden trap door.

Reynolds and Watts just looked at each other and shrugged their shoulders. They had been working together for so long it didn't take any words to convey that they were thinking they were both crazy. Reynolds grabbed the bag of stuff she had requested and they followed her into a small tunnel. Down some old wooden steps that surely hadn't been trod on for decades.

"What is this place?" Reynolds whispered.

"The journals I read don't really say for sure who was responsible for the building of it. The mansion was built by John Porter back in 1819. My history's not so great, but it's likely he was a crony of some of the presidents. You know the oil that makes things run, money and politics. After John Quincy Adams left the White House in 1829, he moved here. During the Civil War, or the War of Demarcation as some of us southerners like to call it, it was used as a Union encampment. That's just two reasons for a president or two who might want to sneak off without being seen. I just connected the dots. I was originally looking for a tunnel one of our more illustrious forefathers might have had made so he could sneak out past his guards to meet his paramours. Lincoln used to come here to visit the Union troops during the war. He usually just slipped away before anyone knew where he was going. Since he was not an easy man to disguise, I think this is how he did it."

"How did you find it?"

"I read a lot and remember it. I just looked in the old records at the Library of Congress. Using journals and old maps, I was able to find it."

Watts looked around, "You're right. This is so cool."

Rachael sent him a grin, "See, I'm not such a bad date after all. Mystery, danger and the possibility of getting shot at. What more could you ask for? Let's get moving, I don't like leaving Mary alone."

"Where does this come out?"

"It has branches. I'm going to drop you all off at the first family's apartments. Then take this equipment to my room. I don't want anything to look abnormal when I leave the apartment after dinner. I'll meet back with you there. We'll all go over the plans. Watch your step, some of the rocks have fallen."

They set off down the tunnel. Both Reynolds and Watts flashed their lights along the walls. The men were trying to hide it, but they were excited. It wasn't often you found a piece of presidential history no one else knew about.

"Where are we exactly?"

"This tunnel runs west of Fifteenth Street. We're almost smack dab in the middle between it and Sixteenth Street. One of the branches originates in the walls behind the first family's apartment. I think the master bedroom used to be used either as a study or extra guest room. I really can't see a philandering husband or one who was sneaking off for nefarious business using a secret passage from the master bedroom. The little lady might get ugly about it. Then when they did renovations to add bathrooms and such, the layout got moved around."

"My guess is they pretended it was part of the water drainage system. Since most of D.C. sits on top of a marsh, they needed to drain it somehow. Anyway, engineering isn't something in my wheel house, but they managed to cover their tracks. When they built it, Meridian Park was mostly trees, I imagine. As the city kept growing someone in the know must have always looked over the plans to make sure the exit remained in an area where there were no out buildings or clearings. Its location has been lost in the changing of the guard so to speak."

"Like I said, I got the President to get me a pass to the Library of Congress allowing me into the records nobody without special clearance can get into. You ought to see the information in there. It's amazing. So, I figured if anyone knew if there was a way out, it would be one of the presidents. Using that hunch, I skimmed through at least six of our illustrious forefather's handwritten notes and journals."

"It would make you blush to hear how randy those old guys were. I had no idea. They even made me turn red. Don't believe all that crap you hear about our Puritan forebears. These guys had sex on their minds as much as they do today. Must have something to do with politics. They're all horny."

"That pearl of history being noted. I finally found this little gem hidden in the outpourings of one of our leaders who was confessing all his sins. He'd found Jesus and needed to get his sins and transgressions off his chest."

Rachael was walking as fast as she could. It would take them at least twenty minutes at this pace. It would be slower going with the older Mrs. Blair. Thank goodness, the First Lady walked every day for exercise. The guided tour continued. Rachael was actually enjoying having a chance to tell someone about the information she had found. After this was over, the Secret Service would have to make it inaccessible. The litter of kittens Johnson was going to have would be a sight to see.

"This tunnel is about one and three-quarters of a mile. The rest that I found let out at Rock Creek Park or somewhere more open. That was too far for Mrs. Blair to navigate all the way to the park and the other was too dangerous. I investigated them just in case. Most of the tunnels have cave-ins since no one has seen to their upkeep. Nothing we couldn't have managed, but I thought it might be too rough for Mrs. Blair. The sad part is, I'm going to have to report these tunnels when this is over. The Secret Service will have all kinds of fits when they find out what they missed. They'll get ulcers over all 'the might have been scenarios' they think up. I just think it's so cool. I wish I could watch."

Reynolds and Watts listened and followed her as she moved swiftly through the tunnel. They looked at each other and grinned. Cade had a sadistic streak. The walls got slightly narrower and appeared drier as they got closer to the White House proper.

Rachael stopped at a tunnel juncture. "We're under

the house now. This connects to the quarters and a small hallway close to my room." She flashed her light up on the wall, and they saw a red slash on the one they were coming down. "I marked the wall just in case we get split up. It's a straight shot from here to the park. Watch the stairs. They're old and rickety. They also have damp areas so whoever has Mrs. Blair make sure she doesn't slip. OSHA wasn't around when they built these, so there's no hand rail.

Follow the GPS in the van and you'll find all-terrain vehicles hidden with coordinates to a hiding place in the woods. Don't wait for me. Just get the First Lady out and safe. I can take care of myself."

They stopped at the small level platform before entering the room. "This is where I want Watts and Mrs. Blair to hide." Reynolds and I will take down the kidnappers when they try to grab her. There's some blankets and pillows in the corner in case you get cold. I left a couple of bottles of water too. I set this up in case I'm wrong. If so, we can all go to bed and pretend we're having a sleep-over."

She stopped talking for a few seconds. Then continued on. "And on that note, we'll all have little birds singing around our heads and there will be no more war and hate as we sing the Alleluia Chorus. When you hear gunfire or lots of thuds and grunts, run for it. Hopefully that will give you all a head start. Whatever you do, don't wait for us. Everything's in place for you to get to a safe haven without us. We'll catch up or be protecting the escape route." She didn't mention the other options. They were both cops and knew what they were.

Mary was sitting in the living room dozing when they slipped into the room. She had changed from her business suit into warm woolen pants, a long sleeve shirt and had a heavy sweater and her walking shoes sitting next to her. Rachael touched her arm softly so as not to startle her. She smiled at Reynolds and held out her hand to Watts.

As he placed his hand in her smaller one, she commented, "You must be Watts, I met your partner rather briefly yesterday."

"I'm pleased to meet you, ma am. I'm sorry it has to be under these circumstances."

"Are you married, Mr. Watts?"

"Yes, I am. We have two boys.'

"Then when this is over, you can come back and bring your family. We will make it a true visit."

"My wife would love that. Plus, I'll get major points in the cool dad department."

"Then it's a done deal."

While they were getting acquainted, Rachael slipped out and went to her room. She came back with some extra armament that she had smuggled in. She handed it around to Reynolds and Watts.

Rachael had a small revolver, a lady's gun. "Do you know how to use a gun Mary?"

"I was shooting as soon as I could hold one. I told you my family was military. I had all brothers. I got my quota of squirrels in my day."

"Your job is to stay alive and free. I don't want you to take any chances. However, that being said, you have the right to defend yourself. If we go down, we'll try to give you time to get away. Hide where ever it is you feel safe. Wilson said it'll be over by zero six hundred. Give it another half hour from then. Call the police or FBI to come and get you."

Mary cupped Rachael's face with her hand, "Child, I trust you and your friends fully. With the Grace of God, we'll make it through."

"Well let's just hope we have a couple of angels riding our shoulders tonight. We'll probably need them."

The men hid when dinner was delivered. Using one of the gadgets from the agency that Jon had included with the weapons, she checked it first for any drugs. Everything was clean. The kidnappers must have a high level of confidence in their ability to get in and out without getting caught. If they didn't think it was necessary to drug Mrs. Blair, they were probably drugging the guards. They also had a plan to take her out of the picture. She really didn't think it included leaving her breathing.

As usual, there was way too much food. They all got plenty to eat. Rachael dug in with the rest of them. She had learned long ago to eat when you could because you never knew when the next time was coming.

After dinner, Rachael made a pallet in the little room in the secret tunnel. "Now I just need to set my room up so they think I'm sleeping there. 'I'll be back.'" She wiggled her eyebrows at the end of the famous last words. Arnold's line was too good to waste.

The agents outside the door nodded when she said goodnight. She closed her door and then hurriedly placed the pillows and blankets to look like someone was sleeping. She placed the packets of cow's blood at chest and head level so whoever shot from the door would see the blood. Hopefully, they wouldn't check too closely when they saw the blood.

She changed into black jeans and a matching long-sleeved tee. Added her black boots and was dressed up and ready to go in assassin chic. Replaced the knives she had removed to change clothes. Thank goodness, the weather was turning mild. The nights could get cool, but not unbearably cold.

Leaving the small nightlight in the room on so the bed was in shadow, she picked up the box that Jon had delivered and was ready to go. Opening up the hidden door in her closet, she scooted down the tunnel to the apartment. She paused at an opening to see into the hallway outside the apartment.

The change of the guard had happened at twenty-one hundred. The agents were still there. They both had a thousand-yard stare, would nod off and then straighten up. The agents had definitely been drugged. It was going down sooner then she thought. She ran the rest of the way to the apartment.

"Okay, boys and girls, the guards are well on the way to la-la land. We need to get this show on the road. I guess the birds flew south, the wars still on and we still have hate in the world." Mary gave her a strange look. Rachael just waffled her hand and grinned. "I'll explain later."

Reynolds guarded the door while Watts and the First Lady went into the tunnel. Hopefully, Mary would get a little rest before they had to run. She had considered just cutting and running. Unfortunately, they needed the opportunity to get information and a timetable. The kidnappers had to think they had a chance at kidnapping their target. If they thought they were busted their plan concerning the President would be implemented.

They needed to catch all of the cells in motion tonight or they would lose them again. Mrs. Blair had agreed to the wait even when it put her in more danger. It might be a high price to pay for a chance of capturing an informant. Her husband and Wilson needed the information for national security. It in itself was an important enough reason for her. Mary Blair was a First Lady in every way.

Rachael turned off the lights and pulled the covers over her. Reynolds took a position behind the door so he could stay hidden.

The kidnappers were patient. It was almost an hour before they entered the apartment. Her eyes had adjusted to the dark. The intruders had donned night vision goggles as soon as they entered. Only the best toys for these assassins. There were two of them. If it was Rachael's op, there were two more in the hallway and a man in the getaway vehicle. They moved professionally. It figured. No such luck for it being amateur night.

Rachael was wrong. There were three intruders. The two men had brought the screw-up fairy with them. Their plan had been simple. Reynolds would take out the man who held back and she would handle the one who made the grab on the 'sleeping First Lady.' Watts and Mary would start to run like the furies from hell were chasing them down the tunnel. They would catch up after dispatching the kidnappers. Hopefully after getting some information from them.

27

"You have a choice. You can maybe have a good day or I can turn it into a living hell... Choose wisely." Unknown

"Bravery is being the only one that knows you're afraid." Tennessee Williams

Man number two hung back in the doorway, out of Reynolds' reach while the other goon grabbed Rachael. The man assigned to grab the First Lady had been a quick study. He knew he had a ringer as soon as he caught a glimpse of her face. Did she also mention he was also extremely large? He was at least six four and around two-hundred and eighty pounds of muscle.

There was the added fact that he also had quick reflexes. Life was so unfair sometimes. Big, bulky men were supposed to be clumsy. This guy didn't get the memo. Grabbing her by her shirt at the neck, he threw her across the room toward the wall.

What happened next held both Reynolds and the second attacker rooted in place. The only explanation they both could have given was that they had the same hallucination. The man that hurled Rachael against the wall had dropped the syringe he was going to use to knock out Mrs. Blair. He already had his gun out. Rachael was drawing hers as she flew across the room. One smooth pull and she shot a split second before she impacted with the wall. Her assailant stood perfectly still for one heartbeat, and then like the proverbial oak tree fell to the floor with a bullet between his eyes. She had hit him in the t-box. He was dead before she hit the wall.

Rachael slid down the wall. Her left hand had slapped against it to absorb some of the shock, but not enough. It hurt like hell. Reynolds hadn't taken out the other kidnapper, and she brought her gun up again as he stopped gaping and started to shoot. The sound of her hitting the wall had snapped him back into the action. The man had finally taken the next step into the room, allowing Eric to get behind him. Before he could squeeze off a round, he was down and out. Reynolds collapsed his police asp, and holstered it. Hopefully no one had heard her impact with the wall.

"Girl, I have never seen a shot like that. What are you?"

"A savant. Let's roll before the others check. Even with a silencer, there's noise. I had planned to do this quietly. Here's hoping they won't pay attention to some of it, they would expect Mary to put up a fight. I don't know how close the rest of their team is. They have a timetable too. These guys are pros. Our guards are drugged, but I don't know how long that will last. Here's hoping they didn't kill them to make sure they stay quiet. I had hoped to be able to question one of these guys. I doubt they knew anything, probably just muscle for hire."

She shrugged, winced slightly. "Guess I'll leave that fun chore to Johnson." They went through the tunnel into her room. The sheets and blanket were covered in blood. The bags must have fooled the shooter. Really sloppy, he didn't check to make sure he had actually killed the intended victim.

She opened the panel, and they both entered. Mrs. Blair and Watts were gone. At least someone was following orders. Rachael was careful to close it and then broke the latch so if the strike team did find their way out, they would have to work at opening it. It wouldn't take long, but every second helped.

They would guess there was a secret way out when

neither the kidnappers or the First Lady's party came out the door. She was banking on it giving them a few minutes' lead time if there was no apparent way out of the room. Maybe they would get lucky and cause some confusion to their enemies.

Hopefully, they would search the apartment first. She had opened a kitchen window that someone could have climbed out of and down. Course they would have to have had a genetic link to Spiderman. It might throw the attackers off for a moment or two. Every second added up in their favor. The longer the team was in the building, the likelier they would be discovered.

You could say what you want, but the Secret Service knew their job. They would not be happy campers to find their "house" had been invaded. The strike team would be up against a bunch of pissed off agents. It was her intent that it would give them time to get out of the tunnel before they started tearing walls apart. They couldn't have bought off the whole White House protection detail. Surely someone would wake up sooner or later and figure out something was wrong.

Rachael grabbed her backpack and slung her rifle over her shoulder. It wasn't her usual sniper weapon. It was a Remington 30 aught 6 with iron sites. It was a good hunting rifle no matter what the game was. Not to hurt any of the gunsmiths' feelings at the agency but, she was just as accurate with it as she was their fancy models. Besides she didn't want to alert anyone at the agency that she had her weapon. She didn't know how many more Ralph's there were running around.

They caught up with the other two just as they got to the bottom of the ladder. Watts had stopped for a few seconds to allow Mary to catch her breathe.

"You two, dump your cell phones. If someone figures out it's you all helping us, they can track them."

They didn't argue, but Watts commented, "How do we keep in touch in case we have to separate?"

She handed a phone to each of them and the First Lady. "Some friends of mine set these up. They can't be traced."

"Not even your agency friends?" This came from Reynolds. He had noticed she hadn't brought any of the guns or fancy gadgets in the duffle bag in her room.

"I have friends in other places besides the agency. No one there knows about these. We have a mole there. I don't trust any equipment from them."

"What about your weapons?"

"They're clean. This is my old hunting rifle I had as a kid. No one would suspect me of taking it to use on an op. I dumped the ones that Jon brought me and the one I got from Johnson. If they are monitoring them, they may think we're still in the apartment somewhere. It may buy us some time. Mary helped me smuggle the rest in."

They walked as fast as Mrs. Blair could move. She was getting out of breath again before they reached the crossover under Q Street. After a short breather, they started moving again.

"Remind me to up my exercise program when this is over."

"You didn't know you were going to have to run for your life when this started."

"Rachael, we all have to run for our lives. It's just that some of us only do it figuratively."

"You're doing great. We're over half-way there."

"Our former presidents must have stayed in better shape than those that followed."

"A lot of them were farmers and soldiers before they took office. Maybe they were just tough old coots. We don't hear much about what their wives were really like. Most of them had to be pretty much hands on when it came to running a home and taking care of children. Not to mention the childbirth thing. I imagine they were as tough as it gets back in the day. Plus, men in those days usually married women a lot younger than themselves."

Mary grinned, sniping back, "A lot of men still do, but not for the same reasons."

When they reached the Meridian Park, Rachael exited first checking to make sure they were clear. She motioned everyone out. They huddled at the base of the trees as she went over the plan again. She knew the men were good. But it gave Mary a chance to catch her breath with some dignity.

"Everyone knows what to do. Reynolds, you, Watts, and Mary take the van and go to the coordinates for the hide out in Rock Creek Park. I hid the all-terrain vehicles where that GPS ends. The ATVs are equipped with GPS units that will get you to the cabin. One of you hide the car and destroy the GPS in it just in case they have a way to track it. Then follow the others. All the cars are pre-computer so they can't put a trace on them. The GPSs are all portable. One of you will have to hike in."

"Mary, I'm hoping you know how to drive the vehicles. If not get a crash course on the way there. I mean that literally, your husband will have my hide if anything happens to you. There's another tunnel behind the lean-to. You'll need to shift the camouflaged netting back to see the opening. It's covered by a steel door. I have another vehicle stashed at the end of that tunnel. Only use it if the noise won't give you away. If it comes down to that, head for the police department and someone you trust."

"I didn't think they allowed private cabins in the park," Watts commented.

"They don't. It's just a make shift lean-to. Calling it a cabin is giving it delusions of grandeur. Since you're not allowed that either, don't tell anyone. It'll be our little secret. If we get charged, I have a contact that may get us a Presidential pardon. If that doesn't work, we'll get a vacation with free room and board." She couldn't help it. Sometimes the sarcasm just snuck right in there. "Mary, you don't go with anyone who doesn't know your safe word. I mean your real safe word. The one between you and the President. This goes deep. We don't know who to trust except for the President and Wilson. I'll meet you there."

"Where are you going?"

"To set up a little distraction. Go and be careful all of you."

Mary gave her a quick hug. Reynolds noticed Rachael's slight grimace as she had her ribs squeezed. She had hit that wall harder than she let on.

Watts and Mary scuttled off to the tree line and disappeared into the dark. He stopped and watched as Rachael closed the hatch to the tunnel. She took a device out of her backpack and attached it to the opening latch before going in. It wouldn't come as a shock to him if whatever it was didn't go off with a loud boom when the door was opened. Cade definitely made use of her toys. He watched her drop back into the tunnel. He figured since she had to come back out, she hadn't armed it yet.

He followed the other two to the waiting car. Watts was in and starting the engine when he got there. He opened the back of the van and rolled the motorcycle out. "You two go on. I'm going with Cade." He lowered his voice hoping only Watts would hear him. "She's hurt and might need help."

He had no luck, hiding anything from Mrs. Blair. She was really sharp. She leaned across Watt's lap. "Take care of her Mr. Reynolds. She's good people."

"I'll do what I can, ma'am. You two get out of here." He grimaced, like Cade needed taking care of. The amount of trouble she got into she'd need a full-time caretaker.

He hid the bike and stepped back into the trees. Stopped to watched to make sure they weren't followed. No other car was in sight as they turned the corner. He sure as hell hoped Cade knew what she was doing.

She suddenly was right next to him. He almost yelped like a girl. "I didn't think you'd obey orders." She actually sounded like she was hissing at him. "Civilians ain't worth shit on an op. I don't know why I care. The only reason I can think of is Wilson would kill me if I let anything happen to his baby brother." She turned and melted back into the trees again. "If you're coming, keep up. I won't come back for you again."

Civilian. Who did she think she was talking to? Christ on a crutch, he was a cop. Lord she was fast, he had to hurry to catch up with her.

Rachael had set the device to explode only if opened from the inside of the tunnel. They made much better time running back through the tunnel to the White House. He followed as she veered left from where they had gone before and came up in a patch of evergreens.

It had taken them less than twenty minutes to reach the White House proper. There was another tunnel under the wall. By the time this was over with, the Secret Service would be tearing the walls down looking for hidden passages. It would drive the curators' crazy.

Considering what was going on inside the building, it was quiet along the perimeter. Rachael punched him in the shoulder. "There! See them? They're trying to sneak out. Bet the time's running out on whoever they paid off or drugged."

"So, what's your plan? You going to let them get away?"

"Hell no! They're pissing me off. Besides, confusion for the enemy is always a good thing. My Daddy always told me the first rule of battle is that incoming rounds have the right of way. Let's see if they know the rules." She pulled her rifle around and settled it against her shoulder.

"Wait! You can't hit them from here without a scope. Besides what if you kill one of the good guys?"

"I don't plan on killing any of them. I just want to sow confusion and give Johnson time to catch them. Nothing warms the cockles of my heart more than raining chaos on the bad guys. Be ready to move." The rifle cracked twice as the men tried to make it to their get-away car. She aimed one more time. One of the vehicles, waiting in the drive, exploded into flames.

"Shit, that wasn't in the plan. Guess that will hold them for a few minutes. Let's move it!"

He glanced back as they headed for the tunnel under the wall. Both men were rolling and screaming on the ground. From the racket they were making neither one sounded near death. He could hear them above the noise the perimeter alarms and the explosions the burning car was causing. The strike team must have been carrying explosives for some reason.

Everyone else was taking cover. Apparently, they also were aware of the rule. Cade was one hell of a shot. She was taking a whopping big chance letting him see her shoot. Whatever faults she had, she took protecting the First Lady seriously. There was no regard about the fallout that might cause her problems. For a killer, she was very protective of other people. He remembered her putting herself between the waitress at the diner and the shooter. Most killers he knew didn't have a strong protective instinct. Maybe he had misjudged Cade.

JOHNSON HAD one hell of a headache. So did the Secret Service agents assigned to watch the door to the presidential apartment. The Marines had gathered up the two wounded men who had been shot according to witnesses, "from out of nowhere." At the onset, since there was considerable turmoil when the shooting first started and the wounded men were first thought to be agents. It became apparent they were imposters due to the lack of proper identification and the fact that no one recognized them.

The first response team had gone to the First Family's apartment due to her being the only "body" they were responsible to protect left in the house. The unconscious guards were slumped by the door of the apartment. It didn't take long to find that the apartment had been breached and the First Lady was gone. There were signs of a struggle and Johnson would have bet his last dollar there was no way Mrs. Blair wouldn't have fought her attacker. But due to the dead body, he'd put his money on Cade. Rachael Cade's room was searched. They found where she had set up the bed to look like someone was asleep. The shooter would have seen the blood bags she had rigged at chest and head level explode and assume he had hit his target. You really had to admire her deviousness. The girl had skills.

Cade must have known something was going down tonight. She had kept it hidden from him and acted on her own. He knew who she was and why she was there. Don Wilson had finally seen fit to work him into the loop. Johnson was royally pissed. He also realized that she was unsure of who to trust. In the end, she had decided not to trust anyone.

He really couldn't blame her. If he had been in her

shoes, he would have done the same thing. She thought he was old school, but he learned fast and had already ferreted out four of the men disloyal to the job. Two were agents and two were part of the Marine guard. As much as he hated to admit it, Rachael Cade had good reason not to trust the security teams in the White House or Secret Service.

Cade wasn't the one, however, who had to call the President. And tell him his wife was missing. It was going to be one hell of a long night.

28

"God gave the three Wise Men a star to follow because He knew they wouldn't ask for directions." Unknown

"I GET LOST easy but I get there fast." Unknown

RACHAEL HAD SEEN the proverbial wheels turning in Reynolds' head. Knew he wouldn't leave her behind. The Lord save her from macho, protective men. After she booby trapped the door to the tunnel, she called Wilson. He would tell the President the news his wife was away and in safe hands.

Unfortunately, Reynolds and she were not in the same position. They had to get away before they were discovered. She didn't like leaving Mary with only one guard. There rest of the night to get through. If she didn't call back by zero six hundred, Wilson would know that their team had been compromised or dead.

They ran back to the end of the shorter tunnel, and back to the park. They covered the ground a lot faster than they had with Mrs. Blair. This time, Reynolds watched their back trail as she uncovered a motorcycle where he had hidden under a tarp covered in vines. This part of the park, ended in some trees that were in front of one of the museums. There were probably security cameras nearby, but she was gambling on it taking a few minutes for Johnson to get everyone up and running.

She pitched Reynolds the helmet that had been strapped to the back of the bike. The extra helmet was part of worst-case scenario and she would have had to get Mary out on the bike. They both got the helmets on and she rolled the bike out. He climbed behind her and tightened his arms as she took off. It was a good thing they were on flat pavement. If it had been a ramp, they would have launched into outer space as fast as she gunned it.

They weren't as lucky as the first time. A car came tearing out behind them. No way of knowing if it was the good guys or bad, and Rachael always erred on the side of paranoia. The odds were, whoever it was wasn't on their team. She didn't see any white hats to give her a clue, which cinched it as far as she was concerned. It made sense to have had teams out searching the surrounding streets. They couldn't have known where or how they escaped, just set out a scatter search and hoped one would hit.

Reynolds had relaxed his hold a little after the take off. Now he pulled in closer to her to help with balance. Even in the heat of the chase, she could feel his arms around her. It felt like he complemented her instead of the usual discomfort she felt when others tried to get close. This was so not a good time to get distracted.

Rachael wasn't the only one reflecting on how good it felt to be this close. She had strapped her backpack down to the bike and the only thing between them was their clothes and her rifle. Both their hearts were beating in double time. He knew his was from excitement, but wondered about hers. Cade didn't seem the type to get worked up over a bike ride. Or being chased for that matter. If he could get his hands free, he really needed to slap his head again. This fascination with this woman was way out of bounds. He needed to get his head back into the game.

Rachael had turned on the headsets in the helmets. Mostly he just heard a running commentary of expletives. He looked behind and saw another car join the parade. When he faced front, he saw the tractor trailer truck roll across the intersection in front of them. A "hold on!" was shouted in his helmet over the intercom.

Before he could even breath out a prayer or an "oh shit" as it looked like they were going to die, in a very messy way. The bike dropped sideways on the pavement and slid under the trailer part of the rig.

Reynolds never figured out how she popped the bike back up on its wheels and then sped down the street. It was either he didn't see it because his eyes were shut or was too busy with his own set of expletives. He was also getting a real, healthy concern about surviving Cade's driving. He glanced back. They were gaining distance as the pursuing cars had to wait for the semi's driver to clear the road.

The driver was taking his sweet time and ignoring the horns and shouted obscenities. Two blocks later, they made a quick turn and were temporarily out of site of the pursuers for a few seconds. Since the truck driver apparently had suddenly developed a hearing loss and hadn't gotten out of the way.

An old panel truck weaved out from an alley. The back doors opened and a ramp dropped out. Rachael ran the bike up the back of the truck as another duplicate of the bike they were on rolled out of the truck backwards and then roared down the street. It would take a while for the cars to catch up enough to notice there was only one rider instead of two. The doors slammed shut, and a few seconds later they heard the honking horns and the squeal of tires as the pursuers finally made it around the truck. They continued to amble down the street for a short time. The truck stopped, and he heard a garage door go up. After the truck entered, there was the sound of the door closing behind them.

Rachael and he had eased off the bike and just gotten their helmets off when the back doors of the van opened up to show a cherry looking elf of a man waiting for them. "You do get yourself in some pickles, little girl." She also heard the sound of a hammer clicking back.

"You know me, Jimmy. It's a weeknight, I was bored. Just reruns on TV and nothing good on at the movies."

"Girl, you never watch TV. Who's the fella?"

"Jimmy, this is Eric Reynolds. He's helping me with a little law breaking tonight. Eric, this is Jimmy."

"You do know he is the law, don't you, little bit?"

"Got me there, Jimmy. You always can tell a badge from a mile away."

"There are just some things you need to know in this world to continue to be able to do business. I thought I'd taught you better."

"I didn't have anyone else to trust, Jimmy. Nobody has a scorecard. Don't have a lot of people I can go to. His word is golden. He won't snitch on you."

"It's a sad day, when the only one you can trust is a copper." Jimmy looked Reynolds over."Guess if you can hang with the way she drives, you might be all right. It proves you're either very brave or certifiably crazy. If the girl here vouches for you, it's as good as done." The gun disappeared.

"Jimmy, we need to go. Someday I'll tell you the story, but we need to run. Sooner or later, the people following us are going to notice there's only one person on that bike."

"I'll hold you to that. You got some heavy hitters after you tonight, child."

"Did you recognize any of them?"

"Don't know no names. Just seen'em around." He spat on the floor before he continued. "Them's the type that wants to convert you or kill you. I stay out of their way. They give people like me a bad name."

"Will Jesse be okay?"

"He's already in the bolt hole. Seeing as you taught him to drive, it'll take the devils own to catch him. They won't find him or that bike. Tomorrow it'll have a new coat of paint and emblems on it. Just like this one will. Your new ride's over there."

"Money will be where it usually is. You take care of yourself, Jimmy. Never know when a girl might need you again."

"Anytime, child, anytime." He disappeared into an office with a wave of his hand.

There was a mud-colored old Toyota SUV in the corner, keys in the ignition. Rachael slid into the passenger side and set up the GPS.

"You two have stock in used cars? And I have to say, I can't believe you're letting me drive."

"I don't question Jimmy's resources. I ask and he delivers. Jon was right about my sense of direction. I get lost at the drop of a hat."

"What was that we just did? I've lived here most of my life and didn't know about half these streets or this warehouse."

"I had a beacon in my helmet. Jimmy had it set up for me. Don't worry about it. This warehouse won't be here by morning either. Jimmy may trust me, but he really doesn't trust cops."

"I wouldn't rat him out over this."

"I know, but he errs on the side of caution, Jimmy does."

"How did you meet him?"

"He was in the service with my Dad. He showed up at my parent's funeral. With both my parents' dead, I guess he thought I might need someone like him some day. He told me to look him up if I ever got to this neck of the woods. So, I did. Now if I need something that can't be traced, I go to Jimmy."

"What was his MOS in the military?"

"He was their supply sergeant and bagman."

"Bagman?"

"Whatever they needed, Jimmy got it for them. No questions asked. Think of him as a real-life Radar."

"That's handy."

"We need to get going." She glanced back at the office area. "Jimmy's given the all clear so we shouldn't be followed."

"You have the strangest friends."

"That's the only kind that will put up with me."

They wandered around the streets for few minutes to make sure there was no tail. She trusted Jimmy, but it payed to be cautious. They had a precious cargo to protect and she wasn't taking any chances. It wouldn't hurt Jimmie's feelings. He would have scolded her soundly the next time she saw him if she hadn't checked for herself. When she was satisfied that they were clear, they headed out to the park to meet up with Watts and Mary.

When they got to where she had hidden the ATV's, she noted Watts had used the camouflage to mask the van where they had it hidden. Rachael knew they would be gone. But she had to check. She hid the car under another vine covered canvas. Jimmy would arrange to have it and the van picked up. They hiked the rest of the way in.

Reynolds almost walked past the lean-to. It was nestled back under an overhang. Vines and various types of growth covered the structure. It would be difficult to find it in daylight. At night, it was almost impossible to see. Rachael pulled him back into the tree line and hunkered down for a few seconds watching the area.

"Do you always just announce to the world, that you're here? If you do, it's a wonder you haven't been shot before now."

"I thought this was a safe place." he hissed back.

"I thought the White House had enough protection that no one could have gotten in to kidnap the First Lady, too. Duh! You saw how that turned out. Stay here. If anything happens to me, get to Wilson and tell him what happened. He'll take it from there. Don't try to be a hero."

"If that isn't the pot calling the kettle black."

"I'm paid the big bucks to do this. You're not."

"I saw your financials. If you're getting the big bucks, you're hiding it really well."

"Next time look under charitable contributions." And she was gone. He had to admit she could skulk with the best of them. She waved him in, a few minutes later.

Watts and Mary were both keyed up and full of questions. Rachael just smiled and told them it had been a cake walk. She made the First Lady a cup of tea and got her settled in the small bed. There were shadows of fatigue under her eyes and Rachael was worried about her. They still had the rest of the night to get through. If they had to run again, she would need all the down time she could get.

The little shelter was set up with a place to sleep and a small stove to heat things. It was a lot more comfortable and cozier than the outside advertised. A little tight for Rachael, but then she didn't like small spaces. They were now hidden deep into Rock Creek Park.

Rock Creek Park wandered over twelve miles. Most of it along the Potomac River. It had been established as a park in 1890 and was a favorite place for hikers and day trippers. Reynolds was willing to bet that even the oldest Forest Ranger didn't know about this place.

Reynolds had found the coffee and had a pot going on the stove. It took him a few minutes to fix it the old fashion percolator way. Rachael sat down on a camp chair and sighed as she held the warm cup in her hands. Her eyes closed. Now, under the light, he could see the bruising where she had been hit. If her face looked like the Fourth of July, he wondered what her back looked like.

"Do you need me to look at your back and see how bad the damage is?"

She didn't even open her eyes as she shook her head no. "There's nothing that can be done about it. I've got some over-the-counter pain pills in my backpack. I'll take some before I go out and scout around."

"You took a hard hit back there. It's a wonder the wall didn't crack. Let me take a look."

She sighed, he wouldn't quit badgering her till she let him. "Knock yourself out." She pulled her shirt out of her jeans so he could assess the damage.

Her back was turning the same colors as her face. The shoulder holster had left some rash burns. He saw the scar from a bullet wound. The scar was still pink, so it hadn't happened all that long ago. She was right. There was nothing he could do for her. She was going to hurt like hell when she stopped moving and let the soreness set in.

The lady had many sides. He wondered when she had gotten the dragon tattoo that twined up her back to the lower part of her shoulder blade. Its body stopped short of her bra line, and its tail wound into regions below her waistline. The person who had made the tattoo was an artist. It almost looked like it would move if you watched it long enough.

"When you're through admiring my art work, we need to set up shifts. One inside, one out. We'll overlap the inside shift so we can get some sleep. I'll take first watch outside. You two duke it out for in here." She placed a hand on the chair seat and pushed to help herself stand. "One hour on, two off so we aren't dead on our feet in the morning." Walking over to the cache in the corner, she grabbed a power bar, tucked a bottle of water under her arm. Left carrying them and her coffee."

"Bossy little thing, isn't she?" Watts observed. "How bad is she hurt?"

Reynolds grimaced and replied, "You don't know the half of it. She's going to have one hell of a bruise. I wish you could have seen it. That goon threw her across the room. She had her gun drawn and shot him between the eyes before she hit the wall. I've never seen anything like it before."

"Girl's definitely got some skills."

"You can say that again." And that's what worried him.

29

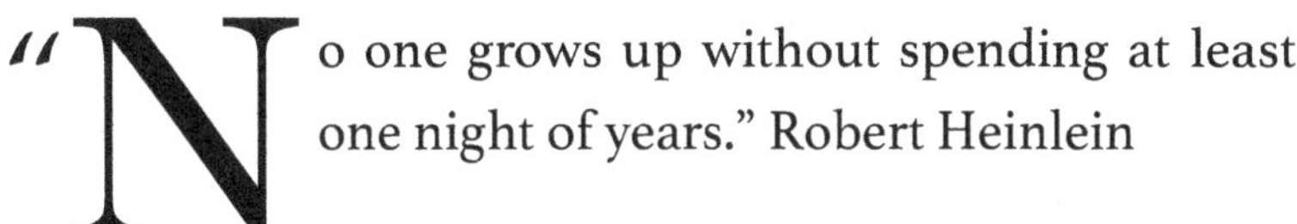

"No one grows up without spending at least one night of years." Robert Heinlein

THE PRESIDENT WAS PROWLING the length of the bunker. It didn't take many strides to cover the distance from side to side. Wilson, had counted up to thirty round trips. He remarked mildly, "Wearing out the cement by pacing will take more time than we have right now."

Blair stopped, and Wilson could see a blistering comment simmering on his lips. He could almost see the thoughts synapsing across his brain as he considered what he wanted to say versus what he should.

"You don't have to rethink everything six times over before you say it to me. I'm a big boy. I can take it."

"Sorry, it's a force of habit. I wonder if I'll ever be able to blurt out what I want to say again. Not without having to think of the consequences seven times to Sunday."

"Rachael says they're safe for now. She wouldn't have said it if it wasn't so."

"I just wish I could have spoken with Mary. She must be terrified."

"I don't know. Having been around Mrs. Blair, she's probably having the time of her life."

A small smile hovered around the President's mouth. He sighed again before answering. "You're right. She would think of it as an adventure. I don't think she realizes how dangerous these people are. Plus, she is trusting. If the traitor is someone we know and depend on, she might unknowingly put her trust in the wrong person."

"Your wife has a finely tuned sense of who people are and if they are lying. I bet if you think back on it, she never liked Jeff Cody. Didn't trust him."

"You're right. He wasn't her first choice. She liked that guy from Montana that had the bad car wreck before we made the selection."

"And if I had been more on the ball, I would have figured out that it wasn't an accident and someone wanted Cody to get the job."

"In this business, there's a lot of 'what ifs?' You'll go nuts if you dwell on them. Sometimes you just have to trust and hope it doesn't come back to haunt you or kick you in the ass. How much longer before we know anything?"

"The teams are ready to go. I had Rachael vet them and our protection detail. She didn't get anything off the ones I picked. The fact they come from a unit outside of Washington is a plus. The kidnappers will make the call soon. They'll try to pull the wool over our eyes about having your wife. They're scrambling right now since their plans fell through. Johnson has at least two of their men, so they're worried about them talking.

When they call, the signal they'll get will show we're in the bunker. Nothing about it will set off any alarms. They'll have to go through the usual unscrambling to get it. They expect it. If we made it easy, they'd expect a trap. We give the go ahead at zero five-thirty our time, and with luck and God willing it's a done deal."

As if in answer to Wilson's comment, the phone rang. The sound was loud in the quiet bunker. Wilson wished he wasn't so imaginative at times. It sounded like a death knell.

The voice on the other end was canned. They had used a voice synthesizer to disguise it so no one could identify it through a voice recognition program. Wilson put it on speakerphone for both of them to hear. "We have your wife, Mr. President, and if you don't stop this take over, we will kill her."

"I need proof of life before I even think about it."

The President's voice had the right amount of anger and concern in it.

"Have the person there with you to go to the web site I will give you, and you will have your proof. Let me know when you're ready."

Wilson nodded his head so the President would know to go on. "We're ready."

"It's resist.freedom.com."

"Catchy title."

"Do not try to get cute with us, Mr. President. We are deadly serious."

Wilson turned the computer so Blair could see it. There was a video of a woman tied to a chair. At first glance, you might have mistaken it for the First Lady. They had done an excellent job. If the President had been overwrought and not paying attention, it might have worked.

The woman's build and coloring were correct. It wasn't Mrs. Blair. Who ever it was had been photo-shopped to look like the First Lady. Even without the blindfold and gag obscuring part of her face, the President and Wilson might have been fooled.

The President finished looking at the picture. "So am I. Deadly serious. So, listen closely. You do not dictate to me on how I run my country. Even if you had my wife, which you don't, I would not allow you to stop me from doing what I think is right. Also, take very, very seriously my next words. If anything happens to my wife. I mean so much as a hangnail. The word vengeance, will be a word you will learn every syllable of, painfully. Do I make myself clear?"

During the President's reply, Wilson could pick up the heavy breathing and agitation of the person on the other side of the line. If it wasn't for the voice over program, the answer would have been in the Minnie Mouse range. The opposition was having a bad night. Mostly due to Rachael Cade.

"You will be sorry for that remark. We had not planned on hurting Mrs. Blair if you had cooperated. Now we will kill her no matter what the consequence." The line was disconnected. Wilson hadn't been able to get a trace on it. The tech people would trace the WEB site but he knew it was probably already down and a dead end.

Blair's face was troubled as he looked at Wilson. "Have I just signed my wife's death warrant?"

"I can assure you, if they go after your wife while she is with Cade, they will fully understand what you just said was not an idle threat. I personally would not go up against her if I had a SEAL team and a dozen operatives with me."

"I know she's good, but she is an awful tiny package to have that much destructive power."

"Do not ever underestimate Cade due to her size. What she doesn't have in mass, she makes up with sheer determination, skill, and pure meanness."

“What do we do about the ongoing threat? We originally thought if we kept Mary safe until morning they would back off.”

“Rachael is scheduled to call two minutes before the operation is a go. We’ll work out a plan and send in a rescue team to coordinates she gives us to get them out.”

“I hope it’s the team of SEALS and agents you were talking about earlier.”

“Even better. Three more hours to go.”

“When I started dating, my dad would get so upset if I came in even a little late. One night I didn’t get home until morning. He was still up, just waiting for me. I expected him to be furious. Instead, he just looked at me for a minute and then said; ‘Someday when you have your own children you’ll understand. When we wait for those we love, we are forced to live one night of years in fear and worry. Sometimes it is hard to care so much.’ I thought it was strange at the time, but now I think I understand.”

When do you leave for the meet?”

“In exactly ten minutes.”

The President shook Wilson’s hand. “Take care, old friend.”

“This is one night that we must all be taking care.”

30

"Service to others is the rent you pay for living on this planet." Marian Wright Edolma

"We don't see things as they are, we see them as we are." Anais Nin

Reynolds decided to let Watts go first on the watch. He wouldn't sleep, but he wanted the time with Cade. He needed to talk to her. Maybe he could get her to see the truth about his brother. Get her away from the dangerous life he was causing her to lead.

Mary Blair's voice came softly out of the darkness. "Awake detective? I can't sleep either. I'm worried about my husband. I'm not the adventurous kind who can defend herself against all odds. I'm scared I won't have the courage I need to get through this. But, that's not why you're lying awake, fretting about, is it? You do know you can't change who, or what she is?"

"I can't help it. You know Rachael's a murderer? She never hesitated when she shot those people back at the apartment or outside the White House. If I had any doubts before, I know now. She was more than capable of killing the Congressman. She has the skills. That and whatever it takes in a person to take another's life. When this is over, I'll have to arrest her."

"What proof do you really have that she did it? It's all circumstantial. The fact that she could have doesn't make it so."

"I can't change what I know."

"Has she told you she did it?"

"No, but I watched her in action. There's no doubt in my mind that she did it," he continued stubbornly. Arguing with the First Lady was not the way to get ahead.

"Even if you had all the proof in the world and a signed confession, you know how this will end."

"What do you mean?"

"Rachael will never go to trial. She will simply disappear or be terminated. A trial will bring out too much information that cannot be shared. It will have political ramifications that would threaten our country.

I have no doubt that she would say that she was responsible. She would never implicate anyone else. Not because it would be too dangerous, but because, she would believe it was the honorable thing to do."

"This is a free country. We have the right to know what's going on."

"Are you really that naïve? Yes, everyone has the right to know the broad strokes of what's going on. If the government told everybody the whole truth and nothing but the truth, the end result would be total chaos. Our enemies would annihilate us. Nothing would get done. To be honest, most people don't really want the whole truth. Keeping this country free is often tawdry work, Detective Reynolds."

"In the past, we have been up against enemies who think as we do. Their honor system and morals are close to the same as ours. If not, they still had a rigid code of ideals and were honor bound to follow them. Their ideologies generally wanted what was best for their people as a whole. It made it possible to work out defensive measures and, in the end, treaties."

"Our enemy now is not Arabs, Middle Easterners, or Muslims, but extremists. Fanatics who truly believe that the only right thing is to be what they are. They will never be satisfied because everyone has to believe exactly like them. They won't tolerate any deviation from what they believe is the way. No one else has the right to exist. They are willing to die a martyr's death to succeed. It is difficult to fight someone who doesn't fear dying and impossible to make a treaty with them."

"They use the pieces of their religion to prove what they do is right. All religions do it, even ours. Think of the witch trials or the crusades in the fifteenth century. Some say their holy books back up what they are doing. You could say that our Bible is the same, that we can justify everything we do if we just find the right passage to back us up."

"There is one big difference. We are not told that we will only be true believers if we take part in some way in a jihad. We may be pushed to spread the word, but not to kill people who chose not to accept it. Before you mention the crusades, Christians agree that though the intention was to spread the Word, there was a lot wrong with them. It was a major cluster fuck, and has been responsible for a lot of the problems today."

"There is no honor to be had in killing innocents no matter what someone's sex or religion is. Do I think all Muslims are bad? No more than I think all Christians and Jews or any other religions are lily white."

"Believers and unbelievers all have black pages in their history. I'm not trying to grandstand for any religion. We've all screwed up in some way through out history. But I believe that God in whatever form you give Him, gave us the ability to have freedom of will. If that is true, no followers of any doctrine have the right to force us to believe as they do. We all have to decide what we are and what we believe."

"I will fight for all religions or for those who don't believe to practice a belief or a lack there of. The responsibility for that type of freedom is that you in return don't force your beliefs on others. You can talk to others about it, but they have the right to say no or disagree. I may be wrong, but the people who are espousing jihad do not want to talk." She sighed before she continued, "I would so dearly love to be proven wrong."

She held up her hand to stop him from breaking into her comments, "When my husband first went into politics, I believed in black and white. I hated this life because to get things done you had to compromise on every little detail. I begged Will to get out and do something else, anything else. You know what his answer was?"

Reynolds shook his head.

"He asked me who else I wanted to do this job. Who else did I think was capable of trying to do the right thing? If good men and women weren't willing to lead, then we would be following idiots and wrong doers. He admits that often the decisions made don't appear to be correct, but he does the best he can with what he has to work with. Are there mistakes made? Often. But we're human beings and not perfect by any stretch of the imagination.

He also admits that politics are rife with people who are in it for the wrong reasons. We can only hope that the citizens of this country will do their job and learn what the candidates really stand for. Then vote for the person who will lead with the best of his or her ability and try to do the right thing."

"But what has that to do with outright murder?"

"The unfortunate fact is that some people don't deserve to live. If they live, they will cause others to suffer and die. Sometimes in horrible ways. I know you will say it's not up to us as an individual to make that decision. But tell me Detective Reynolds, have you ever taken a life in the line of duty? That day, when those two men were going to kill all those people in the restaurant, were you willing to pull the trigger to protect the other customers?"

He sputtered for a second and then nodded yes.

"Would you wait for a jury of his peers to decide he should die before you shot him? Would it have been better for you or whoever you were protecting to die in that person's place? Would your noble sacrifice have been worth the lives of your fellow officers who would have had to hunt him down and bring him in after he killed you? What about the innocent lives he might have wasted before he was caught? Who makes the decision then?"

"It is people like you and Rachael. We need people like you who have the training and knowledge to back up your actions. Those who can make the hard decisions, or take action to protect those who cannot protect themselves. Would you prefer that someone who only has his or her best interest at heart make them, or someone who wants to protect others? Is it wrong to kill someone who is trying to kill you or destroy your way of life and country? Is it only right when the individual is holding a gun to your head? What are the parameters?"

"Believe me, I don't believe in wholesale murder. But where do we draw the line? When is it the safest and sanest thing to do a surgical strike? Take out the disease? When do we let that illness take its course? The jobs both you and Rachael have decided to take on are not black and white."

"No one should have the power to decide who lives or dies. It's too much responsibility in the hands of one or of a few." He repeated stubbornly.

"Power corrupts and absolute power corrupts absolutely or however the quote goes. It is a conundrum. Do we let fate decide, even if it means many innocents may die as a result? I don't know the answer. I don't think any of us do. The fact that we are having this conversation in the middle of the woods. Hiding from someone who is trying to do us harm, is a telling factor. It is telling that as much as we have evolved, we still fall back on killing to solve a lot of our larger problems."

"But Rachael's a nurse! Even taking everything you said in consideration, how can she be both? How can she help save lives on one hand and kill with the other?"

"Ask her. How can she not do both? From what I've been told, she is an excellent nurse and has saved many lives. You should read the reports from the medical unit she was in. Some of the things she did to help save our soldier's lives are just as wonderful as helping to delivery a baby."

"Taking the lives of the enemy saved her patients and the people sent to help save them. And as I have found out in the last twenty-four hours, she has a great capacity to assess a situation and make decisions that can cause other people to live or die. Is she right? I don't have an answer. I asked my husband why he trusts her so much. He said it's because she is neither black nor white, but grey. Her code name is the 'Grey Paladin.'"

"Rachael Cade is one of those rare humans that is able to look at both sides and make a rational decision based on what she finds. She doesn't kill on a whim. She is very open about her belief in God. That cross she wears is not a piece of jewelry to her. It means something. Ask Wilson how many times she's turned down an assignment and been proven correct."

"I don't know how she does what she does, but it's something right now I am very thankful for. I want to live, and she's the main reason I'm still breathing. Don't judge her until you know her."

"Why do I even care? Why do I need to understand and know what she thinks?"

She reached over and patted him gently on the shoulder. "Because Detective, I believe you think that you're head over heels in love with her."

Reynolds heard Watts cough to cover a laugh. He had been listening in on the conversation. He glared at him for a second as Watts turned back to guard duty. His partner knew him way too well.

Mrs. Blair was quiet. He stared at the ceiling until it was time for him to take Watts' place on guard duty.

31

"No one is going to feel sorry for you. So you have to go out there and be FIERCE." Gabby Douglous

"It is what it is." Unknown

Rachael didn't look much better when she came back into the shelter. She moved with the careful grace of someone who was in pain.

Reynolds waited until Watts left for his watch outside. "How much pain are you in?"

"On a scale of one to ten? Probably around four. Mostly just bruised. I think I may have a couple of cracked ribs. Nothing major."

"How long can you hold up?"

"As long as I have to, Detective. There aren't any other options available."

"What are your plans after we hand Mrs. Blair over to the guards?"

"I haven't thought that far ahead. I'm still trying to come up with Plan B in case we're betrayed by our would-be rescuers."

"You really are a paranoid SOB aren't you?"

"Comes with the territory. It's what keeps you alive."

"Do you trust anyone completely?"

"Except God? No, I don't. There're some days I even wonder what He's up to. The only person that comes close is your brother. In most things, I trust him almost implicitly."

"You'll go crazy if you don't have the capacity to trust. How do you relax and recharge?"

"Who's to say I'm not crazy already? I sort of have a Jekyll and Hyde life as it is. Besides that, my personal life has never been all that great anyway. Pleasant for the most part, but nothing to write home about."

"What are you going to do when this is over? Go on to the next crisis my brother sends you to? Then the next. Until you're so burned out that nothing matters any more?"

Rachael snorted and then held up her fist and started holding up her fingers as she counted out her options, "Let me see, my options are...? Oh yeah, we need to survive tonight. There seems to be a contingent of discontents who want us dead with extreme prejudice. They appear to have the greater numbers and resources at this point. Our only edge is they don't know where we are, at least for the moment anyway."

"I have a feeling that whoever is leading this group either knows me very well or has studied me. Which means it's someone in the agency who has a very high security clearance. So, I don't even know how long we'll be safe here."

"What else is there? If you want to enumerate them, then that appears to be number one. Number two would be that you'll have me in handcuffs and try to arrest me for murder. Number three, I get away and you start a massive 'woman hunt' until you get shut down by the powers that be. Number four, you decide to look the other way and you never see me again."

He felt a shutter go through him when he thought of never seeing her again. What was wrong with him? How could he have such conflicting feelings for someone he hadn't even kissed yet? Hell, they hadn't even held hands. That thought made him shiver all over again. Yet visiting her in prison wasn't appealing either. "You don't see a happy ending?"

"This isn't a freaking fairytale land. I'm not going to change what I do or what I am. People aren't going to learn to accept that we're all different. They don't seem to realize that if we just learn to live together, instead of trying to change everyone to fit a pre-conceived idea of what's right, this world we have to live in might last longer. I'm not going to magically fall in love with Jon and have this picture-perfect wedding we've been planning and live happily ever after. Since you're so inured behind your self-righteous outrage that I might kill people as a side job, I don't really see any fairy dust glittering around our relationship either."

"I am what I am. And I never mentioned anything about us having a relationship. As far as I'm concerned, you're a suspect in a murder investigation."

"Don't be an ass. We may not be able to read each other as well as we do most people, but stuff still leaks out around the edges. We're attracted to each other. Deal with it, and we go on with our lives. At least be honest. There's a good chance we won't live through the night. You want to face St. Peter with a lie on your lips?"

"Are you really that cold inside, Rachael? Don't you want to feel and act like normal people once in awhile?"

"...and people in hell want ice water. Not to sound anti-social, but most people tend to suck, especially long term. Part of that reasoning is due to the type of people I'm exposed to on a regular basis. I try to overlook everything except major short comings in the people I know. I know we don't always have sterling thoughts all the time. At least I don't. I'd hate to be the one listening in on my head conferences. I just can't stand the façade of something good hiding a monster. I don't hate anyone. I hate what they do.

I've been taken in too many times when I gave someone the benefit of the doubt and then got screwed. I try not to use my gift on everyday acquaintances. That's not fair. It's an invasion of their privacy. But in my line of work, I can't always take everyone at face value. If I do, then it may mean I end up dead. If I trust the wrong person the people who depend on me get injured or dead. To save things from getting messy, I just distrust most everyone on general principle."

"What about friends?"

"You don't listen. As I said, acquaintances that are friendly are different. It's easier overlooking their fickleness and it doesn't hurt as bad when they betray you in little ways. That's human nature. Sometimes it's even funny. I like to think people are basically good and just have momentary bouts of weakness. I can tolerate people who are mostly good and their bad parts aren't evil, just normal human."

"Back to the original conversation, what are you really going to do?"

"Well, if I'm not in jail thanks to he, whom we will not name, I'm going to take a short break and then another nursing job. I've also thought about doing another bout with Doctors without Borders. They always need nurses. That's a nice thing about having extra money. I can afford to work without pay. I'll do that until I'm needed elsewhere. Think happy thoughts. With the new smart bullets, they're making now, my other job may become obsolete."

"But you'll kill again if my brother gives you the order." He added with frustration.

"Listen Mr. Dudley-do-right, what I do or don't do isn't any of your damn business. I don't have nightmares about my work. I still feel welcome when I talk to God. Can you say the same? About your brother? Let's set the record straight. I will do almost whatever he orders me to do. I trust him fully. If I disagree with him, he actually listens to me. That's more than I can say about some people."

"This isn't about me!"

"Oh yes, it is or we wouldn't even be having this conversation. You hate the fact that you may have any feelings for someone you think is a killer. Just doesn't fit in your scheme of how things should be. I'm not June Cleaver in an apron and happy smile. I'm a female Jason Bourne in blue jeans, who kills people. So, I don't fit your dream of what a wife or significant other should be. Since what might have happened between us isn't going anywhere, let's get back to guarding Mrs. Blair. Maybe if you're lucky, one of us may get killed and you won't have to deal with how you feel about me. Just go get some rest. I have it here."

"You're the one that wanted an overlap," he muttered.

"I've changed my mind. See, I can act like a woman sometimes. I'll wake you in an hour. Now, go away."

32

"The test of people is what they can do when they're tired." Winston Churchill

RACHAEL'S HEAD and stomach were churning. She didn't need this right now. Her symptoms were in line with a concussion. Add to that on top of the fact that the first time she really felt something for a man who actually might return the feelings was a total fail. Maybe the brothers weren't capable of loving someone. She wanted Wilson with all her heart, but he put obstacles around it. His brother used the same tactics. Of course, he just wanted to toss her in jail and throw away the key. Lord, she was tired. Sleep sounded like ambrosia she wanted, no, make that, needed to partake of, and allow herself to heal. All she longed to do was curl up and figuratively lick her wounds.

Moving restlessly around the room, checking the forest sounds and listening. She heard the hoot of an owl. The park was home to three types, the great horn owl, the barrel owl and the little screech owl. They could all be the rock group The Who, and she wouldn't recognize one from the other. Two more hellishly long hours to go.

Watts came in and Reynolds took his place outside. Rachael finally got to settle in one place and close her eyes. Despite her exhaustion, she was too keyed up to sleep but maybe an hour down time would help recharge her batteries. Her body was still, but her mind was racing. They may have won this round, but someone was still after the First Lady. A person who was supposed to be on their side had to have a lot of hate built up to go to this extreme. It had to be something other than money involved. There were more expedient ways to halt an operation then going after the man's family.

She must have dozed for a few minutes when something started vibrating against her hand. It took a few seconds to realize it was her phone. Her phone was supposed to be untraceable and only Wilson had the number. So, it was either good or really bad news.

Rachael sat up and then walked to the edge of the lean-to. The sun's rays were just starting to scatter the night. Taking a deep breath to clear the cobwebs from her head, she answered the phone.

The sound of Wilson's voice was a relief. "The President has given the word, it's done. Bring the package home."

"So, you didn't have to get blown out of the water?"

"Went smooth as silk."

"Someone must have screwed up."

"Ain't that the truth. Morning's still young. There's still time for stuff to hit the fan. We may have many disasters in our future. The package?"

"Sleeping. Who do we make delivery to?"

"Secret Service and a small squad of Marines will meet you at the pick-up point. I sent a familiar back-up just in case. Couldn't do much about the Secret Service. Apparently, Johnson has had an epiphany and cleared all his men. Swears he found all the bad eggs. The Marines are from Cherry Point so they should be clean."

Rachael gave Wilson the GPS coordinates she had gotten from the map she had studied. It was just a mile from the hide-out. She would have preferred somewhere farther away. But, Mrs. Blair had, had a long night and Rachael didn't think she would be able to manage anything much farther.

"Word of warning. The threat against the First Lady is still there. They threatened to take her out in revenge.

The President not giving in to their demands seriously pissed them off."

Persistent buggers. "Tell the President to give Mary's safe word to one of the Marines. I won't turn her over unless I know for sure they're from you."

"Why one of the grunts?"

"Because I don't think these people could have the ability to turn an entire Marine unit from another base in hopes that they might be on the rescue team. The Marines are usually pretty Semper Fi and don't turn that easily. Secret Service I'm not so sure about. Despite Johnson's re-evaluations."

Rachael felt a slight vibration in the air and then a tremor under her feet. "Reynolds, get Watts! Now!" Mary ran across the floor as Rachael yanked up the back curtain that hid the tunnel and opened the door. "Go! Get down the steps and run." She could hear Wilson asking her what was going on. Watts and Reynolds sprinted into the cabin, and she all but shoved them down the ladder. "Run!"

Rachael had already grabbed her backpack and rifle, pulled the metal door to, and was down the bolt hole. She didn't even put her feet on the rungs and slid down as fast as gravity would take her. She took off like the hounds of hell were at her heels as soon as her feet hit the floor. She didn't know if she really heard the sounds through the earth or if the sounds of the whomp of the helicopter blades and the hiss of the missile were simply in her head. The ground above them shook as the missile hit the small lean-to and impacted on the small hill behind it.

Watts and the First Lady had made it to the first initial turn and were around the corner. Reynolds had turned back to wait for her. She screamed at him again to run above the noise over their heads. As usual, he ignored her. Launching herself into a tackle, she took him to the floor with her and rolled around the bend, as the metal door blown off its hinges leading the charge as the hot whoosh of flames came barreling down the tunnel like a dragon's breath.

Rachael was resting on top of Reynolds, when they stopped sliding. "When I say run, I mean run, you idiot!" She was breathless so it didn't come out much like an order, more like a complaint. "I gotta say though, this is going to piss off the Parks Department big time."

Reynolds' didn't answer. He just shut her up by kissing her. Rachael felt like the flames reaching down the walls of the tunnel echoing in her gut. For the first time in her adult life, she welcomed the touch of another person. She couldn't completely read his thoughts, but the clean, joyous flames played through her body like fire sprites and her heart was beating in time with his.

He was as good a man as she had thought he was. There was no greed or ill will in the images she saw. He had known grief and sadness but had tried not to let it color his life. She could feel the shadow of a woman who had hurt him and was still part of his life. She was the person he loved more than life itself. Rachael wanted to erase that pain she felt in him as she wrapped her arms around him, and wholeheartedly returned the kiss. Both of them forgetting for an instant about the danger they were in. It was a bitter sweet feeling because deep down she knew she couldn't take the place of the shadowy woman in his mind and he wouldn't take Wilson's place in hers.

Reynolds hadn't intended to turn one of the nicest tackles he had ever seen on or off the football field into a kiss. Actually, he didn't know what had gotten into him, but once Rachael was in his arms, it was what he had to do. As he had wrapped his arms around her to try to cushion the fall with his body, the momentum had rolled him underneath of her. When he looked up into her emerald-colored eyes, he couldn't help himself. Reaching behind the nape of her neck he pulled her down into a kiss. He was even more surprised when she returned the favor. But the images that flowed into his mind from hers in the split second shook him to his core.

He saw an image of a tattered angel with her gray wings drooping. Instead of white garments, she was in blood-stained camouflage. Her sword was still in the guard position and her eyes were set in defiance. The ghost of his brother behind her, guarding her back.

There was a bond between them that was like a golden cord keeping them together. The pain from her childhood lanced through him, and he felt the love from the wellspring in her heart. She truly believed in what she did with all her heart and soul. The woman he thought heartless, cared about him and thought he was a hero for coming to help her in spite of what he thought she was. He had to wonder what she saw on her end. Their exchange had been a two-way street.

He pulled back, and for a split second they stared at each other. Watts yelled at them from further down the tunnel and they broke apart. Reynolds saw her wince as he pulled her to her feet. "How bad?"

"Well, it didn't help my ribs any, but I'll make it. You make a nice pillow." They both were avoiding discussing the elephant in the tunnel. They had kissed and seen each other for what they really were. "We need to catch up." As she turned to go, she swung back around to face him, causing him to stumble. This time she put a hand out to help. "At least you answered one of my questions."

"Yeah, which one was that?"

"How people like us get together to procreate." She hurried down the rest of the tunnel before he could reply. But for some reason in spite of the mess they were in, he had a silly smile on his face as he followed her.

33

"The thing that's important to know is that you never know. You're always sort of feeling your way." Diane Arbus

"It's not the tragedies that kill us, it's the messes." Dorethey Parker

The President was listening to Wilson's conversation with Rachael. He hoped he might get a chance to talk to his wife. Wilson knew the President was concerned about her, so he had put the call on speaker phone. When Rachael started yelling for the others, he knew things had gone dreadfully wrong. The line went dead, but not before Wilson and the President heard the explosion of the missile hitting close to wherever Rachael and the others were. There had been a hiss and silence.

"I've killed my wife," the President uttered in anguish.

Wilson grabbed him by the shoulders. "Don't give up hope. Rachael had some warning. She wouldn't have taken them anywhere that didn't have a rabbit hole."

"So, what do we do?"

"We'll have a good idea as to location as soon as the reports of a fire come in. You can't cover up that kind of an explosion. Considering the time frame, they were more than likely in Rock Creek Park. The kidnappers just came around to the same conclusion. They probably used heat sensors to find them. They almost made it to the finish line. We just have to believe she'll get her to the rescue team."

"So, we send the team out to do what? Wait and hope they straggle in, safe and sound?" The President's fear for his wife came out as anger.

"That's exactly what we do. Rachael asked me to send in a special team. No one else knows they're on the way. Believe me, who ever gets in their way will wish they had never been born. Rachael has come out of tighter spots than this using her brain and whatever she had on hand. This time she has an edge."

"And what's that?"

"She has my brother and his partner with her."

"Your brother?"

"We have different names. I had him change his name to protect him. He's a detective with the D.C. police department."

"The detective who wants to arrest Rachael for murder?"

"He's the one. But he'll get over it. Rachael went to him for help. She's never been wrong about someone's character before. If anyone can help get them through, it'll be Eric."

"Then I guess we both better pray that they make it."

Wilson grimaced, the President was pulling himself together but he was still agitated. "We need to get back to the others and monitor the operation. You need to pick a Marine to give Mary's safe word to. Not the one the Secret Service has, but the one that's just between you two."

"How did Rachael or you for that matter know we would have one?"

"It's what we would do, if we had some one we cared about. Someone who could ever be in a hostage situation. It's the only smart thing to do. We both know that you and your wife aren't stupid."

The President's smile was strained and brief, but he was beginning to compartmentalize and start to function again. He was still worried. He had to have faith that Rachael would succeed in bringing his wife home. Mary was the one person he wasn't sure he could live without. Rachael knew that. She had never failed him before.

34

"The more hidden the venom, the more dangerous it is." Marquise De Valois

"THERE'S nothing better than a friend, unless it's a friend with chocolate." Charles Dickens (or in some cases, automatic weapons)

THEY HUDDLED by the exit to the tunnel. It would take a while before the attackers learned if there were any bodies in the shelter. The fire would be too hot. If they waited for it to cool down, it would give them an opportunity to get away. The attackers would have to be able to walk to the back of the lean-to to see the hole that led to the tunnel through the hill. Rachael was sure they had people watching to make sure no one had made it out. But they wouldn't be watching the back of the hill. At least that's what she hoped. It wasn't a small hill.

"Okay, here's the plan. Who ever did this can't hang around for very long. The fire will be called in, and the police and fire department will be there soon. The Park Rangers will be in a snit. As soon as they find out it was caused by a missile, every alphabet agency in the country will be there. We need to get to here." Rachael had pulled a map out of her backpack and showed them the place marked on the map. "If anyone tries to stop us, you two will get Mrs. Blair to the rescue team. I'll intercept the others."

"Let me help you. Watts can get her there."

"I'm used to working alone. You agreed to follow orders. Mary, you do not go to anyone until one of the Marines gives you your safe word. You know which word I mean. The one only you the President know. Do not trust anyone, and I mean anyone, until they give you the word. Understand?"

Mary nodded her head. "You be careful, child. We haven't finished planning this shindig for Ida."

Rachael gave her a hug. "You'll make sure it's the greatest wedding ever, no matter what happens." Rachael stepped toward her, "It has been my honor and privilege to have gotten to know you." She whispered something softly in Mrs. Blair's ear.

Mary pulled away, and her eyes were shiny with tears. “I’ll do it, child. You are a daughter to be proud of.”

Watts preceded the First Lady as they started down the trail. Reynolds hung back. “What’s plan B if they don’t know the magic password?”

“Run like the hounds of hell are chasing you. Take her to your department. You have enough people there who are armed and can protect her until the cavalry shows up. Follow your gut, you’ll know if they’re wrong or not.”

“What about you?”

“I’ll either be with you and you’ll have your golden opportunity to throw me in a cell or you won’t have to worry about me anymore.”

“So, what, you kiss me and then leave?”

“You kissed me. My mission is to get Mrs. Blair back safely. You volunteered. It was your choice to see this through, so if I can’t do it, it’s up to you.”

“We kissed each other and sooner or later we’ll need to deal with it.”

Rachael reached up to cup his face and placed a tender kiss on his mouth. She whispered softly, “Thank you for showing me what could be possible.” Then she was gone, melting away into the trees. He headed down the path after the others. Deep down he knew she didn’t expect to come back.

She made an arc around their back trail, and it

wasn't long before she found him. He whirled around as she stepped out of the shadows. "Hello, Jon."

"Rachael, thank God, I found you. Wilson sent me to look for you when he lost contact."

"Really? You're very fast. Considering Wilson didn't know where I was. Your timing is impeccable as always. I thought you weren't to go out in the field until this was over."

"Sometimes we have to change our plans. You're the one who's always harping on the need for a Plan B."

She bowed slightly in his direction "You have learned well, grasshopper. Do you really think you can take me out with you and only six men?"

"You always were hard to fool. I thought I was pretty good at it though."

"I couldn't read you. Which was strange since you weren't that difficult to scan when we first met. We really didn't have that much contact at first, so I thought maybe Wilson had let you in on my talent and you were trying to cover yourself. I believed you must have had a natural shield. You had just worked to make it stronger. It's what I would have done. So, I didn't really suspect you, not in the beginning anyway. Wilson trusted you, and I trusted Wilson."

"This is the first time we've actually had to spend any real time together that wasn't work related. It didn't take long before you starting leaking. You were trying too hard. I knew it had to be someone high up in the food chain to know the information that was leaking out. You fit the bill."

"It could have been Wilson."

"Wilson has a strong shield. But his is genetic. He let his down so I could read him a long time ago. I wouldn't have come to work for him otherwise. Yours, however, is one that has been grafted into your brain. It has a slimy feel to it. I would say it was planted under hypnosis. Since you don't like losing control, I'm willing to bet you fought the practitioner. He was strong enough that you still got some barriers up. But you had enough resistance that there were cracks. Also, I know Wilson would die rather then turn traitor."

"I really was falling in love with you."

"No, you wanted me. That's two different things. Now all you want is to get even and take what you want. I'm really curious. Why did you do this? It couldn't have been the money. You knew your family would cave, sooner or later and you would inherit."

"Power is a more potent aphrodisiac then money."

"You had power. Everyone knew you'd take over the agency one day. You had the choice of that or you could have gone home and tried to buy everything in the world."

"One day is the problem. I want it now. My father is still alive, he's healthy and he holds the reins. Wilson has too many years left and things can always change.

This job is dependent on which ever political hack is in office."

The last administration almost destroyed us. Wilson is a fool. He's actually patriotic. There isn't anything he wouldn't do to keep this country safe. He can't see the way the wind is blowing. This United States is ripe for the picking. It has outlived its time. Why buy the world when you can take it?"

"Did you convert or are you just working for them?"

"Why would I convert?"

"You know as soon as you out live your usefulness, they will kill you. If you are one of them, you might last a little longer, but as an infidel they owe you no allegiance what so ever."

"It's not like you to profile a suspect. You are usually too accepting of allowing people to go their own way. 'Live and let live' as I've so often heard you say."

"I may be tolerant, but I'm neither stupid or gullible. These are not the kind of people who believe in turning the other cheek. They will use you. When it suits them, they will get rid of you."

"What happened to believing in people and giving them a chance?"

"Jesus said to be meek, not weak. I'm working on the meekness part, and I have a long way to go. But at least I try. Then again, who am I to say? As Heinlein once said, 'One man's theology is another man's belly laugh.' I just don't like the way your side swings. So maybe it's a personal problem."

Rachael stepped back into the shadows. She had sensed the other men moving to box her in. Jon blinked and then growled "Don't try anything foolish. We outnumber you, and I don't care how good you are. You can't take all of us."

Her voice whispered out of the trees, "But that's the nice part about working with martyrs. They are so willing to die for their cause. You don't have to get your hands dirty."

"I mean it, Rachael. Come out with your hands in plain sight. We'll let you live. I told them you were my woman."

"Only in your wildest dreams. I'd stay alive long enough for you to get what you want Then you would kill me. I really didn't think rape was your cup of tea, but I guess I was wrong. Besides, I'm too dangerous for you to let me live anyway."

She had felt the two men coming up to box her in. Dropping to lower her center of gravity as they came in to rush her. Using the knives, she had in her arm sheaths she slid the blades through their body armor. They both folded to the forest floor. The idiots hadn't even tried to disarm her. No one expects anyone to be as good with a knife as they are with a gun. Moving further back into the trees to get behind the others, she heard Jon call out her name again.

"This is your last chance, Rachael. I give the word and even you can't get out of the way of a wall of bullets."

That was her cue. She grabbed a low hanging branch and swung up into the trees. They would shoot low hoping to take her alive so she could tell them where Mrs. Blair was heading in hopes of intercepting her. Even the most seasoned agents forget to look up. The bullets whipped through the lower part of the trees, tearing away leaves and twigs. She had kept Jon talking long enough that the others would be far enough out of range of any bullets winging their way through the woods. Hopefully they had made it to either the hidden vehicle or the rescue party, and were on their way to safety. Once out of the area, she thought Blair would be safe. Even Rachael couldn't come up with a Plan B that had that many traitors available.

Jon's men finally stopped their volley to reload, and she dropped out of the branches. She stepped out from behind the trunk of the tree and shot the other four members of the little assassination team. Jon dropped and rolled to cover before she could take him out. He fired as he rolled. He made one of those one of a kind, miraculous shots that sometimes happens on the battlefield. He only got off two shots. One hit her leg and the other got her in the chest.

She rolled back behind the trunk for cover. Jon had the upper hand now. She couldn't run. She was getting down to her last reserves. It isn't fair when the bad guy gets all the fucking breaks. t.

"Slowing down, Cade?" he called out tauntingly.

"You wish," she spat back.

"I tagged you. In a fair fight, you might have a chance, albeit a slim one. You're good Cade, but you don't stand a chance against me. With you wounded it'll be like shooting fish in a barrel."

"Some of those fish are sharks, Jon. You might want to be careful when they decide to bite."

Keep him talking. The wound on her leg normally would be annoying but not life threatening. The one in her chest was a different story. He had missed her heart, but he might have nicked a lung. Colby would be upset that she hadn't worn her vest again. Hind sight's a bitch. Her leg was bleeding like a stuck pig. It wasn't arterial, but she wouldn't last long at the rate the blood was soaking the ground.

God, she was tired. It was becoming an effort to take a deep breath. The others should be safe by now. Reynolds would make sure Wilson sent a team back to help. She wondered if Colby would be curious why they weren't being sent out to pick up his Tiger Kitten any more. She was cold, so cold. The need to move and fight back was there, but the will was seeping away in a red stream into the forest floor. She fumbled at her belt to use it to put pressure on the wound, but her fingers just moved uselessly at the buckle. Fatigue was washing over her like a wave.

She could smell the leafy tea smell of the wood. At least she would die at home, not in some far away land. Here someone would look for her body. Rachael drew in another shuddering breath and felt Jon's shadow as it fell across her body. She must have lost a space in time to allow him to sneak up on her like that.

"So, this is the end of the great Rachael Cade." He squatted down so he could look her in the eyes, "We really could have had some fun together if you hadn't been such a prig about sex."

"I didn't love you." Her voice was starting to slur.

"You told me that. Repeatedly. I think I might have been half in love with you though. That's why you pissed me off so bad. Every other woman was fawning over me, but not you. I even wondered if you had a secret thing for Wilson. You two were so tight. However, the vibes weren't right. Then you fell for that pig of a cop. That really hurt. I thought you had better taste."

"Don't have it in you to love anyone." Rachael was getting fuzzy. Everything seemed so distant. She struggled to lift her weapon.

Jon knocked her gun away easily. "None of that. You lose this time."

She licked her lips and answered, "I won, they got away."

"I'll concede to you on that point, but we'll kill her another day. It doesn't really matter anyway. It might be better this way. A grieving widow at a presidential burial is always a good tear jerker. By now your precious President, his staff and Wilson are nothing but ash, a footnote in the history books. I just accomplished in minutes what you've been doing to the other side for over two years. This war is far from over. The Vice President will do whatever I say. He hasn't a clue what goes on and never has."

"You still lose. Wilson knows about you. They weren't in the bunker."

"No, he didn't know. He trusted me."

"Not as much as he does me. I warned him before I ran with the First Lady. They're safe."

"My men verified the explosion. You're bluffing."

"Just let the bomb go off to bring you out into the open." Rachael was getting colder, her teeth were starting to chatter. She must be losing more blood than she thought and going into shock.

"I should just let you bleed out. It would be sweet to let you suffer and think about how I beat you this time. Draw it out. Unfortunately, they want to be sure that you're dead or under my control. I don't trust you not to pull something out of your hat to save yourself. Nor do I have the time or patience to nurse you back to health. I doubt you would be useful anyway. You'd cause too much trouble and take up too many resources. So, it's goodbye Rachael. Go to hell, knowing you missed the best lay you ever could have had."

"Still an arrogant bastard. I don't think you'd even come close to the best. I wouldn't count on seeing me in hell, I happen to believe in God. Even if that's where I'm heading, you'll beat me there by a long shot. What do you think your buddies are going to think when they find out your neat little plan for world dominance failed?"

"Whatever." He stood up and placed the barrel of his gun between her eyes, and she stared right back into his. She wouldn't give him the satisfaction of closing her eyes no matter how tired she was. "Any last words?"

"What about those Redskins? Think they'll make a bowl bid this year?"

He hesitated a heartbeat, "You hate watching sports." The small red dot settled right above his lip. The shot would sever the spinal cord. The shooter was making sure that Jon's finger didn't spasm as he died and take her with him.

"Not today. Look down." She saw the look of sheer surprise in his eyes, a microsecond before the bullet tore through his brain. The next second, he was lying dead next to her.

"I told you to go with Watts and the First Lady. You don't ever obey orders, do you?"

35

"Don't mess with anybody on Monday. It's a bad, bad day.' Louise Fitzhugh

REYNOLDS CHECKED Jon for a pulse and then shoved him to one side. "Before we got to the car, Mrs. Blair sent me back to get you. Then I ran into these guys. They insisted I come along."

She looked around him and saw Colby holding a rifle and watching the woods. The others had spread out. "And you trusted them?"

"Mrs. Blair told me your safe word. They knew it. I'm not completely stupid except when it comes to you. How bad is it this time?"

"Must have hit a bleeder in my leg. Don't know

about my chest. Can't feel it. "Her voice was starting to fade. "It doesn't hurt. Just so cold."

Colby squatted down next to her, "Hey Kitten."

"You've been practicing how to shoot. I had asked for you, but wasn't sure if you could come. How did Wilson get you here so fast?"

"Can't let a rookie like you out do me, they'd take away my green feet. Glad to know you care. We just happened to be in the area. Just goofing off and getting bored. I need to look at that chest wound. You've got yourself in a mess this time. You should know better than to start a run without us." He applied pressure to the leg wound with his belt, not enough to form a tourniquet just enough pressure to slow the bleeding. But the amount of blood already pooled under it worried him, she was too small to lose that much volume. "Still being too stubborn to wear a vest I see. Stay with me, Babe, I have help on the way."

"I just feel responsible for you. You know the old Chinese adage that you are responsible for those you save. I need you to look good. It's a pride thing. Stop worrying. It's just a scratch. I'll be fine."

"That's what you said the last time and how long were you in the hospital? At least you'll have matching wounds."

"You know how nurses and doctors are. Nag, nag, nag. I only stayed so I could have a vacation. Besides Wilson was hovering like a broody hen. They're safe?"

Reynolds answered. “The Marines met them and scooped Watts and Mrs. Blair up. I don’t think anyone could get close to her now.”

She sighed. “Thanks for your help. I couldn’t have done it without you both. But you never listen.”

“Lucky for you I don’t. You’d be dead now if I had.”

“That would solve all your problems.”

“What do you mean?”

“It’s hard to think you might be in love with an assassin.”

“What makes you think I might love you?”

“I just know. The same way I knew you’d come back for me.”

“And you called Masters an arrogant bastard.”

“The proper word would be bitch.” Why was she having this conversation? All she wanted was to be warm and to go to sleep. “It doesn’t matter. I’m pretty sure I’d love you like a brother, even if you are a pain in the ass.”

“We can discuss this later.”

“I may be wrong, but I don’t think we have a later. Do you have any water? Why is it so cold?”

“Don’t you even think that.” He searched her backpack and found the bottle of water she had put in it. He lifted her in his arms and dribbled some into her mouth. She swallowed slowly.

Colby was pulling medical supplies out of his backpack. He had an IV-line ready to go. Rachael didn’t even grimace as he put the line in. The others were back, and one of the other P.J.'s was starting a line in her other arm. She didn't even notice when they had dressed her leg wound.

"I usually think what I wish." Rachael reached over and patted Colby on the arm, "Take care of the guys for me."

She smiled slightly at Reynolds. "If you're right, I promise to make your life miserable for a long time." But, oddly, for the first time in her life, she wanted to give up. Then she started to let herself fall into the black sleep that had been trying to claim her.

Colby took her from Reynolds arms and gently laid her on a blanket to conserve heat. "Come on Kitten, they called us home to come and get you and you don't have a smart-ass comment for me?"

Rachael didn't open her eyes, but someone kept nagging at her to wake up. The voice was familiar but didn't belong in this place. She roused slightly, "Colby?"

"Yeah, it's me kid. The whole team's been trying to find you."

"It's cold." How can it be cold in the desert? "Is it nighttime?"

"I've got you. We'll get you to a warm place. You're safe now."

"Watch your ass, Colby, I won't be there to protect you."

"Don't worry, Kitten. You'll be back, mean as ever. Now it's our turn."

Rachael was gone. She went down that black rabbit hole that had been trying to claim her, at least it felt warmer there. She was surprised there wasn't a bright light waiting there to guide her. Was that a good or bad sign?

Reynolds had moved out of the way of the rescuers. The team was made up of the elite Navy Para Rescue unit, PJ's and they started working on her as soon as they reached her. Only the best was good enough for the agency's premier assassin. That put her on the same level as astronauts and downed pilots.

Colby had called in a helicopter. By the time they loaded her on board she had IV lines sprouting out of both arms. Normal Saline in one and blood in the other. It said something about her life that they already had cross matched blood for her. Rachael was so pale it was scary. She looked like a child packaged on the stretcher for flight. The team members that stayed on the ground led him out of the forest. Colby was one of them.

Reynolds walked next to Colby. "I take it you two know each other."

The Sergeant gave him a sharp glance. "Yeah, we know each other. She saved my life not too long ago."

"I don't guess you can tell me that story."

Colby gave a cocky grin along with his answer, "I could, but then I'd have to kill you."

"She'll be alright, won't she?"

"Kitten's tough. The wounds aren't that bad, she's just lost a lot of blood. The bullets appeared to have missed anything vital. Get her tanks filled again and she should be fine. What's your story?"

"If I tell you, I'll have to kill you."

Colby's reply was a sharp laugh. Ten minutes later they were at the edge of the forest and there was a Secret Service car ready to take Reynolds to the White House for debriefing. This was getting to be a common occurrence since he had met Rachael. He felt a slight change in the air next to him, and Colby and his men were gone. At least now he knew where Rachael got her skulking skills. Then again, she probably already had them before she met the PJ's. They didn't trust a lot of people.

36

"Faith is not being sure where you're going, but going anyway." Federick Buchner

"I HAVE FOUND out it is not what happens, it is how you tell it and who does the telling." Nancy Willard

RACHAEL WOKE up in an unfamiliar place. She kept her eyes shut to covertly check her surroundings. Nope. She obviously was not in the heavenly singing and chanting department. There were no wings beating unless you counted the sound of her heart beat bleeping on the monitor. She was pretty sure you weren't supposed to hurt after you died. In any event, she knew with absolute surety they didn't use Foley catheters. Opening her eyes, she recognized the accoutrements of a hospital ICU. She didn't much care for seeing it from this perspective. Rachael was happier being on the giving end of hospital care, not the receiving.

"You might as well keep your eyes open. I know you're awake."

Wilson was seated next to her bed. He looked tired with dark circles under his eyes.

"How long have I been out?"

"Around thirty-six hours."

"Can I please have a drink?"

The nurses hadn't put a water pitcher by her bed yet. Wilson had a bottle of water by his chair and gave her a sip from it. Swapping germs with the boss. That was a hoot.

"Mary and the President are both safe?"

"Yes. You didn't ask about Eric."

"I knew he was safe. He was with Colby."

"Right. But you need to make a decision before I call the nurses in here."

"What kind of decision?"

"Between my brother and the First Lady I've been inundated with requests to see you. What your condition is. In fact, my own brother has threatened my life if I don't give up your location. We have made your condition a little dire than it is."

"Why's that? And how dire is it?"

"Once they got some fluids and blood into you, took care of the small hemothorax in your lung, your condition improved considerably. As you already had probably guessed, you were going in hypovolemic shock. We got to you before there was any organ damage. I guess we'll never be sure about the brain. In your case, it'd be hard to tell."

She must have really been in trouble. She actually saw a hint of fear in Wilson's eyes. First, he was willing to swap germs with her, even if it was just his water bottle and now, he was trying to be funny.

"You had surgery for the bullets in your leg and chest. The doctor said you now have a matching set of scars. The insinuation was that it was two, too many. He also said you shouldn't have any residual damage in the leg other than being sore. It missed all the major vessels and basically, just bruised the muscles. It just caught a major vein on the way through and bled a lot. Same thing with the one in your chest. It missed all the important parts. Your biggest problem was loss of blood. You must have had one of your good angels sitting on your shoulder."

"So medically, not so dire."

"No, you'll live. It just looked a lot worse than it was."

"Why was everyone trying to kill me? I thought Jon at first, but he wanted me alive. For the short term anyway. He had plans for me."

"It was his parents. They had found a nice little wife for him. They thought if you were out of the way, they could bring him in line. The first attack was to kill you and leave Jon alive. That was the original plan. They underestimated you and your ability to defend yourself. The back-up plan was to have you raped and killed in your apartment. Underestimating you again. The two men at the burger place were ad-libbing."

"Glad to clear that up. The decision I need to make?"

"You can die here and disappear."

"And if I decide to live?"

"We go back to what you do. The only problem is my brother. He thinks he's in love with you, but..."

"But he's having a major fight with his conscience because he knows I'm the assassin and doesn't know what to do. He also has some unfinished business with someone named Lenore." Rachael paused for a heartbeat. "He still has feelings for her, but is conflicted."

Wilson looked startled, "He talked to you about her?"

"Not verbally, but I caught the gist of it in the tunnel when we were running."

"You picked all that up on the run?" Wilson's facial expression showed he didn't quite believe her.

Long story, short. "Let's just say we had a little down time. I'll tell you about it sometime."

"I'll hold you to that. Anyway, the problem with my brother," he paused for a second time.

She finished his sentence for him. "If I die, he doesn't have to make a decision one way or the other that he may later regret."

"I love my brother. We haven't been close in the last few years because he feels what I do is wrong. But I care. I don't want to see him hurt."

"Can he make a case against me?"

"Without you giving a full confession? No. Even with that, he might have a problem getting it to trial. You have too many people who are willing to speak up for you as a character witness. Having the President of the United States and his wife in your corner is a very strong point."

"Not to mention the fact that I can literally disappear off the face of the earth if it's too embarrassing for me to go before a judge."

"I protect my people, Rachael. I don't sweep problems under the rug."

"I know. That's why I work for you. The big problem is, I think I really like the big galoot, even if he doesn't obey orders. I want to see where that goes. With my so-called gift, I don't think I'll get many chances to meet someone I can love without hiding who I really am. I've only met one other and he's not interested."

"Well, since neither of you are sterling examples of

obeying orders that ought to work out fine. What if it means giving up working for me?"

"You see, if this was a real romance novel, I would be willing to give up anything to be with him. But that's not life. I am what I am. The nursing and what I do for you is an integral part of what makes me, me. If I give it up, then I will eventually resent it. It would be like asking him to give up being a cop or Lenore."

Wilson sat back in his chair and ran his hand through his hair. "Still, what if he makes it conditional on you giving up working for me?"

"Then we weren't meant to be. We may never be together. He's nowhere near giving Lenore up or dealing with that issue. I don't plan on this being my life's work. There are others who can do what I do. If I ever have children, it would change the whole picture. The world is full of ifs. I really like him. Is it love? Can I love him even with my feelings for you? Am I coloring my feeling for him because of my love for you? It would hurt my heart to lose him. If he truly loves me and we're meant to be together, then we will work it out. The bigger issue is whether or not I'm trying to replace you with him. That would be unfair to everyone concerned, especially Eric."

"Ouch, that hurt. If it doesn't? Work out I mean? Love doesn't always conquer all and your still stuck on like. We both know that. And as much as I hate to admit it, Lenore is a problem. He never has been able to let go and she keeps coming back to pull on the leash."

"Then we go back to our lives, bruised but better for having known each other. At least on my part. I love you, but you will never let down your guard and love me back. I want a chance at a life with someone who cares for me. Love would be better, but like is a good place to start."

"You two make a pair. I have had to listen to him justify to himself that loving you isn't the wrong thing to do. He still doesn't know for sure if you are what he thinks you are. I don't think you will be able to make a go of it unless he knows for sure. He'll think it'll be okay, but it will eat at him."

"I plan on telling him, but he already knows. He just needs to hear me say it."

"You don't think he'll try to throw your ass in jail?"

"I think the police department has policies against fraternizing with convicted felons. Not to be crass, but I think he has other ideas about what to do with my ass. He might have to let this one slide."

Wilson let out a surprised bark of laughter, "Like I said before, you never know what's going to come out of that mouth of yours. When you tell him, let him know what Moody really was. You'll be blowing national security just by informing him of your job description, so you might as well go for broke."

"I have a job description?"

"Always a smart ass."

"That's why you love me."

She closed her eyes and felt a light kiss on her forehead. "Well, if you're going to be part of the family, I guess that's a requirement." Yeah, but the question was, what part of the family?

The next time she woke up, Reynolds was in the chair next to her. He had pulled it up close enough to hold her hand. When her eyes met his, he cleared his throat, "I guess we have a lot to talk about."

At the rate they were going it was going to be a long, long time to get everything out that needed to be said. "There's a joke I heard once. A man walks into a bar and asks for a glass of water. The bartender pulls out a shotgun and shoots barely missing his ear. The man says thank you, leaves a tip on the bar, and walks out. What's the punch line?"

"The man had the hiccups."

"So, you've heard the joke. I take care of the hiccups of the world. Now some people would say that the bartender could have just made a loud noise or given him a glass of water with sugar in it and accomplished the same thing."

"Why sugar?" He sighed, "You don't agree?"

"You can sometimes cure occasional hiccups that way. Old country remedy. But if you have a patient who has hiccups you can't stop, even with medicine, they're probably going to die. Usually there's an underlying disease process that is causing the hiccups in the first place. But the point is that until modern medicine can cure the problem, the body will die."

"The job that I do is the only option we have at this time in our evolution. There will always be men of war, corruption, and hate. The only thing they understand is retribution. They won't change or become born again. Maybe the church is correct when they say some people are demon possessed. I don't know why they do what they do. I only know what stops them."

"We can use the rule of law and imprison the wrong doers. We can put them away so they can't cause harm. But that doesn't always work. I've been to countries where the prisoners run the prison. The guards are just there to keep them in. When we find the answer on how to really change people or to take away the aggression that caused man to be at the top of the food chain, then I'll be out of a job."

"I like you, maybe even love you, but the person I am is the sum total of what I do. I can adjust and compromise on most things, but not on what makes me tick. A famous actress once said, 'I'm selfish, impatient, and a little insecure. I make mistakes. I am out of control and at times hard to handle...But if you can't handle me at my worst, then you sure as hell don't deserve me at my best.' Although I am rarely out of control the rest fits. Granted, I'm not in Marilyn Monroe's league, but all I can promise is if this is truly love, I will love, cherish, and protect you. Jon once asked me what the difference is in being willing to die for someone or live for them. Living for someone is so much harder, but I want to try to do that with someone."

"Then you better make good on that promise and always come back."

"So, you're not going to throw me in jail?"

"I love you and making a marriage work is hard enough with our jobs. Trying to do it with you in jail would be a real bear."

"What about your lady friend?"

"Lenore? I've known her most of my life. I thought we had something, but she can't seem to settle down. When she gets in trouble, she calls me. I get her straight. She leaves again."

Rachael didn't tell him that Watts had told her about Lenore and that she was in town again.

"You do know if we try to make this work, you may have to make a choice between the two of us?"

"I don't love Lenore, she's just a needy friend."

"I don't think Lenore sees it that way."

Eric frowned. "We were talking about us. Lenore doesn't figure into that."

Rachael wisely didn't say anything else. But she knew that it was a bigger issue than Eric wanted to think it was.

EPILOGUE

"Love doesn't make the world go round. Love is what makes the ride worthwhile." Franklin P. Jones

"If you reach for something and find out it's the wrong thing, if you change your program and move on." Hazel Scott

The day was gorgeous. The wedding wasn't in the Rose Garden because Ida's family and friends were a lot more numerous than Rachael's. Ida had visited her in the hospital with Mrs. Blair and they had told her all about picking out the flowers. It was one of the planning sessions she had missed. Not that she was complaining. Ida had been ecstatic when Mrs. Blair and Rachael told her the wedding plans were really for her.

The only problem was the logistics of getting all of Ida's and her husband to be's family there. Rachael solved the transportation problem by hiring a pilot to fly her plane, and then flying the whole family to D.C. Wilson had come through with a house they could all stay in. Ida's soldier didn't know what to do about all the brass. The fact that the President of the United States and his wife were going to be at his wedding was a little out there, but he played it smart and just kept quiet. The boy had potential.

Ida was absolutely stunning in the dress she had picked out. Mrs. Blair had ordered it while Rachael was still recovering. She had also ordered the one Rachael had tried on. Mary had simply smiled when she opened up the box and told her to keep it just in case. Then she winked and laughed as she walked away. Maybe she had cracked under the pressure.

Reynolds had come with her and was now helping her get in a pew. She was using a cane and still had a slight limp. "I thought you said you didn't need that thing anymore.'

"I don't, but did you see the dress code? I would have had to been in heels if I didn't have an excuse to wear comfortable shoes. Besides that, Ida wanted me in the wedding party and this was a good reason to be able to wiggle out of it. Have you ever seen so many people in one family?And look at the number of children."

"Don't you like kids?"

"Actually, I think they're aliens left here by their parents for us to raise. Then if they work out well, they take them back. If not, we get to deal with the results."

"How does that explain us?"

"Well, not everybody's perfect, and they leave some good ones behind."

"So, does that mean you don't want children?"

"Is it a deal breaker?"

"I'll be up front about it, I want a few. But since you have to deal with most of the consequences of the care and feeding, it's really your call."

"Yes, I want children, just not right away. I'm not ready yet."

"Fair enough. But back to our original discussion I have to say, despite the lack of proper shoes, you look as beautiful as the bride."

"Bite your tongue, flattery will not get you in my good graces. The bride is the only one who is beautiful today."

"You are an unforgiving wench. I was following Mrs. Blair's orders to come back."

"I would have handled it. You could have been killed."

"I noticed how you had the upper hand holding Masters' gun to your head."

"I might not have made it, but he would have gone with me. I had a knife to his femoral artery. That's why he was hesitating on pulling the trigger. He was more worried about his boys than killing me. It gave Colby time to set his shot."

"You won't ever give it up, will you?"

"Nope"

Rachael saw a movement in the back of the church. Wilson was talking to an agent. He nodded at her and started to walk away. Just then Eric reached in his pocket for his phone. She looked at the screen. The name was Lenore.

Eric looked at it. He mouthed, "I have to take this." He left the wedding. Eric didn't make it back for the ceremony. She watched the bride and groom come back down the aisle and then went to looked for him. She found him outside the church. He wouldn't meet her eyes. "I have to go. I'm sorry. Somethings come up."

Rachael looked down. "Eric, you say you love me. Lenore calls and you leave me for her."

"It's not like that, Lenore is complicated and she needs help."

"Then get her help. That's what professionals are for."

"She won't go."

"I'm sorry Eric, this is one time you need to choose. Her or me? Your choice."

"What? You're going to be a hard-ass and ask me to

walk away from some one I've known for years because you want me to make a choice between her and you? I thought you were above this type of 'girl tantrum.'"

"Don't even go there. We have discussed this and you knew at some point you would have to choose. Is it more important to run and help Lenore or to leave me here with no ride home?"

"I'm sure someone here will give you a ride. The President will probably offer."

"The issue is not a ride home. The issue is who's more important to you. Lenore or me?"

Reynolds glared at her for a few seconds, then muttered something under his breath.

"Would you like to repeat that?"

"No, I'm sorry." Then he shoved his hands in his pockets and walked away.

She watched him go. She waited for the misery of a broken heart to set in. Her heart appeared to be intact. Rachael realized she had wanted so much for her feelings for Eric to take the place of what she felt for Wilson. The brothers were a lot alike. One's fixation on a woman he couldn't fix and the other on his country.

Wilson walked up to her. "Eric get called in to work?"

"No, Lenore called and he went."

"So, I guess you need a ride."

"I guess I do. I'm going home. Don't tell your brother where I went."

"I'm sorry Rachael."

"It was nice while it lasted. I guess I thought it could be something more. I'm a sucker for hopeless causes. But I have learned not to give my heart away to someone who doesn't want or treasure it. Give me time to congratulate the happy couple and I'll take you up on that ride."

Wilson was waiting when she came back. He was leaning against one of the columns of the church. He watched as she walked up. Wilson realized how close he had come to losing her. Not only to a bullet but to another man.

"I'm ready to go. If you drop me off at my room, I'll pack and catch a cab to the airfield." Rachael had moved back to the apartment after she got out of the hospital.

Wilson hesitated for a heartbeat. "Would you like some dinner before you get ready to fly home? Maybe put it off for another day or so? I think it's time we talked about something besides work."

Rachael had been planning her flight home in her head. It took a second for Wilson's request to sink in. Maybe miracles did happen. "Yes. Yes. I think I would like that very much."

ABOUT THE AUTHOR

LINDA PETRILLI has had an amazing life. From retired trauma-triage nurse, commissioned officer in the medical branch of the Coast Guard, firefighter in the mountains of New Mexico, trained as Tactical EMS for SWAT, and is a pilot. She learned to shoot at an early age and is proficient in most weapons and minor destruction like archery, knife throwing, and martial arts.

Born in New York and raised in Kentucky. After joining the service, she never cleaned out her garage because she moved every 5 years. She met her husband in the service when he was her flight instructor. He told everyone he only married her because she'd never salute him and he didn't want to throw her in the brig.

She writes mysteries with a paranormal twist and strong female characters. She now lives in Colorado with her Newfoundland Ace.

Want to know when her next book comes out? Join Plot Duckies Publishing email list: http://eepurl.com/dbLuC5

MORE BOOKS FROM PLOT DUCKIES PUBLISHING

We publish books with strong female characters. Want more? Here's our current list or check out what's available on our website at PlotDuckies.com or search for them on Amazon or other retailers.

Adventure in the Amazon. *Toy of the Gods* (award-winning series - Idol Makers) by Sonja Dewing: Toy of the Gods

Post Apocalyptic sci-fi. *Revelations* (Glyph Series) by Ronin Romero: Revelations

. . .

Super spicy fairy tale anthology with strong women and chiseled bodies. *Dark Fantasy: Spicy Fairy Tales* by ten authors. Dark Fantasy: Spicy Fairy Tales

***

Tween historical fiction. *Meg and the Rocks* by Katy Hammel. Meg and the Rocks

Award-winning middle Grade historical fiction. *Meg Goes to America* by Katy Hammel. Meg Goes to America

Award-winning children's bilingual book. *Gramita's Tortillas* by Maria Gomez. Gramita's Tortillas